A Deadly Vow

ANGUS BRODIE AND MIKAELA FORSYTHE MURDER MYSTERY
BOOK FIVE

CARLA SIMPSON

OLIVERHEBERBOOKS

Prologue

THE SMELL of rain mixed with the scent of stale food and the ever-present stench from sewage. Smoke from the coal fires had seeped through the walls and at the edges of the window, along with another smell more often found on the streets at the butcher's stall, or in the gutters. It was the metallic tang of blood.

It pooled on the floor, a dark stain that spread beneath the young woman who lay there.

How many times had he returned from running bets at the tavern or at the Hall, and heard the sounds that twisted deep inside him, and then saw the aftermath of the black and blue marks?

It had happened too many times, and each time Màili Brodie brushed it off.

"Yer da is a good man. It's just the drink that makes him so."

The last time, the man he knew as his father hadn't returned for several days so the rent on the flat came due and there was no food. There was barely enough coin to purchase bread and a few vegetables. The next time, his father was gone for weeks.

He didn't mind. To his way of thinking they were better off without him. At least the beatings stopped. After that, there were other men. He returned more than once only to have her meet him at the door.

"Ye need to wait downstairs, my darlin' boy. Just a while longer."

Just a while, might mean a few minutes, or more. That was when he went back to the street and returned later. Afterward, there was usually enough to pay the rent and provide food for a while.

One didn't spend as much time on the streets as he did, and not know what went on between his mother and those men who often followed her from the tavern where she worked.

"If anything should happen," she had once told him, "ye must go to yer gran. Do ye ken?"

He hadn't seen her since she and his mother had had a dreadful argument, his grandmother's words harsh.

But this was different.

He stood in the flat then, everything in chaos, the small table overturned, and all that blood.

"M'athair?" he whispered, and caught the slight flicker in a bloodied eye as he knelt beside her and took her hand.

"Was it... Da?" That shadowy figure who came in and out of his life, and usually not in a good way.

He didn't want to believe his father had done this. But all those other times...

"Remember what I told ye?" she whispered, a strange sound that caught in her throat.

"Who did this to ye?" He wanted to know, needed to know, the anger rising as he fought back the tears.

"It's not for ye t' worry over, son," she replied. "Do ye remember what I told ye?" she insisted, barely able to say the words.

He nodded, wiping his cheek with a threadbare sleeve.

"Take this," she told him.

It was the copper pendant that she always carried. For protection she had once explained of the figure embossed there, cruel irony to his way of thinking, yet she insisted.

"It will protect ye," she whispered, her hand tightening over his. "Ye must go now and don't come back."

He held on even as her hand went limp in his.

"No! Doona go!" he pleaded.

But there was only silence and death in that room.

"I will find who done this!" he vowed. "I swear it! And he will pay!"

The constables came then in their black uniforms, summoned by the woman downstairs who collected the rents. She had heard sounds, he overheard her tell them from where he hid in the shadows.

There were questions. He didn't hear them all, but he did hear the woman tell them that there were men who came and went. Then, he heard a name.

"I collect the rents for the landlord. Tobin was the name of the young man I saw," she replied. "He worked for a harness maker and came often. He had some manners. And she has a boy. Not a sign of 'im tho', and the woman was behind on the monthly rents. I won't be able to collect that now."

"Aye, the lad probably took to the streets. On 'is own now," the other constable replied.

His attention was drawn to the shadows... something he saw there. Or someone?

"The dead-house for this one at Greyfriars for those who canna pay. Poor thing. What might be the name?" he asked the woman.

"Máili Brodie. At least that's the name she gave when she let the room."

"Aye, we'll see the name put into the record. We can do that much. Any other relations?" the one constable asked.

"The husband. But like I said he hasn't been here in some time."

The boy watched from the street as his mother's body was

removed, then put into the wagon, merely a thing to be rid of now. Then, he waited until they were gone, and returned to the room one last time.

The old woman had set the lock. He picked it. He was good at that.

He gathered what there was of his few possessions, the medallion tucked into the pocket of his threadbare pants, a threadbare jacket that was too large for him yet, purchased from the second's shop for when it would fit better, and another pair of pants that he rolled into a bundle.

He stared at the dark stain on the wood floor, sadness and anger twisting deep inside him.

"I will find who done this. I swear it!"

Angus Brodie left that room for the last time and made his way alone out onto the street...

One

OCTOBER 1890, THE STRAND, LONDON

"MOST EXCITED TO READ YOUR latest endeavor, Miss Forsythe," my editor James Warren commented as I stood to leave his office after handing him my latest novel.

"The publisher has been very pleased with the sales of Miss Emma Fortescue's adventures and found it most exciting with elements of mystery and intrigue added. And in this one— *Murder on the Stage*, your protagonist is certainly leading a most exciting life."

She most certainly was.

"I often wonder if there is some resemblance," he continued, the question there in his comment.

Resemblance indeed, I thought, as I gathered my carpetbag and stood to leave.

I did like James very much. He was young, quite handsome in a scholarly way, not the usual stodgy sort I had experienced with my editor who couldn't possibly understand the appeal of my first novel and was at least eighty years old.

However, he had been persuaded to publish it due to my "family connection", namely my aunt, Lady Antonia Montgomery, who had ancestors as far back as William the Conqueror, and whom it was said had more money than the Queen.

A favor, it was called, that small publishing run that quickly sold out and had gone on to a dozen more and counting since. Not that my aunt hadn't something to do with that. She had effectively been a one-woman publicity machine insisting that all her acquaintances and business associates— of which there were many— must absolutely read that first book.

Scandal, the dailies had called it, a member of society and a titled young woman— myself, writing common travel adventures that, and I quote: "*Were most assuredly the invention of a bored spinster.*"

Revenge was sweet as my book sales exceeded everything else my publisher put out that first year. By the time my third book was released, I had purchased the townhouse in Mayfair and was living quite independently, thank you.

It was that third book that had been somewhat scandalous, following my heroine's adventures in Istanbul and then Greece, as my adventuresome self in the guise of Miss Emma Fortescue, had taken myself/herself off to a Greek island with her travel guide and...

I frequently found that volume hidden in women's dressing tables, folded with the daily newspaper society page, or secretly read at ladies' afternoon teas.

I was enormously grateful for the success of my publishing career that freed me from the usual expectations for young women my age— namely that of marriage and a tribe of children, along with boring garden parties, society events, and in general following the expectations of society.

It undoubtedly had something to do with mine and my sister's somewhat unusual childhood that included the death of both our parents, then being bundled off to live with our great aunt. That had proved an endless adventure of itself with a woman who had never married— although there were rumors of at least two notorious affairs. She had lived her life as she chose.

My sister had been through her own difficulties more recently and had returned to what she loved and was quite good at— her art, something she was forced to abandon in her brief marriage that had ended in murder and divorce.

I had always assumed the role of protector over my sister, being two years older, and had a specific thought about that as I thanked James Warren for his time.

"When may we expect your next novel?" he asked now as he rounded his desk and walked with me to the door of his office.

My recent plots for Miss Emma Fortescue had been closer to home, with an irascible but handsome man, a Scot no less, who could be stubborn and difficult, but "made her toes curl", as my aunt was fond of saying.

I thought of the note I'd received that morning from an acquaintance of my aunt— a very distant acquaintance due to some difficulty between them in the past that no doubt had to do with a man.

However, the "*difficulty*" was not insurmountable when it came to a situation deemed most serious that involved her daughter and a disturbing photograph, along with the request that Mr. Brodie and I make inquiries on their behalf.

Brodie's office on the Strand, in fact, was my next destination as I assured James Warren that I would have something to him within a fortnight— in the form of a story concept for him to put out with the booksellers as a "teaser" for my readers.

I stepped out of the building into a persistent drizzle that was not uncommon for October as the seasons changed, and deployed my umbrella. My publisher was not far from the office, but a heavier rain had set the street awash, a spray of flotsam from the gutter exploding in the air with each coach and cab that passed by.

"What do you think?" I asked my companion on the street. "Do we wait for a cab or attempt this afoot?"

I ignored the stare of a woman who passed by with her shopping basket hooked over her arm, ducking from one overhang at the front of one building to the next.

I was accustomed to such stares and couldn't give a fig as the somewhat scruffy "gentleman" who sat waiting for me cocked his head to one side as if he actually considered what I was saying.

The hound, that I had named Rupert after a childhood companion, stood reaching past my knees and shook himself off with one of those "hound" comments, clearly disapproval of the weather.

"A cab it is then," I replied.

In that way that drivers are constantly looking for that next fare, a driver pulled up in short order.

"Yer won't want to be out on a day like this, miss. What be yer destination?"

"Number 204 on the Strand," I called out as I climbed aboard. "And there is extra fare for the hound."

I had discovered in the past that most drivers were quite amendable to having Rupert aboard, particularly when it meant extra fare. For his part, the hound climbed aboard and onto the seat beside me. He smelled of all sorts of mysterious things, all quite offensive.

"Right you are," the driver replied, and we were off to the Strand.

We arrived in good time in spite of the weather and the usual congestion of traffic, the hound jumping down as I paid the driver. To say that I was a bit soggy from the ride with a well-soaked companion was an understatement but hardly a concern considering my travels in the past that had taken me to different places in all sorts of weather.

Mr. Cavendish, known as the Mudger on the street, rolled out from the overhang at the entrance to the stairs at Number 204, where he could usually be found in such weather.

He had lost both legs in an accident years before and navigated the Strand and other parts of London with terrifying skill on a rolling platform most usually with the hound alongside.

"Fine morning, Miss Forsythe," he greeted us.

I opened my carpetbag and handed him the paper sack my housekeeper, Mrs. Ryan, had sent along.

"That has the smell of ham," Mr. Cavendish commented with a gleam in his eyes.

"I was hard pressed to keep this away from the hound until I arrived," I replied. "You'll find some of Mrs. Ryan's sponge cake as well."

"Ah, bless you, miss," he said with a wink. "You are an angel sent to watch over this pathetic old cripple."

"Pathetic old cripple" was a bit off the mark, as I knew only too well.

I had no way of knowing exactly how old Mr. Cavendish might be. His hair, under the cap he usually wore was streaked with gray and he had numerous lines on his face and about those sharp eyes.

But as for pathetic? His physical condition didn't limit his ability by any means.

"Are you certain that you are not Irish?" I replied for he certainly spoke like an Irishman, with a gift of gab and a wee stretch of the truth.

"Not as far as I know," he replied, keeping the sack just out of reach of the hound. "Although Cavendish was me mum's name, don't know anything about me father."

"Is Mr. Brodie about?" I inquired with a look over at the stairs that led to the office.

One could never be certain, as he did have inquiries aside from the ones that we had shared since that first case that involved my sister, and those he participated in with Sir Avery Stanton of the Special Services, a somewhat mysterious agency that I knew little about.

"Aye, you might say he's about. But a warning, miss, he's been out of sorts. Something has him stirred up."

I had not spoken with Brodie in several days as I finished my latest novel and he had been off on some business for Sir Avery at the time. That was not unusual in our "arrangement", as some would have called it.

Our relationship had changed from that of working associates making inquiries on the behalf of clients, to something far... more as the best way to describe it.

It was not unusual for me to stay over at the office on the strand for one reason or "another", and more recently until I was working on my latest book deadline, he had stayed over at the townhouse.

Though usually that was when my housekeeper was away visiting her married daughter and grandchildren— to protect my reputation as he put it which I had laughed at since my "reputation" was already quite questionable due to the novels I wrote. Still, he had been most adamant about it.

It was one of those quirks of Brodie's that I found quite endearing— a man who had lived the way he had on the streets of Edinburgh as a young boy, finding his way to London, then with the Metropolitan Police, and now making private inquiries for those whose reputations were quite often genuinely questionable.

"Should I wear armor?" I asked Mr. Cavendish with no small amount of humor as I turned toward the stairs that led to the second-floor office. After all, I was not unfamiliar with Brodie's grumblings and grousing over some matter or another. But Mr. Cavendish's reply took me back.

"You might want to make it another day, miss, though I do appreciate the food, as always."

That seemed quite ominous. "Thank you for the warning." I gathered up my sodden skirt and climbed the stairs.

As I said, I was quite used to Brodie's temperament— occasional outbursts of frustration or anger over some matter or another, occasionally directed at me when I had taken it upon myself to venture out somewhere he disapproved of. However, for the most part we had navigated through our disagreements.

There were other occasions, of course when I simply let him rumble about. That was when I might find him slamming desk or cabinet drawers, having lost something that was right in front of him, then glowering at me when I pointed that out.

For a logical, intelligent man, he could be quite illogical.

Something that he had accused me of more than once. I blamed it on the fact that he was a Scot. As a whole they had the reputation for being stubborn, inflexible, even thorny and with a fierce nature. I had discovered that I liked that fierce nature very much.

But this was different. I sensed it the moment I stepped into the office. There wasn't the usual grumbling or curses over some matter that couldn't possibly have been my doing since I had not been there in several days. Nor was there the usual comment about something someone had failed to do, or some aspect of a case that he wrestled with.

There was only silence, brief acknowledgment as I arrived, then he looked back down at some paperwork on the desk. In fact, there were two pieces of paper that he folded out of sight, a tablet where he had made notes, and an envelope marked with the name of the owner of the building on the Strand where the office was located.

The rent for the office, a full seven days before it was due?

I greeted him in the usual manner and made a comment about the weather. There was only the briefest response.

"Aye."

He was obviously preoccupied over something.

"I've received a request from a woman in a matter she would like us to make inquiries, Althea Mainwaring, on behalf of her daughter," I commented as I removed my long coat and set the umbrella in the stand.

Once again there was that silence as Brodie wrote an additional note.

"She included a photograph that was received along with a note. She was quite disturbed by the contents." I waited for a response, then frowned when there was none.

"She's concerned over the nature of a photograph regarding her daughter that was included. I have made contact with her, and assured her that we will meet with her as soon as possible."

Still no response.

I went to the coal stove. The coffeepot that sat on the mantle above was cold, something else that was unusual. Coffee was usually the first order of the day, however obviously not this morning.

"I'll make coffee and then we can discuss when we might meet with her."

The only response then was the scratch of the pen on the paper in front of Brodie. He obviously wasn't listening.

I decided on another tactic to gain his attention and possibly determine what it was that had him distracted to the point of ignoring everything else about him.

"Fire!" I exclaimed, which considering the fire several months before at the office, it had the desired effect, although a bit drastic.

Brodie suddenly looked up. "What the devil?"

His expression said far more.

"I thought that might get your attention," I started to explain. The expression on his face stopped me. He looked quite haggard, the lines deeper at the corners of his eyes, those dark brows drawn together.

"Possibly a poor choice," I admitted. "There is no fire. I wasn't at all certain you were listening about an inquiry we've been asked to make..."

That dark gaze met mine briefly, then angled away. "I will be away for some time, a matter I need to attend too."

"Is it something I can assist with?"

"No." His voice quiet now. He laid the pen on the desk. "It's a matter that has needed to be taken care of... for some time."

"Very well," I replied. I thought of that "situation" that had led to his leaving the MP a few years back.

I knew that it was between him and Chief Inspector Abberline, though he'd never spoken at length about it. Whatever it was, it seemed most serious.

"Is it Abberline?"

God knows the man had been a thorn in Brodie's side from the beginning of our association. Even further back according to things I had learned, that had to do with a case Brodie was on at the time when he was with the MP.

"No."

Blunt and to the point, with that same thoughtful expression.

"It has nothing to do with Abberline."

"If it's something for Sir Avery then perhaps I can assist..."

"I said, no," quite sharp this time.

There was something more, but he didn't share it, instead he simply said, "I'm the only one who can do this. I was going to send round a note, but since yer here..."

Send round a note? I glanced down at that envelope. Like paying the rent? Or leaving instructions in his absence for Mr. Cavendish?

What was he talking about?

"I don't know how long I'll be gone." That dark gaze didn't quite meet mine.

"Very well," I replied. Mr. Cavendish had warned me.

And then that dark gaze softened for just a moment.

"I need ye to understand. There are things, private matters from... before."

I didn't understand at all. I hadn't a clue what this was about.

I set the coffeepot back on the mantle. As I did. I glimpsed the battered leather suitcase on the bed through the partially open door that led into the adjoining bedroom.

"Of course," I replied.

That dark gaze followed mine, to the bedroom door.

"There are reasons..." he started to say.

"Reasons that you cannot explain." Or would not, I thought. That much was obvious.

"I will arrange to meet with Mrs. Mainwaring myself," I said then, returning to the coat stand. I pulled on my coat. "Perhaps I can assist her in some way."

"Mikaela..." Brodie came around the desk.

"I understand," I continued somewhat frostily. "Of course,

you must take care of the matter, whatever it is. We can discuss her situation when you return."

"I don't expect ye to understand," Brodie said then.

"You could help me understand," I replied.

He pushed his hand back through that thick dark hair. "It's you here. This."

Which explained absolutely nothing.

"Me?"

"It's the way you are, the way you come here and..."

"And? Just what is it, Mr. Brodie? How is it that I've offended you? It's obvious that you're angry over something. However, I would point out that I have not been here the past several days therefore it is impossible that I'm somehow responsible for something that you will not explain..."

"This isna for ye!" His voice rose. "This..." He made a sweeping gesture of the office.

"It isna for ye, Mikaela Forsythe."

He was angry and I didn't give a fig! Let him be angry. I was angry as well.

Bloody hell! *Not for me?*

What the devil was that supposed to mean?

We'd had our disagreements in the past. It would have been impossible not to for two strong-willed people. However, to say that I was put out by this sudden change in him was an understatement.

I made my own choices and decisions about what was right for me. I had been doing so for some time now, and for him to make an announcement that this was not for me?

He tore off the notes from that notepad, then folded them and tucked them into his pants pocket, then picked up the envelope with the rent.

"I don't know when I'll be back," he said then, in that unexpected, even solemn way, that tightened my throat with its finality.

"Ye must go, and not come back. Tis best this way."

Two

"BEST THIS WAY?"

For whom?!

I parried with the rapier and dagger, then went on the offensive, parried high again, and attacked in two lunging steps.

The tip of the rapier embedded in the target— the dartboard on the wall of my front parlor that also served as my writing room when I was working on my latest novel.

There was an audible groan from the general area of the fireplace, my current houseguest the hound. My housekeeper, Mrs. Ryan, had set the morning fire against the chill that came more frequent in the mornings now with the change of seasons and Rupert had made himself comfortable. It seemed that my morning practice had momentarily disturbed him.

I had first become acquainted with the art of fencing— some would argue that it was a sport, however, my somewhat reluctant instructor at the time, referred to it as the *art* of inflicting death. Something, I found most intriguing at the time.

My fascination with the *"art"* had obviously been inspired by the gallery of portraits of my ancestors in the home of my great aunt where my sister and I were raised.

One portrait depicted an ancestor in an elaborate wig and

long dead for some one hundred fifty years, in a stance with his rapier propped before him. Aside from the wig, I was very impressed. According to my great aunt, that particular ancestor was responsible for the deaths of no less than a half dozen opponents over some matter or another.

I was fascinated and while at private school in France had undertaken lessons with Monsieur Fontaine. I was notably his first female student, something he frequently reminded me of and clearly objected to. However, he did not object to the substantial fee he received from my aunt for his instruction.

It had been some time since I had practiced the basic moves due to one thing or another, and I felt a drop of moisture slip down my back from my physical exertions as I attacked my "opponent"— said dartboard, once more.

I heard my housekeeper's greeting for someone at the front entrance, then refocused my attention, parried, cross-parried and ended the "dartboard's" life with a perfectly executed riposte.

"Here you are!" came the announcement from the entry to the parlor, agitation quite obvious as my sister, Lady Lenore Forsythe, swept into the room.

"I've sent round several messages with no response! I was afraid you might have taken yourself off on some adventure again." This with a frown and a glance at the corner of my desk where said messages lay unopened. Then a startled exclamation.

"Good heavens! What is that?" she demanded.

I glanced in the direction she was staring, hand at her throat as if the next sound might in fact be a terrified scream as she had suddenly gone quite pale.

"*That*", had raised its head at the disturbance to his morning nap. I made the introductions.

"That is Rupert."

Rupert the hound to be precise. He had returned with me that morning from my most recent visit to the office on the Strand. I had gone there and found that Brodie had still not returned from some "*matter*", he had gone off to attend to.

I had no idea what that private matter might be as Brodie had said nothing about it beforehand, nor had he indicated anything to Mr. Cavendish.

That was three weeks earlier.

"Rupert?" my sister repeated, somewhere between disbelief and horror. "It has a name?"

The sound of his name brought a groan of acknowledgement from the hound and then he settled himself once more to his nap on the rug before the fire. There was little that might move him, unless of course we were attacked or there was food involved. He was quite fond of my housekeeper's sponge cake.

"The same name as our family pet when we were children?" she added incredulously.

"I thought he resembled him," I explained. "And he does seem to recognize the name."

"He looks nothing like him, and the smell..." Linnie pressed a handkerchief to her nose as if to make her point.

"Hmmm. I suppose that he could use a bath," I admitted.

My housekeeper had been threatening to give him one, but had decided against it. It might have had something to do with the hound's size, like that of a small horse, or his attitude regarding the subject.

"Is it safe to be around him?" my sister asked.

"Perfectly safe, unless he is provoked," I replied, which seemed highly unlikely considering he was presently snoring.

"I also rang you up this morning..." Linnie replied somewhat skeptically as she walked a wide circle around him, then added in a more critical tone, "the least you might do is respond."

She was in bit of a temper as I turned and listened, rapier propped before me.

"Since you are here now..." I suggested.

I loved my sister dearly. At one time it had been just the two of us, if not for the intervention of our aunt. Linnie was talented, intelligent, and quite lovely but she did have a habit of going on about things.

"Good heavens, Mikaela. Are you perspiring?" she commented with a hint of disgust. "And must you play with that dreadful thing when I am attempting to have a conversation with you?"

Playing?

Admittedly, my sister's idea of participating in sports of any kind was similar to that of most young women of her acquaintance— croquet, walking about the gardens at Huntley Park, clipping roses in the private garden of her new residence, or attending afternoon tea with her circle of ladies.

I found it all quite boring, and it did seem the number of her so-called friends had dwindled somewhat after the scandal.

Not to say that Linnie was one of those shy, reserved types. Not at all. Her reticence in all things that might include a member of the male species, was out of self-preservation. Since her divorce and the scandal that accompanied it, she was quite determined to *not* make the acquaintance of any marriageable man. For myself, I was much of the same opinion though for other reasons.

Our collective experience with the institution of marriage— hers with a philandering husband, both of ours with our parents' unhappy marriage and then the loss of both, was not a story with a happy ending.

"This '*dreadful thing*,'" I pointed out somewhat *pointedly* regarding her criticism of the rapier in my hand, "is most effective as a weapon and has been known to end the lives of certain persons. Particularly in the hands of a rather notorious ancestor of ours."

"Yes, I'm well aware of our colorful ancestors," Linnie replied. "The apple certainly did not fall far from that tree. You might have collected butterfly specimens on your travels, or pieces of art," she continued. "But no, you pursue the most bizarre skills."

Linnie was the artist in the family, a talent pursued during our private schooling in Paris amid endless tours of the Louvre and other galleries. I could have pointed out that pursuit was quite mind-numbing, however I was not a cruel person.

18

"But no," she continued. "You prefer swords, practicing personal defense as you call it, and carry a revolver as you go about these cases you've undertaken with Mr. Brodie. And then there are your adventures as you call them. I wouldn't be at all surprised to find you with a shrunken head or severed hand that you've collected along the way."

I left severed hands to Mr. Brimley, the pharmacist who assisted Brodie and me from time to time in our inquiries. He acquired specimens for his anatomical examinations that I found to be quite fascinating.

As for her pithy comment about a shrunken head, I had already decided that might be a bit off-putting for my house-keeper, Mrs. Ryan. Particularly as I was not fond of cooking my own meals or spending hours pushing around the carpet sweeper should she decide to leave me over such a thing. However, there was the hand...

"It is because you are just like *her* that I wanted to discuss this latest episode with you..." Linnie continued.

I had no doubt who she was referring to. She suddenly stopped. "You are alone this morning?"

It was my sister's polite way of inquiring if I had a guest, Brodie perhaps.

"You were saying," I replied, responding by not responding to the obvious.

"You really must do something about Aunt Antonia," she continued, pulling off her gloves and then throwing both along with her reticule onto the desktop, a clear indication this was not to be a brief visit.

"Her safari to Africa?" I ventured, which had come up in conversation several times over the past months.

Our aunt had been planning to go off on safari for well over a year, waylaid briefly when she broke her ankle. However, the latest I was aware, everything was on for her departure quite soon, even though I had cautioned her the weather might be questionable this time of year.

She had waived off my concerns in her typical fashion and informed me that she would simply wait out the weather at the private lodge in Kenya where she would be staying.

"The safari has been cancelled," Linnie announced. "*That* is the problem."

Months earlier it had been a "*problem*" that our aunt *was* planning on going off on safari. Now, it was a problem that it had been cancelled?

"I did warn her about the weather," I replied, setting the rapier back in the stand alongside the medieval sword my aunt had given me from our family collection.

There were several such weapons at her residence at Sussex Square, acquired over the centuries after our first ancestor had arrived with William the Conqueror.

Several were mounted on the wall of the game room where I had spent hundreds of hours after we went to live with her, admiring the collections, my imagination running wild over the gleaming swords along with other weapons.

"She has called the whole thing off!" Linnie informed, quite distressed which I found most interesting since she had not wanted to accompany Aunt Antonia when the initial plans were made.

I had to admit it was not at all like our aunt. Once she decided on something that was final.

Had she decided she wasn't up to trekking across the savannah? That seemed highly unlikely. It had to be something else.

Her age perhaps? At almost eighty-six years old, it was possible that she had simply decided that she was not up to a prolonged trip abroad. Or...?

"Has she taken ill?" I asked, quite concerned now.

"You might say that!"

"I did say that," I pointed out. "What are you saying?"

Linnie paced back and forth across the parlor, abruptly encountering the immovable object named Rupert, and immediately changed course.

"I don't think you're ready for this," she announced.

"Ready for what?" I demanded, wanting very much for her to get on with it.

"It's a man!" Linnie announced.

A man. Well, that narrowed the possibilities down by half.

"She has a new acquaintance," she continued.

"She has several acquaintances," I pointed out. "It happens when one lives as long as she has."

"Not like this."

"How 'not like this?' What are you trying to tell me?" I demanded. "For heaven's sake, get on with it."

She took a deep breath. "She has asked me about... protection."

"Protection? What sort of protection?" I asked.

There were all sorts of protection— knives, a revolver, or in our aunt's case a few well-chosen words usually did the trick.

I had witnessed that on more than one occasion. She was quite good at it. It was something I aspired to.

"Good heaven's must I spell it out?" Linnie replied. "Protection, as in when a woman sleeps with a man!"

I wasn't certain what was more entertaining, my sister's flustered response— considering she had once been married and knew about such things, or the fact that our aunt might be keeping company with a man as they say.

"What did you tell her?" I asked, struggling to keep a straight face.

"I told her to ask you."

That was certainly passing things off.

I immediately thought of Mr. Munro, manager of her estates, whom our aunt was most fond of. However that seemed to have been lusting from afar or at least one-sided as Munro had been keeping company with my good friend Theodora Templeton for the past several months.

"How long as this been going on?" I asked, as I tried to imagine our great aunt having an affair.

"Apparently for some time," Linnie replied, keeping her voice low with a glance toward the doorway to make certain we weren't overheard by Mrs. Ryan.

"It's only recently that things have... progressed," she continued.

"*Progressed*", as in sharing a bed? That of course, created all sorts of images which I chose not to think about.

"Good for her," I replied, then asked, "Has she mentioned anything about her toes?"

"Good heavens, what does that have to do with anything?"

Everything, I thought, but didn't say it. Instead, I reminded her, "Your mouth is hanging open."

"Is that all you have to say about the situation?" she asked incredulously.

"I'll be certain to tell her that she has no need for protection if she should ask, as there is undoubtedly little chance at almost eighty-six years old of finding herself '*caught*' as they say," I explained. "However, she might want to be mindful of certain diseases."

"That is precisely the point," Linnie replied, quite flustered.

In spite of the early hour of the day, I offered her a dram of our aunt's very fine whisky to calm her nerves.

"She is so like you!" she continued, taking the glass I held out to her. "Or possibly it's the other way round," she said. "And I don't want to know where that bit of wisdom about diseases comes from." She quickly emptied the glass and set it on the desk.

"You haven't asked who the man is."

"I have every confidence that you will tell me." She ignored my sarcasm.

"His name is John Waverly Atherton."

"The architect?" I replied.

He had designed several notable buildings and residences about London as those in high places were obsessed with modernizing London as they called it.

"It seems that she has decided to add a wing onto the house at Sussex Square," Linnie explained.

That was something an architect might be involved with, I thought.

"And," she added. "He has been spending a great deal of time with her, presenting his design drawings as she describes it."

"That might be useful in his profession," I pointed out.

"He is fifty-six years old!" Linnie then added. "Almost thirty years younger."

"Bravo for her," I announced, if in fact there was any truth to her suspicions.

"There's more, and I blame you for this," she continued.

I could hardly wait for this.

"She has a tattoo!" my sister announced. "I can only imagine where she got the idea for that!"

"Most interesting. What does it look like?" I had two tattoos, acquired in my travels. I waited for my sister's indignation. She did not disappoint.

"Is that all you have to say?"

"*If* your suspicions are correct, then I say that it is her business and none of ours."

"Have you considered that she might have become...?"

"What?" I demanded.

"That she might be getting a bit... dotty. It has been known to happen to those of her age."

She had my full attention now. "You're talking about a woman who speaks four languages fluently, provides political advice to high-ranking officials who seek her out, and plays cards with a vengeance including recently taking several hundred pounds in wagers from you, as I recall. I would not call her dotty under any circumstances."

"Aren't you the least concerned for her with this new...? I don't know what you would call it!"

"Acquaintance? Companion? Someone who holds her interest?" I suggested. "Lover, perhaps?"

"I might have known that would be your response, considering..."

"Considering what?" I demanded.

I had a fairly good idea where she was going with this. It was not the first reference to my single status or that I might be familiar with methods of "*protection*" when sharing the company of a man.

And by the way, where the devil was that man? I frowned as my thoughts returned to the question of where Brodie had disappeared to.

"It's just that you seem to understand her very well," she replied, taking a more diplomatic approach. "As I said, you're very much alike."

"I don't see the harm in her having an acquaintance with a man," I announced. "She's an excellent judge of character, and quite capable of looking out for herself."

"Please say that you will have a talk with her," Linnie begged. "I don't want her to be taken advantage of, a woman of her position."

More likely the other way round, I thought. However, I did love my sister, even though she had become somewhat overzealous in things of late. The thought occurred to me that what she needed in her life, in spite of her protests, *was* a man.

"I will speak with her," I assured her, then added, "by the way, how is James Warren?"

I had introduced her to my editor. He was well educated, quite handsome, with a sense of humor, and had a keen sense of appreciation for art.

"What about him?" Linnie demanded, suddenly distracted from the reason she was there.

"Nothing," I replied. "He seems to be a very fine person and he mentioned something about attending a private viewing of a new art collection."

"Yes, well... Yes, he is a fine person." Linnie continued then. "I really must be going. Please do remember that you promised to speak with Aunt Antonia. She does listen to you." She headed for the front entrance.

"Your gloves?" I reminded her as she seemed to have suddenly become quite preoccupied.

"Yes, of course."

I handed them to her, and she was off, bidding good-day to Mrs. Ryan as she let herself out.

I was enormously grateful that Linnie was concerned about our aunt. However, I also knew my aunt very well. A good many of her acquaintances had passed on. If she had found someone she enjoyed keeping company with, as I said... Bravo!

I changed my clothes and ate the luncheon Mrs. Ryan had prepared. Anxious to be off, I had passed a good deal of it to the hound under the dining table.

I would speak with our aunt eventually. In the meantime I was far more concerned about Brodie.

Something wasn't right. Not that he owed me any explanations where he went or what business he conducted. However, over the past several months we had established a routine, most particularly when it had to do with a case we were working on.

I might stay over at the office on the Strand, or Brodie might find some reason to accompany me late of an evening back to the townhouse.

Whatever Mrs. Ryan might have thought about the matter, she chose not to comment, and merely went about her way.

She and Brodie got along, as she called it, in spite of the fact that he was a Scot and she was Irish.

He had assisted in finding her daughter's murderer and she was grateful, not that she wouldn't argue with him over some matter or another. Brodie participated but always with that amused expression in his eyes.

In spite of their differences, they had a great deal in common, coming from humble backgrounds. More than once I had simply left them to their bickering and taken myself off to the parlor to work on my notes or my latest novel. Brodie would then appear sometime later and announce that Mrs. Ryan had taken herself off to bed.

"She can be a handful," he had commented once. "But a good woman."

Now, that *"good woman"* announced that the cab I'd called for had arrived.

I donned my long coat and grabbed my umbrella. Rupert had roused from his nap and fell into step beside me.

"Should I hold supper, miss?" Alice asked as she accompanied me to the door. The unspoken being, should she wait supper for Brodie and me.

"I will let you know."

"And this for Mr. Cavendish," she handed me a brown paper bag that by the smell contained some of her sponge cake.

She had an uncanny way of knowing where I might be going. She said it was the Irish in her, that way of knowing something before it happened.

Who was I to argue? My good friend Templeton spoke to the spirit of William Shakespeare all the time. And, oddly enough, there were too many instances when it seemed he had responded and was correct in the information he passed along.

I tucked the bag of food into my carpetbag where it would be safe from the hound until we arrived at the Strand, and we were off.

Mr. Cavendish was in his usual place as we arrived at Number 204 on the Strand. He rolled out from the alcove at the entrance to the building. He tipped his cap.

"Afternoon, miss."

The hound jumped down from the cab, his nose pressed against the carpetbag as I asked the driver to wait.

"Is there any word?" I asked.

He shook his head. "But not to worry, miss. Mr. Brodie has been known to take himself off on some matter or another."

"Do you remember anything else he said before he left?"

Mr. Cavendish shook his head again. "As I recall, he told the driver there would be extra fare if he made good time to the Tower."

The Tower of London? And possibly the offices of the Special Services?

I handed over the food Mrs. Ryan had sent.

"Bless the woman," he said, taking the bag as the hound followed the scent of food in eager anticipation, abandoning me for a sponge cake. So much for loyalty I thought, as I returned to the cab.

Brodie had been spending a considerable amount of time at the offices of the Special Services in London Tower in between our recent investigations.

As near as I could determine, the Special Services was separate from the usual constabulary. It had far more authority, in matters of British interests that often extended into other countries when necessary, and without the usual restrictions from other parts of government.

As Brodie had explained it, that independence allowed them to operate far more expeditiously when necessary. However, Brodie never discussed precisely what *necessary* meant. It all seemed quite secret and clandestine.

Upon reaching the Tower, the driver let me off at the High Street and I walked the rest of the way to the river entrance where I had accompanied Brodie in the past.

The usual guards were at their posts and nodded in recognition. I was escorted inside those imposing stone walls and signed in at the warder's desk. Within a very few minutes Alex Sinclair arrived.

He was quite a brilliant young man whose acquaintance we had made in a previous case, responsible for developing a machine that was capable of coding outgoing messages then decoding incoming messages, although it wasn't clear where those incoming messages came from.

I had learned however that Sir Avery Stanton, now head of the Special Services, had connections in other places beyond

London. Our previous case that had taken us to France came to mind.

"Miss Forsythe!" There was a slight hesitation as Alex greeted me. "It is good to see you again."

He escorted me into the office of Sir Avery Stanton instead of his own office that contained his latest machine that he was developing, files spread across his desk, and that wall of maps.

Sir Avery rose from behind his desk, quite formal, and greeted me. We exchanged the usual pleasantries.

"How may we assist you, Miss Forsythe?"

"Mr. Brodie and I have been asked to make inquiries on behalf of a potential client. I'm aware that he has spent a considerable amount of time here. Have you had word from him?"

The expression on Sir Avery's face was one that I had seen before. It could more accurately be described as no expression at all.

"I was told that he directed his driver here some time ago. I am aware that he has been working on some matters on your behalf. However, I do need to speak with him..."

"If you will provide us the information, we will see that he receives it when he returns," he replied.

Ah, so they were aware that he had been gone for some time.

"When might that be?" I asked.

"That is unknown at present," he replied.

"Can you at least tell me where I might contact him?" I asked.

"As I said, it's a personal matter. He did not share the details with us."

"Did he say when he might be returning?"

"I'm sorry that I cannot tell you more," he continued. "Now if you will excuse me..."

That appeared to be the end of our conversation. I caught the look Alex gave me. However, I couldn't resist a parting comment.

"You've been most helpful, Sir Avery." When the door had closed behind us, I turned to Alex.

"What do you know about this? Did Mr. Brodie mention where he might be going and what it was about?"

Alex Sinclair was quite adorable with that shock of hair that constantly spilled over his forehead and glasses that gave him a very serious demeanor. I could see why my young friend, Lucy Penworth, was quite taken with him.

He motioned me to follow him into his office. He closed the door behind us.

"He did say that it was about something that had happened some time ago."

That was certainly far more than Sir Avery had been willing to share.

"He received information from one of our people in Edinburgh. Afterward, he asked me for the timetable for the express leaving London."

Three

"DID he say what it was about?"

"No," Alex replied. "However, it was right after he received that telegram."

A personal matter. A telegram Brodie received, and then he had taken himself off to Edinburgh.

I knew that he had lived there as a boy and then made his way to London after living on the streets for a time after the death of his grandmother. He and Mr. Munro had arrived in London together some time later.

In the years since, he had acquired an education of sorts and worked whatever job could be found. Along the way he had made himself into the man he was now, whom I greatly admired for his hard work and his refusal to accept the lot he'd been handed in life.

However, he never spoke of those early years before he arrived in London.

"What about the information he received?"

Alex shook his head. "It was from one of our people in Edinburgh. He's been making inquiries on Mr. Brodie's behalf some time ago."

It was obviously something that was important to Brodie, important enough that he had immediately left for Edinburgh. And, something that he chose not to discuss with me.

Not that he owed me any explanations. However, his behavior was quite unusual, and I couldn't help but think it might be something serious.

"I don't suppose he shared the contents of that telegram with you," I commented.

Alex shook his head.

"Who would have received the telegram here?" I then asked.

"That would be Edward in our communications office," he replied.

I was aware that the Special Services agency had their own telegraph communication separate from that of the Electric Telegraph Company that crisscrossed London and a good part of the rest of Britain. It had been an enormous advantage in our last investigation when we needed information.

"There would be a record of that telegram," I commented.

"Yes," Alex hesitantly replied. "However that information is confidential." He squirmed at the look I gave him.

"I cannot divulge that information, Miss Forsythe. It would be worth my position here. You must understand."

I understood perfectly. However, that had never stopped me.

"There would be a logbook, of course," I continued. "It would show the date and time the message was received, and when it was dispatched to Mr. Brodie, along with the contents. And as it was a personal matter, it wouldn't involve the agency or be your responsibility."

I then added, "A quick glance is all it would take."

He groaned. "If Sir Avery was to learn that I gave you information..."

"I certainly won't be the one to tell him," I replied.

I told him that I would wait at the High Street as he escorted me to the river entrance, so not to put him at risk of any suspicion on Sir Avery's part. I placed my hand on his arm and thanked him. He blushed profusely, dear young man.

I retraced my steps and waited at the cab station where drivers left off and picked up their fares.

Alex eventually arrived, looking quite anxious. "I had to wait until Sir Avery went into a meeting before I was able to speak with Edward at the communication office," he explained.

It seemed that Brodie had made inquiries several months earlier through the agency regarding a man by the name of Tobin in Edinburgh from thirty years earlier.

The name meant nothing to me, not that I expected it to. He had never spoken with me about his past. Then, very near a month ago, he had received word that information about the man. That was about the time of my last meeting with Brodie, just before he had taken himself off to Edinburgh.

"It seems that the man was dead, but Brodie contacted a man we work with from time to time, Sholto McQueen, to see if there might still be family in Edinburgh. That was when Brodie left."

He had used the concierge office at the Waverley Hotel to make inquiries and to receive information.

I knew Edinburgh quite well due to my aunt's property at Old Lodge. The Waverley Hotel was very near the rail station. When we traveled north we stayed at the Waverley before traveling on to Old Lodge by private coach.

"Mr. Brodie let us know when he arrived and that he would get back with us about when he would be returning," Alex added and then hesitated, his expression quite serious. "We haven't heard from him in some time."

That was not like Brodie. He was meticulous when investigating a case. His exactness for detail was one of the things I found most fascinating about him, and something we very much had in common. It was not like him at all to not communicate when he said that he would. I couldn't help feeling that something might be wrong.

I checked the time on the watch pinned to my shirtwaist. It was midafternoon, too late to catch the express train north. Any other train would take hours longer, making a half dozen stops along the way.

"What can you tell me about the man he contacted?"

"McQueen knows the city and other people we've worked with on certain matters in the past although the man is a bit of a rough sort. I know that he's given Sir Avery a bit of a go from time to time. His brother-in-law owns a tavern in the Old Town. The White Hart Tavern. Brodie was to contact him there, I believe."

I now had more information than when I started. I signaled for a cab.

"Miss Forsythe!" Alex followed me to the curb as a driver arrived and I climbed into the cab.

"What are you going to do?"

He really was quite adorable in that scholarly sort of way. I could imagine that my young friend, Lucy Penworth, was quite a fascinating challenge for him. I squeezed his hand reassuringly as I closed the gate to the cab.

"I do appreciate your assistance, and I promise not a word to Sir Avery that you shared the information." I signaled the driver.

"Wait! Miss Forsythe..." Alex called after me as I left him standing at the curb.

I argued with myself that this was Brodie's personal business, and obviously not something he wanted me to know about the entire way across London. If it was anyone else, I would have accepted it and told him to take a flying leap off the nearest bridge for all I cared.

A visit with my aunt seemed in order and it occurred to me a way to kill two birds with one stone as the saying goes, as there was one person who might be able to tell me something about the reason Brodie had taken himself off to Edinburgh in secrecy and after all these years.

Mr. Munro, my aunt's manager of her estates, was the one

person who perhaps knew Brodie better than anyone as they had lived there together as lads and then made their way to London together all those years before. And it was an opportunity to see my aunt after that conversation with my sister.

I had moved from my aunt's residence at Sussex Square a handful of years earlier as the success of my novels provided me the means to purchase the townhouse. It also provided me privacy for working on my novels, and planning my next adventure.

However, driving through those gates was like coming home. It would always be the place I called "home", for two young girls who suddenly found themselves orphaned. As for our aunt, she would always be the touchstone, an unconventional woman ahead of her time who had righted the course of our lives with love, bits of wisdom, and somewhat eccentric ideas.

"Good day, Miss Forsythe," Mr. Symons, her head butler, greeted me at the entrance.

"A pleasure as always to see you."

"Is my aunt about?"

She had long ago dispensed with formal titles. She had several and it was always cumbersome.

"*For Heaven's sake,*" I recalled her saying once. "*I can't remember them all. Why should I expect anyone else to remember, and it makes me feel like some doddering old woman who should be walking around with a fluffy dog in her arms.*"

Enough said, even though it gave some people quite a turn, particularly among her circle who impressed themselves with their titles.

"*Arrogant fools all of them,*" my aunt had commented, never one to hesitate with an opinion.

"I believe that she is supervising the removal of the jungle from the formal drawing room," Mr. Symons replied now.

Removal? That was something unexpected as she was quite fond of the "jungle", which was in fact her version of the African jungle installed several months earlier in preparation for her safari to the subcontinent so that she could become accustomed to living in the rough as she put it.

Although, in the rough, might have been a bit over the top considering her staff of servants and the lack of wild, dangerous animals. Which brought to mind...

"And the monkey?" I inquired.

"Dispatched to the London Zoo as it was going about destroying the china and causing great havoc in the kitchens, a much more suitable environment."

I had to agree, and it would have companions there.

I thought of Ziggy, my friend Templeton's five-foot iguana that had recently taken up residence there as well. At last report, he seemed to be doing quite well, although a bit lonely. I wasn't at all certain how she might have determined that.

"I hear a familiar voice," came from the formal drawing room that had been transformed with a profusion of potted palms that reached the ceiling and all sorts of jungle species acquired from the botanical gardens.

"I did wonder how long it might be after your sister's visit before you came calling. How are you, my dear?" my aunt commented, having traded her jungle attire of pants, jacket, boots, and pitch helmet for a brilliant purple dressing gown even though it was well into the afternoon.

And Linnie had suggested that our aunt might be slipping a bit mentally. I believe she had mentioned the word, "dotty." I refused to believe it, however, there was the purple dressing gown.

"She is simply concerned about you," I replied, handing over my umbrella and gloves to Mr. Symons. "And I have a perfectly good reason to call on you."

My aunt slipped her arm through mine. "I've decided to take your advice regarding the weather and put off my trip. Africa has been there for thousands of years. Certainly it can wait a while longer for my visit.

"In the meantime, I must show you something I am quite

excited about. And then you can tell me the other reason for your visit. We'll share a dram. It's near enough that time of day."

Of course, much like my aunt, I considered just about any time of day the right time.

The formal drawing room was transformed, revealing once more the portraits of ancestors on the walls, a somewhat austere group that I was grateful I was not too closely related to. The carpet had been returned and laid out on the slate floor, along with the Louis XV furnishings.

Another servant appeared with a decanter along with two glass tumblers— my aunt's version of afternoon tea.

I also noticed a crystal ashtray along with a humidor with cigars on a side table. Unless our aunt had taken up smoking, which was entirely possible, it seemed that my sister's suspicions regarding a certain gentleman spending a significant amount of time at Sussex Square might be correct.

"Linnie mentioned that you've engaged an architect for some changes you're thinking of making," I mentioned.

"John Atherton," she replied. "The man is absolutely brilliant. The work he's done about the city... Incredible! Everyone wants to engage his services."

There was a sigh in there that made me wonder precisely what "services" she was referring to.

"He completely redesigned Olivia Stanhope's country house," she continued. "And he's agreed to assist with some ideas I've had for some time to add on some rooms. He is just the person to design the addition so that it blends with the rest of the house."

I might have asked what those ideas were since there were already an abundance of bedrooms, a formal parlor, and two smaller parlors, not to mention the game room, and library? However, she was quite a ways into the whole thing and continued enthusiastically.

"A gymnasium," she announced. "You gave me the idea with your membership of the one here in London. I thought, why not? And my physician has mentioned that it would do wonders for my health and mobility for when I decide to proceed to Africa, of course."

Of course, no mention of specific sporting routines, perhaps of an intimate nature? I thought.

"John is designing it complete with a walking track as he calls it and machines recommended by Dr. Gustav Zander. There will be a vibration machine to stimulate muscles, a back strengthening machine, one for chest enlargement although I thought that might be a bit over the top."

Something for every part of the body. "And a vibration machine for one's riding position," she added. "It's all very exciting."

It was impossible not to imagine the various machines at work — and a machine for one's riding position! I was beginning to think my sister's suspicions might be correct.

"How very clever," was all I could manage at the moment.

"It will require adding onto the west wing as that is the most logical place and near my private rooms where I can change into the appropriate costume." She beamed excitedly.

Never let it be said that my aunt wasn't into her own adventures.

"I am having Madame Juliette design an entire wardrobe of athletic costumes." She leaned forward like a conspirator sharing a secret and patted my hand. "Including walking skirts very much like the ones Templeton brought back from her tour of the United States for you."

It was all so exciting! And it certainly had the color in her cheeks. Or possibly that was John Waverly Atherton's doing.

"Is he about?" I casually asked.

"Oh, no. He left hours ago. He'll return later with some new sketches."

Hours ago would be quite early in the morning. And sketches to show her. I could have sworn my aunt, considered by everyone who knew her to be unflappable, had just blushed.

"You seem pleased about the arrangement," I commented.

"Oh, yes, quite."

And that was all that mattered. As for John Waverly Atherton, I had no doubt that my sister was already using her considerable resources to determine precisely what Mr. Atherton's intentions might be, aside from designing the new addition to Sussex Square

"You may report back to your sister, that John is most capable..." Aunt Antonia added. "As I am certain that she asked you to inquire with me."

I took another long sip.

"I won't take advantage of his generous nature," she assured me. "I have every intention of compensating him for his services. Now, tell me, besides Linnie's concerns about John, what brings you to Sussex Square?"

"It's something I thought Mr. Munro might be able to assist with," I explained without going into details about Brodie's disappearance.

He knew Brodie better than anyone. He might be able to provide some insight as to the reason Brodie had chosen to return after all these years.

"I believe that he's in the cellar, something about checking the household inventory. The man is quite meticulous at keeping everything in order." She leaned forward again.

"However, I should warn you that the staff has complained that he has become quite the tyrant of late, muttering to himself, most often in Gaelic, and quite short-tempered."

I was familiar with that sort of thing. I emptied my glass, then went in search of Munro.

I found him in the wine cellar, note board in hand, pencil pointed much like a saber at a shelf filled with bottles and counting to himself.

My aunt was correct. There were several curses in Gaelic as he seemed to start over. If my translation was anywhere near accurate he had just cursed the bottles of wine and whisky, himself, and muttered something else I possibly didn't need to know the translation of.

I hesitated to interrupt. However, I did need to ask if he knew anything about Brodie's disappearance.

"Good afternoon," I greeted him.

There are several things I was reminded of as his shadow loomed up out of the larger shadows that lined the walls of the wine cellar.

He was not quite as tall as Brodie, with dark hair, but clean shaven as my aunt insisted upon for all the men in her household, and with that striking blue gaze. However, he had that same wariness, that same guarded expression, that I suppose came instinctively considering the way he and Brodie had lived before arriving in London. And then, like Brodie, it was quickly hidden as he turned and walked toward me.

However, quite different from Brodie who had acquired the somewhat more refined manner of a police inspector and then one who made private inquiries that might take him anywhere including offices of high-ranking officials, Munro looked more like a wild Highlander with his scowl and that sharp gaze.

The only thing missing might be a claymore sword at his side and a clan plaid, boots whispering across the stone floors, his shirtsleeves pushed back on muscular arms, and that icy gaze.

"Miss Forsythe," he greeted me in that broad Scot's accent not quite as thick as Brodie's. He cocked his head, that gaze sweeping the aisle between those stacks of barrels, then back to me as if he thought someone else might be lurking there. Watchful was the word that came to mind.

"What brings ye here? Is my assistance needed by her ladyship?"

Mr. Munro reserved his polite manner for my aunt and myself, but there was an edge that I knew appealed to my friend Templeton, that unpredictable if somewhat dangerous demeanor that was always just beneath the surface.

"I need to speak with you about Mr. Brodie."

"Aye?"

He was quiet, thoughts hidden in a way all too familiar in another, so that I thought he would politely inform me that he had work to do and send me on my way. Instead, he nodded and gestured to a nearby barrel that sat at the end of a row racks filled with bottles of whisky, with two chairs beside.

I knew that my aunt liked to sample the latest shipment of whisky when it arrived. I could just imagine the two of them, opposites in the extreme, seated across from each other opening random bottles, to make certain the contents were up to her standards.

He pulled a bottle from a nearby rack. "The latest of her ladyship's thirty-year stock sent from the Old Lodge." He gestured to one of those chairs, then took the other one.

I watched as he removed the cork then poured, a long scar on his arm gleaming in the light of the overhead electric. A reminder of the life he had lived on the streets and other places before his position in my aunt's household?

The cork removed, he closed his eyes briefly and inhaled the scent that escaped the bottle.

"The angel's share," I commented.

"Ye know of it?" He poured two tumblers and handed one to me. "He did say that ye have an appreciation for it."

I took a sip. It was rather wonderful.

"Mr. Brodie has been gone for some time," I began. "To Edinburgh." I caught the flicker of a reaction. However he said nothing.

"I was told by Sir Avery at the agency that it is a personal matter."

"Aye." He took another sip and nodded, which might mean anything or nothing at all.

Our conversation was very much like expecting a comment from the hound— almost impossible. I tried again.

"It's not like him to take himself off without a word to anyone and for quite some time now. The Agency has not heard from him. I was hoping that you might know something about it. "

"What did he tell ye before he left?" he replied.

I explained our last conversation, how very odd it had seemed, particularly with the prospect of a new case.

"He told me to handle the inquiry myself. That is also very much not like him. I thought that you might be able to tell me something about the business that has demanded his attention."

He frowned and tossed back the last of the whisky in his glass, and seemed to be considering what to tell me.

"There are things, that a man carries inside him that only he can do." He shook his head. "If he's gone back now, it's the matter of a promise he made, a vow if ye will, a long time ago when he was a lad."

"What sort of vow?"

That sharp blue gaze met mine as he obviously considered how much to tell me.

"How much has he told ye about the time before we came to London?"

"I know that he lived with his grandmother before she died."

"Aye, and his mother? What do ye know about her?"

I didn't know anything more than what I had just told him. Brodie had always been somewhat vague about it. I shook my head.

"I thought perhaps not," he replied when I said nothing. "He only spoke of it once when we were lads after he took to the streets. His mother was murdered. He returned one night where they lived and found her dyin' in her own blood.

"It's one thing never to know who yer parents were. It's another to have a mother and then have her taken away from ye. That was the vow he made, to find the one responsible for her death. Some would say it was simply a child's reaction. But not fer him.

"As I said, miss, there are things a man carries deep inside him.

41

He's waited a long time to make good on that vow, and ye need to leave it be."

"I was told that a man by the name of Sholto McQueen is assisting him."

"McQueen!" he spat out.

If ever a word, or name in this case, expressed a comment, the name of Sholto McQueen most certainly had. Mr. Munro obviously didn't like the man.

"You know of him?"

He nodded. "He has a certain reputation about Edinburgh. He works both sides of the street, if ye get my meanin'."

I had heard that comment before about someone from Brodie.

"You've had past dealings with him?"

"In a manner of speaking. It involved a shipment from her ladyship's estate at Old Lodge that went missing when it was delivered to Edinburgh. I was able to find the shipment and the man responsible for attempting to sell it at a profit for himself."

"McQueen?" I ventured.

He nodded. "He insisted that he had paid good money for the shipment, that it was the driver who offered him those dozen cases. He threatened to call in the authorities in the matter."

Both sides of the street— both law-abiding citizen and criminal.

"The driver has worked for her ladyship for over twenty years at Old Lodge. He's as honest as the day is long," he went on to explain. "So, Mr. McQueen and I had a conversation about the matter when I finally found him. I was able to convince him that he didna want to involve the police."

"I can imagine how you did that."

He smiled. "There are some ways that are more efficient than others."

"You don't trust him."

He didn't reply the obvious. Still the Agency used him for acquiring information.

He nodded. "Aye, until someone offers him more coin. Brodie knows the sort well enough." That sharp blue gaze narrowed. "He's more than capable of taking care of himself. Ye need to leave it be, miss. Leave this to him."

I thanked Munro for the information, far more than I had ever guessed. Brodie had most certainly kept his secrets.

~

I looked up as my housekeeper made a sound for the second time. She stood beside the breakfast table with a disapproving expression.

"Yes?" I asked, since it was obvious she was not going away, but very much had something to say.

She frowned with a glance directed at the breakfast she had prepared, still untouched on my plate.

"Is the food not to yer liking?" she inquired.

"It's perfectly fine," I assured her.

"That is most surprising how you would know that it's *fine*, when you haven't touched it," she pointed out.

Never let it be said that Mrs. Ryan was shy about speaking her mind. She peered at my current work in progress— my notes about my meeting with Alex and Mr. Munro.

"I've seen it before when you are in the middle of one of your books, or one of those inquiry cases with Mr. Brodie. And you're wearing your adventuring clothes," she added. "My friend, Mrs. Hudson, has spoken of it as well when her employer is off and about."

It seemed that Mrs. Hudson's employer, a somewhat eccentric though brilliant fellow in the same profession, had a penchant for odd habits, even disappearing from time to time, then returning after some foray into the criminal world.

I had found the train schedule the night before from the last trip I'd made north with my aunt. Along with a quick check of the daily that lay on my desk, I was able to confirm that the northern express departed King's Cross station at ten o'clock of a morning, arriving at Waverley Station in Edinburgh approximately six o'clock the same evening.

The Waverley hotel, where the agency's man had sent Brodie that telegram, was only a short distance from the station.

I went into the front parlor, checked the carpetbag beside my desk that held clothing items I might need, and the revolver Brodie had given me. I slipped the notebook inside as well.

"King's Cross station?" Mrs. Ryan remarked with more than a little surprise. "The north country this time o' the year? The weather can be dreadful."

I looked up at the sound of the bell at the door that announced that the driver I had called for had arrived.

"I will be gone for a few days." I had no idea how long I might be gone, but didn't say it.

She followed me to the door as I pulled on my long coat and seized my umbrella, a necessity if ever there was one for traveling this time of the year.

"What should I tell her ladyship or Miss Lenore if they should inquire where you've gone?" she asked.

"I have left notes for both my aunt and my sister on the desk. You will need to contact the messenger service to have them delivered. And there is more than enough coin for market and the coalman's next delivery." I then stepped out into the morning drizzle, Mrs. Ryan frowning as she stared after me.

I arrived in good time at King's Cross station. I paid my fare for the express to Edinburgh, then found the platform for my train. A porter directed me to my compartment as other passengers boarded other cars, steam billowing out into the frosty morning air.

The compartment was the usual sort with an inside door that opened onto a narrow passageway that led to other parts of the train, and an outside door with a drop window. The long-cushioned seat could easily have accommodated two additional passengers, with room for three more at the opposite side.

However it seemed that I might have the compartment to myself.

I had just removed my coat when there was the shrill sound of the train whistle— the last call for any remaining passengers to immediately board as we were about to depart.

I had taken my notebook and pen from the carpetbag and just settled myself for the long train ride ahead when the outside door was suddenly pulled open.

A man dressed all in black— black wool coat over a black wool turtleneck jumper, pants, and boots— with a frosty blue gaze slammed the door.

"Mr. Munro?" I commented, quite surprised. But on second thought I supposed that I shouldn't have been.

"Miss Forsythe," he acknowledged, however said nothing more.

I might have inquired if he had perhaps lost his way? Taken the wrong train to visit old friends? The usual sort of congenial patter between travel companions.

However, it was obvious that it was neither. It was also obvious precisely the reason he was there after our conversation the previous afternoon.

"You completed your inventory at Sussex Square," I commented.

"Aye." A man of few words.

He then settled himself on the upholstered bench seat opposite, folded his arms across his chest, closed his eyes, and promptly went to sleep.

So much for conversation. Or any objections on my part.

I made an entry in my notebook.

It seems that Mr. Munro has decided to join me. I can only speculate that he considers the situation most serious. Murder he has told me, and that B has vowed to kill the man responsible for his mother's death.

. . .

I had just finished making the note and settled myself for the long train ride north when the inside door to the compartment was opened by the porter. An elderly man and woman stood in the passageway with him.

"You will find this more comfortable," he was telling them. "And there is more than enough room." He stood aside as the couple entered the compartment.

"Good morning." The woman smiled and greeted me, then glanced questioningly at my companion who had roused at the sound of the door being opened.

I had to admit that Munro appeared a bit intimidating with the frown on his face and the look he gave the couple.

"I'm Mrs. Cogdill and this is my husband, the Reverend Cogdill," the woman said hesitantly.

I exchanged a greeting, then glanced over at Munro. He nodded, his expression— one that I had seen on more than one occasion with the usual results. A bit intimidating, and no doubt meant to prevent conversation.

Mrs. Cogdill sat beside me while the Reverend sat on the long seat across at the far end from Munro.

"How far are you traveling today?" Mrs. Cogdill asked attempting to strike up a conversation.

"Edinburgh," I replied.

"We're returning to just beyond," she continued. "After visiting our daughter and her family," she added congenially, then glanced at the notebook on my lap.

"You're keeping a journal? That is most fascinating."

"In a matter of speaking," I replied and closed the notebook to prevent potential shock should she catch a glance at the latest entries I'd made that included the word *murder*. It might be a bit off-putting.

"It's so very nice to see a handsome, young couple traveling about," she continued.

"Oh, we're not married," I replied. "We're merely traveling together."

I caught the shocked expression Mrs. Cogdill's face.

"I see," she said, color creeping into her cheeks, then, "oh, my."

I could have sworn there was a flash of amusement in that sharp blue gaze that stared at me from across the compartment.

And that ended any further conversation.

Four

THE DIRECT LINE from London to Edinburgh passed through the English countryside, including York and Durham, and then along the Northumberland and Scottish coasts.

The brief appearance of the sun that afternoon disappeared altogether the farther north we traveled, the weather typical for Scotland this time of year— heavy rain, with thick clouds pressing down.

It was well into the evening when our train pulled into Waverley Station with its web of a dozen or more rail tracks, lights gleaming through the rain along the expanse of the enormous bridge across that confluence with Princes Street in what was now called the New Town in one direction and the Old Town in the opposite direction.

The first order was to find Brodie.

As we parted, Mrs. Cogdill leaned in and whispered. "If you should need to speak with someone while in Edinburgh, the Reverend and I will be staying for a few days before proceeding on."

No doubt to confess my sins, traveling with a man I was not married to. I thanked her.

"Miss Forsythe."

Munro appeared at my side. He nodded to Mrs. Cogdill, then took my arm.

"He did warn me about ye," he commented, the fierce downpour sending passengers scattering to seek shelter and effectively ending any further conversation.

I deployed my umbrella for the short walk into the main station, and from there we headed for the carriage park.

The Waverley Hotel was only a short distance away, however that distance was not for the faint of heart nor those without a stout pair of boots. Or a boat, as it appeared that it had rained for a good part of the day and the streets were awash.

The hotel was an eight-story building on Princes Street. The telegrams Brodie had sent and then received from the Agency were from the concierge office. I had hoped that we might find him there, but that hope was quickly dashed as I was informed at the front desk counter there was no one by that name registered at the hotel.

I was then asked if I needed accommodation.

"Two rooms," I informed the desk attendant, since I had no idea how long it might take to find Brodie. I signed the ledger and handed one of the keys to Munro since it seemed that he was there for the time being.

I couldn't very well expect him to stay on the street, although from the stories I'd heard about their time there, I suspected that he undoubtedly knew of places where he might stay.

"Ye have that look," he commented with a suspicious expression. "What are ye thinking, Miss Forsythe?"

I now had someone with me familiar with all parts of Edinburgh, including the area known as Old Town.

"Are you familiar with the White Hart Tavern?"

"Aye," he replied. "I know of it."

"I've been told that it's owned by Mr. McQueen's brother-in-law. It seems that Brodie has met with him there. He might be able to tell us where Brodie is."

"This is Brodie's business," he reminded me. "And none of

yer own. He would not want ye interferin'," the conversation interrupted by our companions on the train. That brotherhood between two men who had fled the streets of Edinburgh.

"Nevertheless," I replied.

He made a sound I was quite familiar with, and I wondered if all Scots came with that, a sound of disapproval worth several words— no further explanation necessary.

I headed for the lift.

"Miss Forsythe..." He caught up with me at the lift.

I entered the cab. "Yes?"

"What do ye intend to do?"

"I intend to put on dry clothes, then go to the White Hart Tavern."

It was just before nine o'clock at night when I returned to the hotel lobby in a dry walking skirt, stout boots, and my long coat, umbrella in hand. I was not surprised to find Munro waiting at the concierge desk.

"I suppose it would do no good to tie ye up, to prevent this foolishness," he muttered.

"Someone a few years ago said that I should always carry a knife for personal protection," I reminded him. "Or in the event of being tied up."

He shook his head. "Even so, ye'll not go alone."

The White Hart Tavern was at Grassmarket at the end of Princes Street in the old part of Edinburgh that had once been a stockyard where farmers brought cattle and horses for sale along with corn and other crops to market. It had also once been the location for public executions. Have a pint or two, I thought, then a hanging!

It was the perfect location for a tavern with a sordid reputation. Although, according to what I had learned years before, there hadn't been a hanging there for over a century.

The ride into the old part of Edinburgh didn't take long as the driver expertly navigated past the hotel, a bank, the exchange, City Hall, and various business establishments into the older part of

Edinburgh where streetlamps were fewer, and the roads plunged into misty darkness.

Much like the East End of London the shapes of tenement buildings, old rooming houses, and shops closed for the day loomed up out of the darkness. A mixture of taverns with three-story darkened buildings, and vending stalls lined the road. Stone arches lead into back alleys and the occasional four-legged shape that much reminded me of Rupert the hound skittered out of the path of the cab.

Then there was the usual business encounter on a street corner, negotiations quickly made, a reminder of the desperate plight of women who lived here with that looming hulk of the castle on the hill behind us.

This was where Brodie had lived as a child, experienced that horrible loss, and had now returned.

Our driver pulled to a stop. "The White Hart Tavern," he called down from atop the cab.

Munro stepped down and held out a hand to me. He looked across the walkway to the entrance of the tavern.

I had paid the driver, and asked him to wait. This would likely be a very brief stop to inquire if Sholto McQueen was about and if he knew where we might find Brodie.

I had been in such places before in inquiries with Brodie. The Old Bell and the George Inn came to mind. The scene was much the same— patrons at the bar, others at tables where a game of dice was underway with the sound of a cup being slammed down to a chorus of groans and hoots of laugher amid a call for more ale.

"What does Mr. McQueen look like?" I asked.

Before I could stop Munro or ask how he intended to handle this, he pushed past me and made his way to the bar.

"Stay here."

With a look at the patrons inside the tavern, a rough sort that I knew would put me at a disadvantage, I was inclined to agree.

The man behind the bar shook his head. Munro slammed a

hand down. When he removed it, a coin lay on the bar. More conversation followed on Munro's part and the man behind the bar— McQueen's brother-in-law according to what Alex had told me— seemed to be somewhat more cooperative.

"Yer a bonnie one, aye."

I turned to the hand on my shoulder, a leering grin on the face of the man who stood there.

"What might brings ye here? Some coin to help pay the rent? Yer a bit up-class from the usual kind. Bert keeps a room," he added. "What say you and me go upstairs."

I glanced to the bar where Munro was still in conversation with a man who had to be Bert.

"I'm with someone," I explained.

"Aye, and now yer with me," the man replied.

Not the first time, I had found myself in such a situation.

"Come along." He grinned. "Ye might like it."

Not bloody likely, I thought, as I stomped down on his foot with the heel of my boot as hard as I could then took advantage of his surprise and brought the knife up and thrust it at his throat.

"Is that the way of it?" he asked. "Ye like it rough, do ye?"

There had been a great deal of discussion about the use of the knife when Munro first gave it to me. Most usually the sight of it was enough to deter someone. I pressed the tip of the blade more firmly.

One look at the man standing before me, the stench of him almost overpowering not to mention his obvious drunkenness, it was clear that he was not the least put off. In fact, he roared with laughter.

In spite of his drunkenness he was surprisingly quick as he brought one arm up and pushed me back against the wall then slapped the knife from my hand with the other.

I pulled back my arm back and drove the heel of my hand into the man's nose. There was a crunching sound as the shock of the blow shot through my arm.

However, that brief shock was nothing compared to the

expression on the man's face as he staggered back, eyes watering as he let out a bellow of pain and cursed as blood spurted across his face. He came at me again and made a grab with a bloodied hand.

Not bloody likely! I thought, as I swept his feet from under him, no mean task given his size, and dropped him to the floor.

I caught a brief glimpse of Munro as he looked up and started back across the tavern toward me. As I attempted to move out of the way another man was thrown against me and what could only be described as a brawl broke out.

The table where the game of dice had been in progress was upended, one of the players thrown backward in his chair as dice and coins scattered on the floor. Another player dropped to pick up the coins only to be seized by the scruff of the neck and landed with a solid blow.

Munro was somewhere, caught up in the melee as the chaos swarmed toward me and then pushed me out onto the walkway.

The shrill sound of a constable's whistle was distant in the night air, then came much closer as a fist closed around the front of my coat amid a string of curses. I brought my fist up once more only to have a hand wrap around my arm.

"What the bloody devil?"

It wasn't so much the curse— it wasn't as if I hadn't heard it before. It was the sound of it, that growl that wrapped around the Scot's accent. It was the familiarity of it, both a warning and surprise as the constable's whistle sounded again, very near now.

It appeared that I had found Brodie. And to say that he was not pleased to see me was a bit of an understatement. There was another curse, in Gaelic this time, then he demanded, "What are ye doin' here?"

There were several things that came to mind. At the top of the list was telling him that I was trying to help his arrogant ass. However, now was possibly not the time to go into all of that.

"Munro!" was all I managed to get out as constables swarmed into the street.

"What are ye blathering about?" Brodie demanded.

"Mr. Munro is here! We cannot leave him!"

By the expression on Brodie's face upon hearing that Munro was there as well, along with more curses and something else rather colorful by the sound of it, I thought that he might leave us both to our fates.

He dragged me toward the recessed alcove at the entrance of the darkened building next to the tavern.

"If it's at all possible for you to do as I say just once, which I doubt, stay here! Unless ye want to spend the rest of the night in the gaol!"

Not of a mind to do so, I rubbed my bruised fist as there was another sound from more than one police whistle.

The driver who had brought us was long gone when Brodie emerged with Munro who was somewhat disheveled with a bruise on one cheek. However, his cap was still in place and in spite of the color that was already appearing on one cheek, he grinned from ear to ear.

"Just like the old days, aye!"

∾

Brodie was furious to say the least while I was quite soaked through as we had escaped an encounter with the police afoot with no opportunity to deploy my umbrella. We made a mad dash through the streets of Old Town as if the devil was in pursuit.

Or perhaps the devil was in my hotel room in the form of an irate Scot, I thought, a bit soggy as well but not the least bothered by it.

I removed my coat and hung it on the tree stand by the door, then crossed the hotel room and turned up the gas at the fireplace.

I glanced over at Brodie, silent as a gathering storm. Then the storm broke.

"What the bloody hell were you thinkin'?" he demanded. "After I told ye that I didn't want ye here!"

As heat slowly filled the room, I pulled the pins from my wet hair to let it dry.

I knew from past experience that it was best to let the "storm" have its way. I wouldn't have been able to get a word in as it was.

"Bloody hell, woman! What would have happened if ye had been taken in by the police? And did ye have a thought about Munro? It would not have gone well for either of ye!"

As it was, it seemed that Munro had handled himself quite well, and had even enjoyed the encounter. He was presently in his room across the hall no doubt tending to his bruised cheek.

The "storm" seemed to have worn itself down a bit. But that was the danger with storms, one never knew when they might erupt again.

"It was not my intention that Munro accompany me," I explained. "He decided that on his own, and it isn't as if I could have persuaded him otherwise, which I am certain you can appreciate."

There was a look about Brodie that was different; the workman's pants, boots, and jacket, the jumper buttoned high at the neck. But there was more, the faint lines at his mouth more pronounced, the expression in that dark gaze even darker.

"Ye will go back to London in the morning."

I wanted to smooth those lines, to touch his face, to feel the softness of his beard, but now was not the time. There was too much anger, and the reason he was here. Something still unfinished.

"Alex was able to find information about Mr. Tobin," I replied, for two reasons. One, to distract him. And the second, because he had had been looking for the man, and it was somehow connected to what Munro had shared with me.

"It seems that he's been dead for quite some time," I paused. "Very near as long as..." I didn't say the rest of it.

He looked at me sharply. "What else did Alex tell ye?"

"He told me that it was personal, that you were looking for someone." I hesitated.

"And ye came here to tell me about Tobin."

"I thought you should know, and since no one had heard from you or knew how to reach you other than the telegrams which you had not answered..."

"Aye." He looked at me then. He shook his head.

"Dead these many years," he repeated.

The room was quiet then except for the hiss of the fire. His disappointment was obvious. Then he seemed to push it back.

"Aye," he said again, as if he'd made a decision. But not the one I hoped for.

"It's not that I'm not grateful, but I don't want ye here. Where this will take me now, ye canna be part of."

I stared at him. What I'd told him hadn't changed a thing! And with that look about him— the disappointment, the anger, anyone else might have taken fair warning.

He turned to leave. "I'll speak with Munro. He's to take ye back in the morning." The door slammed behind him.

That went well, I thought more than a little sarcastic. And that whole rant about what I could and could not do?

It was past midnight as I finished undressing, hung the rest of my clothes to dry, then crawled under the covers of the bed.

I had never developed the skill for following orders, something that some people no doubt considered a serious flaw in my character.

But there you are, I thought. Whether he wanted it or not, I was already part of it.

It was early when I rose the next morning and departed the hotel before there was the opportunity for any encounter with either Brodie or Munro.

There was a coffeehouse just down the way from the hotel that also served breakfast. I sat at a corner table where I could see guests as they arrived as I had no intention of causing a scene for the proprietor.

I ordered coffee black, a great deal of it, along with shortbread biscuits and strawberry jam while I made my notes from what I'd learned the night before and made a plan.

From Munro, I knew the approximate date Brodie's mother, Màili, was killed and the location, a place called Bleekhouse Close at Canongate.

Even that long ago, I was convinced there had to be some record of it and that record might provide information.

From copies of the Scotsman newspaper that I'd had read on previous occasions, I knew there was a crime page just as there was in the Times of London. With any luck, they had a film archive of past issues. It was a place to start.

The newspaper offices occupied an impressive four-story building made of red sandstone block in the baronial style on Cockburn Street just off the Royal Mile. The clerk on the ground floor directed me to the third floor.

When I inquired about a photographic archive at the third-floor desk, the man smiled. "They're making progress on that," he said enthusiastically. "The most recent issues archived are now back to 1872, and presently working on archives for older ones."

Wonderful, I sarcastically thought, and prepared myself for a long day of searching through old editions of the newspaper near the time Brodie's mother was killed.

I submitted a request ticket for copies of the daily beginning December 1, 1860, as I thought that might be the best place to start from the information Munro had provided and that Brodie had given Alex.

The clerk eventually returned with a thick bound leather volume stamped with the dates December 1 through 15, 1860.

Experienced in researching information for my novels and then the inquiries Brodie and I had made in the past, I sat down at the table with my notebook and pen, and opened the first issue. It was going to be a very long day.

It was late afternoon when I stood, stretched from sitting for hours and massaged my brow where a headache had begun. And only two more archives to go, I thought.

I returned to my chair and opened the next volume beginning with the date December 19, 1860. I scanned through the issue, found the crime page for that date, with the same result as each one before— nothing that contained any details that matched what Munro had shared with me.

He had mentioned that it was just before Christmas holiday when Brodie returned to the room he shared with his mother and found her dying. I was rapidly running out of dates.

The incident, when I found it, referred to Number 28 Canongate, attended by two officers of the police. Reading through past the first line, I saw the address, Bleekhouse Close!

I reread it more slowly. It had initially been reported as a crime of prostitution, then it had been changed to murder.

The victim, a young woman, whose name was not listed— *A single woman, age approximately twenty-five years, was discovered to have been badly beaten, deceased, and then transported to the death house at Greyfriar's kirkyard.*

An additional notation mentioned: *"child, approximate age ten years, not present at the time"*, along with the names of the two constables who had arrived that night and made the report— *Constables A. Meeks and M. Graham!*

It was then the clerk reminded me that it was near the end of day and closing hours. I returned the archive to the desk then left the Scotsman newspaper building. There was one more place I wanted to see.

The streets were darkened, the days shorter this time of the year with misty rain ever present as I waved down a driver and gave him the address.

"Number 28 Canongate? That's at the bottom o' the Royal Mile," the driver cautioned. "Not a place most people ask to go this time of the day, if ye get me meanin', miss. Most of them buildings are set to be torn down."

"Nevertheless, if you please."

The ride through the Old Town reminded me of the East End of London with buildings that were three to four hundred years old, and streetlights fewer and far between the farther we went.

There was an occasional carter with bundles of rags or hog heads of ale making one last stop at a tavern for the night before returning to a warehouse somewhere. And amid those buildings built of sandstone on streets that wound away from the Royal Mile, a young boy had been orphaned thirty years ago.

I had no idea what I might find if Bleekhouse Close was still there as we passed other buildings that had been marked for removal. Signs were posted at windows and doors much the same as the City of London with their improvement projects. The driver turned down another street where most of the buildings were still standing.

The letters were etched into the carved entrance of the alley that led from the street at Number 28— Bleekhouse Close. A fitting name, I thought, as I stepped down from the hackney. A sign posted in front indicated that this building too was to be torn down.

"Are ye certain, miss?" the driver inquired.

I nodded in spite of the darkened, empty building that loomed up out of the darkness with a single pale light shining at the end of the passage that led from the street. I nodded and asked him to wait.

The building at Bleekhouse Close was three stories with crumbling stonework and rows of darkened windows. Some were broken out, except for one on the ground floor.

In spite of that sign the street that the building was scheduled for demolition, it appeared that someone was living in that ground floor room.

I hesitated. I had lost the knife I carried, in the brawl that had broken out the night before at the White Hart Tavern. However, I did have the revolver that Brodie had given me, a useful precaution since I did not know who might answer the door to the room.

I climbed the stone steps to the front landing where that light shone from the first-floor window, knocked at the door, and waited. I was about to knock again when the door slowly opened far enough to reveal a face.

There was a thorough inspection from my head to foot by the person who couldn't have reached to my shoulder, eyes sharp in the woman's wrinkled face.

"What do yer want?" she snapped.

In the past when making inquiries, I had found that it was best to keep an explanation simple, one that wouldn't bring more questions.

"I'm a writer and I wanted to see if it might be possible to see inside before these buildings are torn down." True, as far as it went. "And I'd be willing to pay."

There was that thorough inspection again. The door promptly slammed in my face. I then heard what sounded like a piece of furniture scraping across the floor, and the door opened once more.

"Ye don' look as if yer with the police."

"I assure that I'm not." Another thorough inspection followed. "A friend mentioned apartment Number 12," I added. "Someone he knows use to live here."

Again, not precisely the truth. She made a sound that might have meant anything.

"Ye say there's coin in it?"

I nodded. She didn't retreat behind that door again, but opened it a bit farther.

"How long have you lived here?" I asked, curious to find someone there at all. There was that narrow-eyed look again.

"A while. Better than livin' on the street when the weather sets, and not as if anyone comes around to collect the rent."

She indicated the stairs. "Number 12 would be the next floor up and at the back. And ye'll need this." She handed me a lantern she had brought with her from her flat.

"Mind the stairs though. They're a bit dodgy in places."

I thanked her for the use of the lantern. The door slammed once more as I turned toward the stairs.

More than a bit *dodgy*, I thought, as the stairs creaked and groaned underfoot. I kept my steps to the inside wall that seemed to be more stable.

Numbers were carved into the door frames of the empty rooms. I easily found Number 12.

I had no idea what I hoped to find by coming there. After all it had been almost thirty years since that horrible night that had orphaned a young boy after his mother was brutally murdered.

Perhaps some understanding of it, I thought as I placed my hand on the knob, and of what Brodie had set out to do now. The damp had had its way, the door sticking at first then giving way. Whatever I had imagined was quite different from what I found as objects came into view in the beam from the lantern.

The first thing that occurred to me was that it looked as if someone might return at any time with the wood table and chairs that were still there. There was also a washstand, the basin long gone, with papers and food tins strewn across the floor where rats, common in abandoned places, had scavenged.

A sudden movement drew my attention as one of those inhabitants fled the intrusion of the light from the lantern, pausing briefly to glare back at me with beady eyes, before disappearing through a crack in the wall.

My throat tightened as I swept the light across the room, then the floor, as I recalled the brief description from the crime page of the newspaper— *"Woman found beaten, deceased, blood on the floor; a child according to the woman at flat Number One."*

Details and facts that made no mention of the sadness and grief for the young boy who had returned to find his dying mother.

I held the lantern aloft, the light pooling on the floor, as if I might find something there. But after all this time there was no sign of bloodstains, only those bits of paper and rubbish left by the last person who had lived there.

I tried to imagine what that was like for Brodie, returning to find her there, just as I had found my father, though the circumstances were different— the horror, the blood, the attempt to understand something for which there was no understanding. Then, the pain of that loss, and the anger that followed.

I thought then of the saying that time healed all wounds. I had heard it often enough, words for those left behind in an effort to make them feel better with the expectation that the pain of a horrible experience would eventually fade away.

I knew different. It was always there, hiding for a while, making you almost feel as if it was finally over, gone, then creeping out when you least expected it.

I turned at the sudden creak from the floorboards behind me.

Even before he stepped from the shadows at the doorway, I recognized the tall, lean frame, that dark gaze that caught the light from the lantern, the lines at his face that seemed deeper.

And the pain, like a wound that had been reopened.

Five

"HOW DID you know I would be here?"

"Munro guessed as much when ye didn't return to the hotel." He shook his head.

That dark gaze swept the room in the meager light from the lantern, and I wondered what he was seeing now? The way it was that night when he returned and found his mother dying?

"Ye couldna leave well enough alone," he said, that gaze fastened on me once more. "After I told ye that ye had no part in this."

I had never been the shy sort, easily intimidated, put in my place. Certainly not by a man... Not even this man.

I felt my own anger rising. "You may think what you like," I continued. "But I don't deserve that. I have proven myself most competent in the past." When he would have made a comment, I refused to let him speak.

"You assisted me once at a very difficult time. I wanted to help you now. You might be interested to know the names of the constables who were here that night."

I took the lantern then and left him standing in that darkened room with the smell of rubbish, the animals that now lived there, and the past.

I returned the lantern to the woman at that ground floor flat and paid her for the use of it, then climbed into the hack. For a half second I thought about leaving him there.

He eventually appeared and climbed in beside me. It was a long, silent ride to the hotel. I paid the driver and Brodie immediately went to the front desk to inquire if messages had been received for him.

"Miss Forsythe."

It was Munro. He had obviously been waiting for our return.

"Yer all right?"

"Yes, quite all right."

He looked past me to Brodie. "When it became late, it was necessary to tell him where he might find ye."

I nodded. It served no purpose to be angry with him. One angry Scot was more than enough for one day. I told him where I had gone before that.

"It took most of the day, but I learned the names of the constables who were there that night."

He nodded. "That could be important. And then ye went to Canongate."

"I needed to see it."

"Aye, but that place, the dreadful memories. In all the years, I've known him, I've never seen that look about him before, when he realized that ye might have gone there. Ye need to understand."

I understood that I was tired, hungry, and cold from the weather that had set in, not to mention that long silent ride back to the hotel. And whether Brodie liked it or not, I was not going back to London.

I turned toward the restaurant where I eventually caught the attention of the head waiter and inquired as to the fare for evening supper. I made my selection then gave him my room number as my aunt had on previous occasions. I also inquired about the hotel's selection of alcoholic drinks and was informed that they did indeed have my aunt's very fine whisky on hand in the men's smoking room.

"Served in yer room, miss?" he inquired with more than a little surprise when I made the request. "We don't usually..."

"My aunt, Lady Antonia Montgomery, frequently stays at the hotel before traveling north to her estate at Old Lodge, and she often makes the request."

"Oh, of course, miss," he stammered and assured me that both my supper and a bottle of whisky would be sent up to my room as soon as possible.

With that, not wishing for another encounter with Brodie at the moment— it could be dangerous for both of us as I was quite ravenous— I thanked him and headed for the lift.

I passed a couple who had apparently just arrived at the hotel.

"Beastly night out," the man commented to the attendant at the entrance as he shook off his umbrella.

Beastly. Now there was a word, I thought, that described several things.

The bottle of whisky arrived promptly, along with Brodie.

As I said, beastly. However, the "beast" seemed to have calmed himself somewhat, possibly for the sake of the young waiter who delivered my supper and that bottle of Old Lodge, named for my aunt's residence in Scotland, along with two tumblers.

I thanked the young man and provided him with several coins' compensation. He glanced from Brodie to me, then quickly excused himself and left. I had the same thought, however this was *my* room.

I opened the bottle and poured a dram.

"Yer angry," the "*beast*" commented.

That was an understatement, and when angry possibly not the best time to be indulging in the drink. However...

I emptied my glass and poured another.

"You're very observant," I complimented him and took a healthy swallow. "You may help yourself," I announced, then took my glass and the carpetbag into the adjoining bedroom, to indulge myself in the clawfoot tub, and slammed the door.

I fully expected him to have taken himself off to wherever he had been staying when I eventually emerged, somewhat less angry now that I'd had a warm bath not to mention a dram of whisky.

He was still there.

He had turned up the gas at the fireplace and the room had begun to lose the chill. I ignored the fact that I was dressed only in my nightshift— he had seen me in far less— and descended to the table.

There was more than enough food for the both of us, but I was not of a mind to extend an invitation and ignored him as much as possible as I sat at the small table and proceeded to eat my supper.

He poured himself a dram, then crossed the room and poured me a glass as well. Then, he returned to the fireplace once more. Wise choice, I thought, refusing to look at him.

"Ye don't understand," he repeated in a tone quite different now.

Before he could launch into another lecture or excuse to put me in my place—

no doubt preferably on a train back to London— I calmly laid down my fork.

"How dare you say that I don't understand," I replied. I emptied my glass, poured another dram, and pushed back the plate, quite fortified now. I stood, ready to do battle if it came to that.

"I was very near the same age when I found my father in the stables where we lived with the back of his head blown off from the dueling pistol he'd used to take his own life."

I had never spoken of it before, however, considering his acquaintance with my aunt it was very possible he knew of the sad, pathetic tale of my father's death.

"I realize that it's not the same, but I do remember that feeling of loss, the anger, and the need for answers."

When he would have spoken, I held up my hand for him to let me continue.

"There never were any, of course. There wasn't any way to

change what had happened, no one to blame. There was only the anger. It's still there. I suppose it always will be.

"As I said," I continued, "not precisely the same, but do not tell me that I don't understand what it is to lose someone! And don't you dare say that I cannot help."

"Are ye finished now?"

There was more, but I didn't say it. I didn't remind him that I had more than proven myself when it came to our past inquiries, some of them quite dangerous. And then there was that other part of our relationship...

If he lectured me once more, I was prepared to have him removed, or take his head off with a well-aimed bottle.

"That isna what I meant, when I said that I didna want ye here," he said, his expression softening in that way I was familiar with and that always had an effect on me. Or... it might have been the whisky.

"I know very well about yer father." He crossed the room then and set his empty glass on the table. He reached out and touched my cheek.

"I know that must have been verra hard for you, and no doubt accounts for some of yer reckless ways."

When I would have argued with him, he pressed his finger against my lips.

"Yer fine and brave, the most remarkable woman I've ever known. And ye have proven yerself more than once." He laid his hand against my cheek.

"When I said that ye didna understand... what I meant is that I didna want ye to be part of this, and what I have to do."

I was prepared for him to argue, perhaps even shout at me. I was quite used to that when that Scot's temper got the better of him. But this...?

He closed his eyes and lowered his forehead against mine. "Ye make me want things, Mikaela Forsythe. Things a man like me can never have."

"What things?" I asked.

He returned to the table and refilled his glass. He turned and looked at me.

"Someone who is fine and good, someone who understands even when she argues with me, and other things." He frowned and emptied his glass. He stared down into it.

"God knows ye have a mind of yer own. But ye canna stay. Ye must go back to London."

There was more. I sensed that in that way that I had come to know him, but we'd already been through this. I wasn't going anywhere, and he would have to accept it.

"You haven't asked about the information I found today." There was more than one way to prove a point.

"Constables Graham and Meeks were there that night. It might be useful to speak with them. Of course, after almost thirty years they may have retired by now, or moved away. If they're still here, they may remember something from that night, something mentioned by one of the other tenants."

"Mikaela..."

"You didn't have that information." It was obvious from his expression that he hadn't.

Point in my favor. And as far as I was concerned, that was the end of the conversation and any further discussion about my returning to London.

"Good night, Mr. Brodie."

I left my room early the next morning, notebook in hand.

I had no idea where Brodie had gone after our conversation the night before, nor did I care.

However, it was apparent that he was not in the hotel as I reached the main floor and inquired at the main desk who I might speak with regarding a chalkboard for my room.

My request was met with understandable surprise, however the desk manager was most accommodating.

"Of course, Miss Forysthe. I'm certain we can assist with yer request."

I then went to the concierge office where I encountered Munro. Brodie was not with him.

Just as well, I thought. I was not up for another confrontation. There was work to be done.

Munro looked up from the desk where it appeared that he was in the process of sending off a telegram as he gave the clerk the message, then looked over at me.

We exchanged greetings. The bruise on his cheek had become quite colorful, giving him a slightly more interesting appearance. Certainly not the first such injury was my guess considering his history and Brodie's.

"I see ye missed yer train," he commented with a slightly bemused expression. Not that there was any question that I would depart.

"It departed quite early," I replied.

"No doubt the first time in history."

"No doubt," I replied. "No ill effects from last evening?" I then inquired.

He shook his head. "No bother. Not the first, nor the last." He pushed a coin across the desk to the clerk.

"Mr. Brodie is not about?" I inquired.

"He took himself off this mornin' on information where he might find Sholto McQueen."

His opinion of Mr. McQueen had obviously not changed by the sound he made.

"I've sent off a telegram to her ladyship, to let her know that I will be here a while longer, and then perhaps make a trip to Old Lodge before I return."

There was a glint in his eyes that suggested that might very well have been the excuse he gave my aunt, while remaining in Edinburgh to assist Brodie.

"Ye have business here, as well?" he asked.

"Something Alex Sinclair may be able to assist with, in the

matter of Mr. Tobin," I replied as I picked up a pencil and tablet to write out the note I wanted to send.

"Making inquiries of yer own in spite of Brodie?" he commented.

"Merely information that might be useful, before the next express leaves for London, of course."

He obviously caught the sarcasm of my response.

"Ye have a devilish way about ye, Miss Forsythe."

"Thank you, Mr. Munro."

I handed my note, marked urgent, to the clerk to send off, then turned to Munro.

"Will you join me for breakfast while I wait for a response?"

At the restaurant, I requested a table where we might have some measure of privacy apart from other tables as guests arrived before departing for the day, or heading out to other destinations. A waiter promptly delivered coffee.

"She said that ye were not one to be trifled with," Munro commented over the rim of his cup.

"She?" I asked as I could hardly think he would have such a conversation with my aunt. Although anything was possible.

"Miss Templeton," he replied.

Ah, my good friend. And in spite of the rumored "difficulty" now between them after what could only be described as a most unlikely but an impulsive and hot-blooded affair— there was that mural that Brodie and I had discovered in the course of one of our inquiries— Mr. Munro hardly seemed distraught over the separation.

I would call his expression on the subject of Templeton as somewhat mysterious. And with a certain gleam in that blue gaze. It seemed that Templeton, after numerous rumored liaisons, some quite high-placed, might have finally met her match.

"I can see her meanin'," he continued. "Ye do have a way of settin' Brodie on his ear."

"Yes well..." I would have pointed out that he usually deserved it.

"He's not used to that in a woman." Munro lifted his coffee cup as if in a toast with that amused expression.

"My compliments, Miss Forsythe. Now tell me, if ye will, how we are to proceed? Himself would never forgive me if I were to allow you to go about on yer own."

I was quickly discovering that Mr. Munro possessed many qualities, not the least of which was loyalty to a friend.

"I believe it may be helpful to find either Mr. Meeks or Mr. Graham."

"The constables who were on the watch that night in Canongate."

I nodded. I realized that out of all the situations they might have encountered over the years, it might be unlikely that they remembered anything at all. But it was a place to start.

He accompanied me back to the concierge office where a return message from Alex was waiting for me.

POLICE CHAMBERS BUILDING, 192 HIGH STREET, FOR INFORMATION ON TWO CONSTABLES STOP
CENSUS RECORDS AT THE REGISTER HOUSE STOP

"Miss Forsythe?"

I looked up to find Munro watching me. I saw no reason not to share the information since it seemed that we were both going to remain in spite of Brodie's objections.

"According to Alex Sinclair, I might be able to find the information I'm looking for at the Police Chambers offices."

"Aye. However, ye will need to make yer inquiries on yer own, for reasons I'm certain ye understand," he replied. "But I will go as far as the High Street and wait for ye there. I won't have Brodie thinkin' that I sent ye off alone," he added. "I leave the arguments for yerself. Ye seem capable of handling them quite well."

"Thank you so much," I replied.

I returned to my room, grabbed my long coat, and umbrella in spite of the fact that the weather seemed most promising, including sunshine that broke through the clouds.

It occurred to me that Brodie was very like the weather in Scotland— quite unpredictable and prone to outbursts.

The Police Chambers were located at 1 Parliamentary Square on the High Street, an imposing six-story structure with a glass cupola on the roof. It filled the square and according to signage included the public court on the first floor with tall sash windows, timber paneling, molded cornice and ceiling with electric fixtures. Also according to the signage, there were prisoner holding facilities on the second floor.

I entered through the timber-framed-and-glass entrance and approached the clerk's desk, having left Munro at the High Street, that ran along the square.

There was an assortment of business establishments on the street that included a hat maker, a brush shop, and an office that provided legal assistance— no doubt to assist those at the court— with other offices and tenement flats above.

In my association with Brodie I had made several trips to the London Police for information, and was most familiar with procedures as I signed in then made the request to speak with someone who would have information about two constables whose names I was given, and where they might be found so that I might speak with them.

When asked the reason for my inquiry by the young constable at the desk, I stayed somewhat close to the truth.

I say *somewhat* as I have found it to be necessary in the past to reveal as little as possible to get the information needed, and a slight exaggeration often went a long way. And in consideration that I was beyond either my aunt's circle of influence or mine, limited as that was, it also very much depended upon the person I was put in contact with.

There was a history of unpleasant experiences regarding a

certain Chief Inspector in London. I was not of a mind to repeat that sort of encounter.

I will admit that I might have exaggerated the situation somewhat as I explained that it was for an assignment my editor had given me for an article on the Edinburgh police and the exemplary actions of two of their constables in long, outstanding careers.

"I simply cannot return without material for the article," I added with just the right emotional touch. "It would mean my job."

Poor young man. He was quite beside himself as I gave him the names of the two constables.

He blushed profusely, reminding me of Alex Sinclair, and then went in search of someone who might assist me.

"I am Sergeant Malcolm. May I help you."

He was older, obviously of some authority by his title, and approached the desk.

I explained what I was looking for. He frowned.

"Yes, I see," he said.

I was encouraged by what appeared to be familiarity with the names of the two constables.

"I will see what information we have if you have time to wait," he informed me. "Or perhaps return tomorrow?" he suggested.

I thanked him and told him that I would wait as I was returning to London in the morning. Another slight stretch of the truth. I was getting quite good at it.

I was prepared to wait for a certain amount of time and thought of Munro at the High Street waiting my return. I needn't have been concerned as Sergeant Malcolm returned in next to no time at all.

"I'm sorry to have kept you waiting."

Which seemed somewhat uncalled for as he had been gone less than ten minutes according to the wall clock behind the counter.

"There are no records for either of these persons," he informed me.

No records? That was impossible. I had found the information just the day before in the newspaper archive.

"There must be some mistake," I replied. "Are you certain?"

"Very certain." He handed the paper with the names of the two constables back to me.

I was being politely dismissed.

"Is there someone else I may speak with?" I asked.

"I'm afraid not, miss." And then as if I was hard of hearing or possibly impaired in some other way and did not understand, in a somewhat louder voice, "As I said, there are no records for these individuals. You must be mistaken."

Not bloody likely, I thought. However it was obvious that I was not going to obtain any information from the man.

"You have been most helpful."

I sincerely doubted if he caught the sarcasm, his expression flat and emotionless.

"Good day, miss."

I returned the note with those names to my notebook and left.

I was not wrong. I had caught that brief moment of recognition when I handed him the note. Then, something far different in Sergeant Malcolm's demeanor when he returned. And then no records of the two men?

Not that I was an expert in human nature, however I was certain that Sergeant Malcolm was lying. But for what reason?

Something was very wrong with all of this.

I found Munro outside the tobacconist shop on the High Street.

"I would say by yer expression, that didna go well," he commented.

"No, it did not," I replied. "It seems that the police have no record of either Constable Graham or Constable Meeks, or at least none that they're willing to acknowledge."

"Most interesting," he commented with a frown. "Brodie needs to know."

I agreed. However, there was another place Alex had mentioned in his telegram that might have information that could be important.

Munro wanted to see about finding someone he knew from certain business dealings for my aunt who might be a source of information, while I waved down a cab as the weather turned and it began to rain.

The General Registry Office was in the New Register House at the east end of Princes Street. It was an enormous building where an archive of records had been gathered from about Scotland and were kept under that distinctive Dome on the skyline.

The Dome was surrounded on the outside by staff and research rooms. According to the clerk where I made my inquiry about the information I was looking for, there were records of births, deaths, and marriages, some going back to the time of the Conquest— very near a thousand years, including extensive census records that had been taken every ten years since 1840.

Most records were on film with only the oldest and most fragile, many of them several hundred years old, kept in glass encased archives on the third floor, including that marriage record of Henry VIII— obviously one of several in existence considering his penchant for wives.

I was directed to the second floor of the main building where I was required to submit a ticket for information to the clerk at the Registrar General's office.

Without an address or date of birth, marriage, or other information, I was informed this was the best place to start, searching by an individual's name.

I filled out the ticket with the name of Constable M. Graham according to the information I had found in that crime page of the edition of the daily of the Scotsman newspaper when Brodie's mother was killed.

Who could have guessed how many Grahams there were?

The task was daunting. However the clerk who retrieved the archived information for me which included a date of birth for each individual as well location, showed me how it cross-referenced with census information. That was also archived on film and included a person's profession at the time the census was taken.

That meant I had only eighty-three persons named Graham to research in the records in hopes of finding the one who was a constable of the police in December of 1860.

I thought of Alex Sinclair and his inventions, capable of sorting information in a matter of minutes.

How marvelous, I thought, as I sat at a table with a reading machine and several rolls of archived documents, and began my search the old-fashioned way, one page at a time.

Several hours later I had a blistering headache from lack of food and reading through the archives. When I stepped out of the registry offices, I discovered that it was well into the late afternoon. In fact it was well on the way toward evening.

However, I had been successful, a reminder that perseverance often wins the day. I had found the reference for M. Graham, more specifically, Mr. Martin A. Graham, with the occupation... police constable.

It had included his date of birth which would have put him at thirty-two years of age in 1860, along with an address also at 24 Carnegie Street.

I had found something else in the census that was taken ten years later in 1870. Constable Martin A. Graham no longer lived at that address, although a wife and two children were shown there as of the next census. Searching further in other archives, I found a record of death for Martin A. Graham, police constable.

It included his marital status, and the name of his wife, age, along with the date and location of his death: 8 January 1861, Edinburgh. The cause of death was shown as mortal injury while carrying out the duties of his profession.

From our past inquiries in some of the poorest parts of London, I knew the streets of London and no doubt Edinburgh as well, could be exceedingly dangerous.

For a young man to die while carrying out his duties, and leaving a young family behind, was so very sad.

However, there was more. The date he died— 8 January 1861. Only a handful of days after Brodie's mother was killed!

A coincidence? I didn't believe in them, and working with Brodie had only reinforced my thoughts on that. What appeared as coincidence too often was some other aspect at work. Was that true now?

If so, what was it? And more important, it begged the question, why was I told there was no record of Constable M. Graham available at the offices of the Edinburgh police?

Most interesting, I thought, as I stepped back after almost being run down on the sidewalk by those hurrying to get out of the rain.

Not only was it the beginning of the evening hour, but it had started to rain in earnest, the street crowded with hacks, cabs, and pedestrians who ran across to get out of the downpour, while the sidewalk was crowded with those who had ventured out late of the afternoon or those trying to get home amid the congestion and weather.

I spotted a driver who had just left off a fare at the shop next door and waved him down. As he pulled to the curb I held tight to my carpetbag and my hat and ran from the shelter at the entrance to the registry offices.

The collision almost upended me. However, I am quite strong and agile, and prevented myself going down as the man I collided with, dressed in a long black coat, reached out and steadied me.

There was a hastily muttered, "Pardon, miss," and a bit of untangling of ourselves. As I collected myself he was gone just as quickly, disappearing into the congestion of others on the sidewalk.

When I would have gone about my way to the driver who

waited, I caught a glimpse of some sort of medallion or insignia on the pavement. By the proximity it had apparently been dislodged and fallen in the encounter. It could only have belonged to the man I had collided with as it was not something of mine own.

I picked it up. It was made of brass with a letter and two numbers in an efficient scroll with an insignia underneath. Perhaps some sort of military emblem, I thought, recalling such things worn by an acquaintance of my aunt who had served in the military in India, decorations all about his uniform at formal events. Most impressive if one was into ribbons and emblems. But possibly something that someone would regret losing.

The driver called out.

I dropped the brass insignia into my jacket pocket, then ran to the hack and gave the driver the name of the hotel.

Six

I WAS RAPIDLY DISCOVERING that while it might be somewhat challenging associating with one opinionated, stubborn Scot, two such individuals glaring at me from the open door of Mr. Munro's room raised the question— not for the first time in history, just how the devil had an entire country full of such people managed to lose their independence.

The only thing I could think of as I stared back at Brodie and Munro— and it had been suggested by notable authors and historians, was they couldn't stop fighting amongst themselves.

It seems they were having an argument and I had managed to step into the proverbial hornet's nest.

"Good evening," I greeted both as I removed the somewhat sodden scarf from about my neck, and went to my own room.

Not that I was trying to avoid anything— well possibly. Experience with one temperamental Scot had taught me that absence was better than an argument.

I was not surprised when Brodie appeared at the open doorway. However, rather than the usual tirade, he leaned a shoulder against the door, that dark gaze narrowed on me. I did my best to ignore him.

"I see that ye missed yer train again," he commented, hardly with surprise.

"Yes, well there was something I thought might be informative. A few days more wouldn't hurt," I added just to tweak that Scot's curiosity.

I didn't look at him, but went about hanging my scarf to dry and removing my jacket that was also quite damp in spite of the umbrella, possibly from my encounter as I left the Registry Office.

There were several moments of silence, then from Brodie, "Mr. McQueen was able to find Mick Tobin's widow."

Was this the proverbial olive branch being offered? Not, *"I thought perhaps this could be useful, or I thought you should know since I value your intelligence and part in our inquiries..."*

I still made no comment, but gave the appearance of straightening the sitting room, untying the string around the paper-wrapped package with the hotel emblem that no doubt contained my clothes from the day before that I'd sent out to be cleaned.

Brodie found it before I had the chance as I turned on the electric that lit up the room— my chalkboard including chalk sat against the far wall, courtesy of my request.

It was currently blank, but I had several comments and questions to add. I still said nothing as that dark gaze narrowed even farther, if that was possible, as he crossed the sitting room appearing to inspect the chalkboard.

"Ye, haven't written anything."

"I've only just returned," I replied. "Good of the hotel staff to provide it."

There was a typical Brodie sound, however rather than launching into every reason plus a half dozen more that he didn't want me there, he quite surprised me.

"Perhaps longer than a few days," he commented.

I was quite accustomed to his comments that often were not comments at all, but something vague. It appeared that we had reached an agreement of sorts about my remaining in Edinburgh and assisting with his inquiries into his mother's murder.

"The location of Mick Tobin's widow should definitely go onto the board," I replied. "Where is she living now?" The unspoken of course, being that we should pay her a visit and try to learn if there was anything she knew or remembered about that night.

"He was able to find an address in Leith."

"It could be productive to speak with her," I suggested.

I had discovered that it was always far more conducive to cooperation to gently prod the bear, as it were. The bear, of course, being Brodie.

"Perhaps tomorrow," he suggested also treading carefully, I realized. "Since ye will still be here."

"Of course," I replied as I went to the board, picked up the chalk, and entered the information about the widow and her residence.

"Probably the sooner the better, since you overheard that he was there the night of the crime." I then casually asked about Munro.

He had joined our conversation as he appeared at the doorway. He glanced over at the chalkboard and made what could only be described as a sound of disgust.

"What the devil is that?"

"It's a chalkboard," Brodie replied. "For information during our inquiries."

I smiled to myself at his explanation and his reference to "*our*" inquiries. It was a small thing, but another point in my favor—not that I was keeping score.

"Looks more like a teacher's lesson board," Munro added with disgust, which raised the question how he might know about that sort of thing, given his education of sorts on the streets.

He looked from Brodie to me. "Well it does," he defended. "Teddy uses a similar thing for her lines..." He suddenly stopped as if he had shared more than he intended.

"That would be Miss Templeton. I noticed it when I had occasion to visit her once in Surrey."

Which of course, brought back that very interesting artwork Brodie and I had discovered on the headboard in her bedroom, during one of our previous inquiries.

I could tell by the amused look on Brodie's face— an expression that was rare and quite... Let me just say that it was an expression that I preferred and much enjoyed. However, it was obvious that he remembered that discovery as well.

And in an effort to move the conversation along, he asked, "Were you able to learn anything at the Offices of the Police?"

Before Brodie could make a comment, or another argument break out, I added what I'd learned to the chalkboard. It was brief, as the information had been brief and initially disappointing.

"No information?" Brodie commented.

"According to the Sergeant I spoke with they have, and I quote, 'no records available of either Constable Graham or Constable Meeks.'"

"Impossible," Brodie replied. "There are records of every man who has ever served. It canna be any different here as the police are under the authority of the Home Secretary in London."

"Nevertheless, I was told there are no records," I replied. "I then followed the recommendation from Alex Sinclair and went to the New Registry Office, where all records of birth, deaths, marriages are kept along with the census that's taken every ten years."

I deliberately let that bit of information dangle as I went back to the board, and made an entry for that office and inquiry I'd made. It was always good to let things out there and then wait.

There was a sound, from Munro this time. One of those typically Scottish sounds that might have been a comment or an exclamation of some sort.

"Does she always do this?" Munro said just loud enough for me to overhear. I glanced at the adjacent windows where I caught Brodie's reflection.

"Aye, all the time," he said with what appeared to be a grin.

There was another Munro sound. "Well?" he then asked, obviously directed at me.

I set the chalk down on the nearby tea table, as it was a small chalkboard, not of the quality or size of the one at the office on the Strand. But it had served more than one purpose.

"It took considerable time as I had to go through dozens of pages of documents. I must say that they do keep excellent records..." I looked back over my shoulder to see two men waiting impatiently. And rather than tempt fate or the providence that had prevented Brodie from growing impatient, I told them what I had learned.

"I found records for Constable Graham, date of birth, his profession with the police, and a date of death." I paused, turned, then told them— particularly Brodie, the rest of it.

"The date of death was less than one month after December 20, 1860. He was only thirty-two years old at the time."

I caught the change of expression in Brodie's face, the way I had seen it a dozen times, the mask that immediately came down hiding his thoughts. Or in this case, attempting to hide them. But I knew him well enough now through several difficult instances, and knew better.

"Was there a cause of death listed?"

"According to the notice of death, it was '*in the course of his work.*'"

"What about the other constable?" Munro asked.

"I found a record of birth and marriage, with an address in Murrayfield as of 1862. However, there was no name or address shown at the address in following census in 1870, or at any other address. Do you know where that is?"

That dark gaze met mine. I knew what he was thinking. Two men who responded the night his mother was murdered, one died shortly after, and the other had disappeared.

"I know of the place," he replied.

I had put another piece of information in what was now a list of possible clues and things that needed to be followed up on.

"It might also be useful to see if Constable Graham's widow still lives at Carnegie Street," I suggested. I knew that could be painful for Brodie, very near where his mother died, but it could also be important. In the very least we might be able to learn where she had gone if she no longer lived there.

"Aye," he replied.

"I'll make inquiries in Murrayfield," Munro spoke up.

When Brodie objected, reminding him that he could be putting himself at risk in doing so, Munro made a comment in Gaelic that was more sound than anything I might have understood.

"Ye forget I know the streets as well as ye do, perhaps better than most of the Peelers, along with a few places..." He looked over at me then and winked. "A few places to hide.

"And there's someone who may be able to assist, knowing those on the street."

It was Brodie's turn to make that sound, obviously one of disapproval.

"MacNabb?"

"I know yer thoughts on the man, but he's been good in the past with me, and he goes back a long way in the city. I'd trust him over Sholto McQueen any hour of the day," Munro replied. "And," his blue eyes sharply gleamed, "he owes me a favor or two.

"When I find him," he continued. "I'll see what he can learn about Constable Meeks. Ye know as well as myself that those on the street often know more than the police or the high mucky-mucks in their offices here or in London."

And he set off to begin his search for Mr. MacNabb, preferring the streets at night where certain "individuals" could be found who might be able to tell him where MacNabb was.

I could tell that Brodie was not pleased, however, he didn't argue or attempt to stop Munro. Not that it would have done any good, I sensed, one stubborn Scot against another.

For my part, I thought that any additional assistance was an advantage even though it seemed by Brodie's response that there was some history there from the past.

Wasn't there always? I thought of our own history together. However, that was another story.

"It might be helpful for me to accompany you to Leith to speak with Mr. Tobin's widow," I suggested. "A woman often responds more openly with another woman."

It was a fact and also a way of assisting in matters. "Aye, yer right, of course," he finally conceded, which was another point in my favor. That dark gaze narrowed on a spot on the floor.

He knelt and picked something up. "Somethin' ye dropped, perhaps?" he commented.

It was the brass insignia that I had retrieved from the sidewalk outside the Registry Office. He turned it over in his fingers.

"It was an encounter outside the Registry Office," I explained. "There was a mad dash about because of the weather and I collided with a gentleman on my way to the cab. I found it on the pavement afterward." I looked at him with growing curiosity.

He was thoughtful. "Outside the Registry Office, ye say?"

"Do you recognize it?"

That thoughtful expression turned into a frown. "Aye. It's an emblem and number, worn on police constables' uniforms to identify the station they're posted to."

"Police constables? I assure you the man I ran into was not..." I stopped and thought back to that encounter.

The man had worn a black long coat and no hat, which seemed very strange now that I thought about it considering the driving rain. And the coat prevented me from seeing anything else that he wore.

"What did he look like?" Brodie asked, the insignia in his hand.

I described what I remembered. "It all happened very quickly. I didn't think about it at the time."

"As if he might have followed ye?"

I started to say that was ridiculous, but didn't.

"Which police precinct?" I asked.

"It's similar to what we wore on our uniforms when I was a constable in London," he replied. "It's for the central police office here in Edinburgh."

The same place where I had made my inquiries about Constables Graham and Meeks.

My gaze met his. Our thoughts were the same— the possibility that I might have been followed by a police constable, his uniform hidden under that black overcoat. And no hat in the pouring rain, which might mean that he had left his constable's hat behind as he set off to follow me.

"Ye seem to have drawn someone's attention," Brodie commented.

"It could have been lost some other time in the past," I speculated.

"And ye just happened to be the one to find it? Yer more intelligent than that, Mikaela Forsythe."

While I appreciated the compliment, that raised the next question— what was the reason I had been followed? Particularly after the Sergeant I had spoken with denied any information regarding Constables Graham and Meeks.

The answer, of course, was there in what I had discovered in the official records at the Registry Office. Constables Graham and Meeks had most definitely been constables with the Edinburgh police— supported by the newspaper archive and additional records that I had found showing their professional status.

What then was the reason the Sergeant I had spoken with had said the files were unavailable?

And what did it have to do with our inquiries into what happened the night Brodie's mother was murdered?

It was there in the expression on his face, his thoughts were the same as mine. If he was correct that I had been followed after my inquiries at the police station, what did that mean?

"Have ye had supper?" Brodie then asked.

"Not yet. I came straight away to the hotel to find out what you and Munro may have learned," I replied.

"Aye, well no food since morning, that could be dangerous for anyone you might encounter."

I laughed out loud. He should know well enough, I thought. It was most unlike him the past several days to be concerned about such things.

"Will you join me then in the hotel dining room?" I asked. "Or I could have supper sent up."

He hesitated. "Perhaps best to have it sent up to yer room, since it appears there are some about who now have an interest in yer presence in the city, and yer questions."

He was right of course. No sense in drawing undue attention. Particularly since we didn't know yet what my encounter might mean, if anything. It was possible it was nothing more than a chance encounter. However, I instinctively knew that it wasn't by chance. And Brodie knew it as well.

He accompanied me to the first floor and the restaurant where I put in my request with the head waiter for supper for two persons, once more delivered to my room.

He looked askance at me and then Brodie, but assured that my request would be handled promptly.

"Can that be done?" a woman seated nearby asked.

The head waiter informed her that it could be done provided there was enough staff to accommodate.

"That is a marvelous idea!" she exclaimed.

It seems that I may have started something.

Brodie and I returned to my suite and shared what was left of the Old Lodge from the previous evening.

"It seems that the head waiter may already have made the assumption that we are sharing a room," I commented. Not the first time in our professional, or personal, relationship.

However, I was very aware, given our initial conversation before he left London and conversations since, that something had most definitely changed. And then there was that ridiculous comment he made about *"not wanting any of this to touch me?"*

Good heavens! What was that supposed to mean? As if I hadn't been in difficult even dangerous situations before. What was different now, I wondered?

Brodie was quiet. He smiled, but it was the sort of smile that didn't reach his eyes. Granted, those were rare enough, still I sensed an undercurrent of something else.

"How is yer sister getting on?" he asked.

Something else that was quite unlike Brodie, casual conversation, chitchat if you will. And most particularly in the midst of an inquiry. I frowned. There was definitely something more going on behind that dark gaze.

"She is quite well, although somewhat perplexed by Aunt Antonia."

"And how is her ladyship?"

I knew him well enough by now. Definitely something else stirring in those Scottish thoughts.

"That is what has Linnie concerned. It seems that our aunt may be keeping company with a gentleman," I replied and watched for his reaction.

"Aye?" he commented somewhat distracted.

"She's concerned that the gentleman may take advantage of her."

"And what about yerself? Are ye concerned as well?"

"I've not made his acquaintance yet, however I'm certain that my sister will take care of that. Our aunt has hired him to design an addition to the house at Sussex Square. She seemed quite taken with him, when we spoke." I paused, still watching him over the edge of my glass.

"I might rather be concerned that she might take advantage of him," I added.

That brought a faint smile to one corner of his mouth, then it was gone. "I'm certain that Lady Montgomery can well take care of herself. Like someone else I know."

It was then that our supper arrived. We ate in silence except for a few additional casual comments, a question about the Mudger and how he was getting along, then Brodie asked about the inquiry that I had received.

"Lady Mainwaring is an acquaintance of Aunt Antonia. It seems there have been some odd occurrences regarding her daughter, Amelia Mainwaring, some photographs of questionable taste as Lady Mainwaring described it."

Brodie listened as he ate sparingly, and I thought of the Mudger and the hound who would have greatly appreciated the substantial remainder on his plate.

I was starving when I returned to the hotel and proceeded to do justice to the Beef Wellington, along with another dram of Old Lodge.

Afterward, I went to the chalkboard and added a note about my encounter outside the Registry Office, as well as what Brodie had learned from Sholto McQueen— who had finally emerged from wherever he had been keeping himself, and provided information about Mick Tobin's widow.

For his part, Brodie was mostly silent, his expression definitely one of distraction by whatever those thoughts were that bothered him. At least, he wasn't ordering me to the train station in the morning for my return to London.

Not that it would have done him any good. It seemed that a stubborn Scot was capable of understanding the word "*no*."

"We should most definitely pay a visit to Mick Tobin's widow in Leith," I said, standing back from the board that had now started to look like our past inquiry cases.

"There may be something she can tell us about that night." Although admittedly I realized the topic could be most delicate— her husband visiting another woman for an encounter that most probably wasn't to discuss the weather, or to share a drink.

"And then, we need to find out if Constable Graham's widow is still at Carnegie Street. There might be something important they remember from that night," I continued, taking the next logical steps as I had in the past when on a case and making inquiries.

"I'll be leaving now," he abruptly announced. "I'll wait in the room across the way for Munro's return, so not to bother ye."

I have to admit, that I was somewhat disappointed, considering our more personal relationship.

"It's no bother," I replied, setting the chalk on the tea table. "You are quite welcome to remain here." I made a gesture that took in the settee or either of the two wingback chairs.

"It would hardly be a surprise to the hotel staff since we've already shared supper."

"I need you to understand..." He started to explain, hesitated, then began again. That faint smile that was starting to concern me.

"I suppose there is no arguing the matter further with ye about remaining here in Edinburgh."

"No, there isn't," I replied.

"Ye can be as stubborn as any Scot when ye have yer mind made up about something."

True enough, I thought. I would give him that point.

"I meant it when I said that I didna want any of this to touch ye... what I have to do."

"Yes, I know. Munro explained that to me."

"What I didna say is that I canna be with ye, not in that way. Whatever I learn, whatever I have to do will change everything."

I wanted to tell him that I understood, and it didn't make any difference to me. But now was not the time nor place.

I had never been the sort to plead with a man to stay. I had never needed to, and I didn't now even though Brodie was the only man who had ever been important to me. And that was saying a great deal, all things considered. And because he was important, I told him what he needed to hear.

That dark gaze met mine and for just a moment I glimpsed the sadness and pain that he'd carried almost his entire life. It was a thing he needed to be done with, one way or another.

"I understand," I replied. Because I did understand about the need to be done with something.

He swore under his breath as he hesitated, then caught me by surprise as he took hold and pulled me against him. His hands went back through my hair and the kiss that followed... definitely toe-curling, and so much more.

When it ended, he briefly rested his forehead against mine.

"You are so fine to me..."

And then he was gone, the door clicking shut behind him.

More than any man I had ever known, he had the ability to undo me with just those few words. Not gifts, nor flowers. Not promises of undying love, which could be highly suspect.

I had been called stubborn, high-minded, reckless by others and by Brodie as well. But no one had ever told me how fine I was.

Damn bloody Scot, was all I could think!

How could something so simple have me undone. It must be the whisky.

When I had finally collected myself, I turned back to the board and added additional notes. Whatever the outcome, I was determined to find out just what he meant by what he'd said. Fine, indeed!

It was a long time before I retired for the night, and when I finally closed my eyes and drifted off there was the taste of cinnamon and Brodie.

So, very fine.

Seven

IN THAT ODD way that reality often finds its way into one's dreams, there was suddenly the sound of voices that brought me up out of sleep, and it was coming from across the hallway heard through the door to the sitting room.

Wearing only my nightshift and with nothing proper in my haste to leave London, I grabbed my jacket from the coat rack and slipped it on. I then went to the door.

The muffled conversation came from behind the door across the hall. It seemed that Munro had returned and there was a great deal of conversation between he and Brodie. I crossed the hallway and knocked on the door.

Brodie pulled the door open, both men looking at me with less than hospitable expressions.

"Has something happened?" I asked.

Brodie nodded. "Aye, there's been a... situation," he replied, his mouth drawn in a taut line.

I glanced over at Munro, however he was not forthcoming with whatever the "situation" was. I then saw the knife that he slipped inside his boot.

A situation. That seemed to be quite serious.

"And no," Brodie added. "Yer not coming along. Yer to stay here."

There was that look that I was familiar with. However, considering that I was standing there in my nightshift— which I might add he took in with what could only be described as an appreciative glance, I was not in a position to argue, even if it would have only taken me a few minutes to dress.

The truth was that I was ill-prepared to go wandering about the streets of Edinburgh at night.

That appraising look disappeared as he checked the revolver he always carried. It was obviously something quite serious.

There were all the obvious questions that occurred to me, however one look at both of them more than indicated that now was not the time. There was then a brief comment between them, Brodie grabbed his jacket, and I was left standing alone in the doorway in my nightshift as they took the service lift at the end of the floor.

Fine, I thought. Now, there was a word that was taking on all sorts of new meanings. At present, it meant that I had to be "fine", until they returned.

There was no more sleep to be had after I returned to my room. The only thing I could do was wait. And it was far too late or early as the case may be, for the restaurant to be open for service. I nibbled at the vegetables that Brodie had pushed aside— obviously not a fan of green things, in favor of the Wellington.

I was inclined to agree regarding cold, green vegetables.

I turned up the fire in the fireplace, then dressed— just in case. Although in case of what I wasn't certain, as I had been given clear instructions that I was not to be part of whatever it was they had gone off to take care of.

I dozed in one of the high-backed chairs before the fireplace. I will admit that it might have been due to the whisky that Brodie and I had consumed over supper, along with only two hours of fitful sleep before Munro had returned earlier.

It was still dark beyond the windows of the hotel room when

I was roused from sleep by a persistent knocking at the door to my suite. I immediately opened the door to find Munro just beyond in the hallway.

"I need yer assistance, miss," he said in a quiet but urgent manner as he returned to his own room across the way.

I had learned to expect, and had experienced, almost anything in my association with Brodie regarding past inquiries on behalf of clients. Working in the East End out of the office on the Strand, not to mention my foreign adventures, I was hardly surprised by anything. And that included the sight of dead bodies.

Most assuredly not ever pleasant, but I was able to separate the horror of coming across a body, or a foot as the case may be, from the responsibility on behalf of a client. And I had to admit there was that curious aspect which Brodie found to be most unusual.

The sight of blood hadn't bothered me since I was a child and found my father dead by his own hand. Nor when I was injured—shot to be precise, during one of our inquiries.

However, I now discovered that it was quite different when the blood was all over Brodie.

I didn't stop to question the reason for that at the moment. There was so much blood everywhere as Munro closed the door behind me.

"Bloody hell!" I exclaimed, which seemed a bit of an understatement under the circumstances. There were several other words, most colorful, as Brodie looked up at me from where he sat at the table, his jacket gaping open, a bloody stain at his jumper underneath.

"I told ye not to bother her with this," he growled at Munro.

"Aye, ye did, however from what ye've told me she's not one to faint away at such things and this will take more than my two hands." Munro looked over at me, quite obviously took in my state of undress, then simply nodded.

I was fairly certain it was not the first time he had seen a woman in her nightshift, or less as the case may be. I was also certain there was more Brodie would have said to him, however, now was not the time as I went into the adjacent room and bathroom and seized several towels.

"How bad is it?" I asked.

"Bad enough," Munro replied. "He fair soaked my shirt as well getting back here."

I returned to the sitting room where Brodie sat at the table. "His jacket and shirt will need to be removed."

Brodie glared at me. Munro merely nodded and stepped in to see the deed done.

Together we managed to remove Brodie's jacket, then his jumper which was much the worse for wear with blood soaked through low near the waist of his pants from the wound. More specifically a bullet wound.

Not that I was an expert, but having been the recipient of just such a wound in one of our previous cases, I was familiar with them. I looked up at Brodie as I gently wiped around the wound that was just below his ribs on his side.

My first concern was the bullet. Munro shook his head.

"It went through, and came out at the back," he replied to my question.

"How fortunate," I replied with no small amount of sarcasm as Munro brought a washbasin with water. That dark gaze narrowed on me.

"Did you forget to stay out of the way?" I couldn't resist.

"The man came out of the shadows. There was no way to know what he was about, nor time to take precautions," Munro explained with a look from Brodie to me.

I continued to clean around the wound. Brodie winced more than once, but remained silent for the most part which was possibly a good thing, since I had a comment or two I would have made.

"And where was Mr. McQueen when all of this was happening?" I asked, since I knew they had set off to meet with him. Their silence had me looking up.

"McQueen is dead," Brodie finally replied.

That set me back a bit. I had questions but those would have to wait.

"You need a physician," I told him.

"No! No physician. There would be too many questions, and it would likely get back to the police straight away," Brodie replied. "That would bring them into the situation."

What precisely was the situation? I looked over at Munro since it was obvious Brodie was not going to be forthcoming with the events of the evening.

"This needs proper care with disinfectant." I thought of Mr. Brimley and his care in the past, particularly with my own wound.

"If we were in London it would be different, but..."

"I said no." Brodie's voice had gone low. "It would be dangerous for all of us until we know what this is all about." That dark gaze softened then in that way that was familiar. I knew there was no arguing the matter further.

He looked up at Munro. "We will make do. There's a bottle of her ladyship's whisky in Mikaela's room." He explained as Munro left the room and crossed the hallway to my room.

"Ye learn to make do when ye live on the streets. Mr. Brimley has prescribed it more than once."

It was a reminder that there were still many aspects to Brodie's former life that I was not aware of, including the sources of the handful of other scars he had.

Munro returned and handed me the bottle of my aunt's very fine whisky, and I had the ridiculous thought that she might be highly amused that it was being used for medicinal purposes.

I soaked the corner of one of the towels from the adjacent bathroom. I had admired Brodie without a shirt in the past. He was most handsome with muscles lining his shoulders and arms, from the places and things where his work took him in our inquiries. And then there was the light dusting of black hair just across his chest.

He was not of the pale, paunchy sort given to complaining

about lifting a heavy carton, or wasting away to drink as so many among those I knew.

I suppose it was a flaw in my character that I had often admired the sight of him when he was about to pull on a clean shirt and set off somewhere during our inquiries.

I thought of that now and hesitated, as a little voice whispered that my hesitance was more than my admiration of him physically. The truth was that I didn't want to cause him any more pain.

"Ye'll need more than that, lass. Ye need to wash the wound with it. If ye want Munro to do it..."

"No," I snapped, surprising even myself at the bluntness of it not to mention the anger I heard in my own voice. "I'll do it."

Once, just once I had experienced the effects of the whisky in a cut on my hand. It was a minor thing, yet it had burned like the very devil. I could only imagine the pain this would cause on not only one wound, but the second one where the bullet had passed through.

"Get on with it then, lass," he gently told me as Munro came to stand beside him, a firm hand at his shoulder.

I muttered something very near a curse, then placed a towel beneath the wound to catch the excess, and poured a good portion onto the wound.

I thought that I was familiar with most of the curses Brodie had muttered from time to time. Clearly, I was not, as he gritted his teeth and still managed to invoke a half dozen in English and the rest in Gaelic, including something that included Jesus, Mary, and Joseph. To say that it was quite colorful is an understatement.

"The other wound as well, miss," Munro told me. "Best to get it on with it quickly."

There was another round of curses from between clenched teeth, then silence, which was even more frightening as Brodie hung his head, eyes closed as he fought the pain. But it was done, for now.

"We'll need bandages," I told Munro. "A bed linen will do." I was confident of his skill with a knife.

In short order he had torn one of the bedsheets into strips that I then folded into thick pads. He held both in place over the two wounds.

Brodie's head was very near mine as I leaned in to wrap another strip of cloth around his waist to hold the bandages in place. His breath brushed my cheek.

"Ye are a rare woman, Mikaela Forsythe."

Now, I was *rare*?

"Be quiet," I told him. I would have preferred to curse him for being such a fool as to get himself shot.

I supposed that was a bit like the pot calling the kettle black, truth be known. And then there was the fact that I could not say anything more at the moment for the sudden tightness in my throat.

As I finished tying off the bandage and would have sat back, the task done, that dark gaze met mine with just a hint of a smile.

"Damned fool," I finally managed. The smile twitched slightly.

"Ye've a fine hand."

"Courtesy of Mr. Brimley," I replied, and wished that he was there. But he wasn't. "I've always been a good student of things."

So here we were, torn bedsheets, an empty bottle of whisky—I certainly could have used a drink and Munro as well by the looks of him, and one well-bloodied Scot.

It was just after two o'clock in the morning. Daylight was still a few hours away. Yet, no one was tired. Except for Munro.

He had pulled one of the high-backed chairs in front of the settee, then propped his feet up, head back against the back of the settee while Brodie was propped up against the headboard of the bed with several pillows including the ones from my room.

I sat beside the bed, making good use of the sheet that had now been appropriated for bandages. I knew well enough that we were going to need more when it came time to change them, daily according to Mr. Brimley's previous instructions.

I would have thought that Munro had dozed off by the look

of him, eyes closed, arms folded over his chest, the slow rise and fall of his breathing. However, looks could be deceiving. He was obviously still awake.

"I'll find Archie in the morning," he said, his voice low so that I might have been mistaken that he said anything at all.

"He'll be able to learn the word on the street about what happened tonight," he added, eyes still closed, yet fully awake it seemed.

"What did happen?" I asked. Had it been a random encounter? Some other "business" Mr. McQueen was conducting that went wrong when Brodie and Munro came upon him and whoever the other person was? Munro had said that the man worked both sides of the law.

"I had word from Archie McNabb where McQueen could be found last night. He had been with a woman named Clarice and had just left her flat."

I sensed there was more. "Please continue."

His eyes opened and that sharp blue gaze met mine.

"We were havin' a conversation about the information he learned about the man Brodie was looking for."

"Mick Tobin?"

He nodded. "Aye."

I could tell that he was considering how much to tell me, and then finally seemed to make a decision.

"The man who shot McQueen and Mr. Brodie, came out of the night verra near the Tollbooth Tavern. Not unusual for that part of Old Town. It does a fair trade in the drink.

"It happened quick," he continued. "He fired his revolver at McQueen, then at himself." He nodded toward Brodie.

"Brodie fired twice."

"Did you see who it was?"

"It was too dark, and the man ran off." This from Brodie who had either been wakened by our conversation, or hadn't been dozing at all. That dark gaze fastened on me.

"Ye need to get some rest," he told me.

There was that "*kettle and pot*" again. However, I had not been shot.

As I knew all too well from our past adventures and inquiries, there was a point where exhaustion set in after going through unexpected, even dangerous situations.

"Go back to yer own room," he told me then. "There's nothin' more to be done tonight."

I lifted the edge of the blanket that covered the lower part of his body to inspect the bandage on his side. There was no indication of fresh blood. Still...

"Perhaps later," I replied. "I can rest just as easily here."

"Mikaela..."

Not a warning, or even angry, his usual response to most situations we encountered.

"You need your rest," I replied, and pulled the blanket back over the bandages.

Bloody stubborn Scot. And this time, it was quite literally, the truth.

I would like to believe that I hadn't dozed off. In my adventures I often slept in a variety of places that necessitated being able to drop off or simply drop from exhaustion. Traversing the Sahara by camel or traversing the Kalahari by boat and afoot, slipped through the fog of sleep as I slowly awakened from a movement beside me.

Then, more fully awake, the events of the previous night returned, and I realized that Brodie had pushed himself up into a sitting position, albeit with great effort and no small amount of pain by the expression on his face.

"What are you doing?" I demanded, pushing back the fatigue from only a couple of hours sleep. "You shouldn't move about."

He looked at me with the barest hint of amusement. "If I don't move, there will be more than a wee bit of blood to mop up."

His meaning slowly sank in along with the memory of how I had navigated the first days after my own injury.

"Oh, of course."

However in this particular situation, Munro had returned and was already up and about and crossed the room to give assistance as it were.

They slowly retreated into the adjacent accommodation, where I overheard a several curses, including *"Jesus, Mary, Joseph"*, followed by, "Leave off, man. I can well enough do this part myself."

I had never fully considered or appreciated the efforts it took for a man to conduct such business, given the layers of petticoats, skirts, and overskirts that women had to pass through for such necessities. I had been known to curse that situation on more than one occasion.

It was simply a matter of fewer garments, fewer complications. Hence my preference for my walking skirts that made life far easier under such circumstances.

There was another muttered curse. Quite inventive, I thought, and I supposed that if a man could curse so thoroughly, then it was very likely that he would survive.

In spite of the circumstances— I was fairly certain that Brodie had survived worse— I forced back a smile more from appreciation, at the sight of two Scots returning from the water closet, one muttering that he could well walk on his own while the other muttered a warning about starting the bleeding up again.

Sound advice I thought. Brodie was obviously of a different opinion as Munro returned him to the edge of the bed somewhat unceremoniously then retreated to the sitting room.

"He is correct you know," I commented, making a quick visual inspection of the bandages about his waist.

"Dinna lecture me, woman," he replied.

"Not at all. I was merely pointing out what anyone with a grain of sense would understand."

That dark gaze narrowed as I stood, aware once again that I wore nothing more than my nightshift.

"A grain of sense?" he repeated.

"Which you seem to be lacking at the moment." I was not of a mind to argue with him. There were more urgent needs.

I was hungry and no doubt they were as well. And I wanted coffee, not to mention a visit to the accommodation in my own room.

I made that suggestion more to Munro as he returned to stand in the doorway to the bedroom, since it was obvious that Brodie was determined to argue over everything. I retrieved my jacket.

"Thank you for your care of him," I told Munro as I passed him at the doorway. "I might have been tempted to pitch the ungrateful sod out the window."

"Aye," he admitted. "It takes a strong will to be acquainted with such as that one. And yerself as well, miss?" he added.

"Hmmm. Perhaps." I glanced at Brodie who was presently frowning at both of us.

In spite of only a few hours' sleep, I refused to be tired. There were too many things to do and take care of.

The first order of the day was to dress. The second order of the day was breakfast. As the restaurant was not open, I waved down one of the hotel staff and inquired about the nearest coffee establishment. I was directed across the way to a small coffeeshop tucked back from the street.

Morning traffic was thin due to the time of the morning, and I crossed Princes Street and entered the public house. The bustle inside and the smell was familiar from the public house just down the way from Brodie's office at the Strand.

I placed a double order of breakfast including cheese scones. Coffee was another matter. The woman behind the counter offered to put in a flask. I purchased the breakfast, coffee, and the flask.

"Yer want to purchase it?" she exclaimed with more than a little surprise. "And yer want to take the whole thing with ye?"

"For traveling," I explained. The flask would do until the hotel restaurant opened.

"We have tins and confectioner's boxes for the food. But that will cost extra."

My breakfast order was prepared and soon ready, two tins and two candy boxes all neatly tied together. I tucked the flask that contained the hot coffee under my arm.

On my way back to the hotel, I stopped at the front desk and put in the request for coffee to be delivered to my room as soon as the restaurant opened. To say that I received a somewhat curious look at the packages in my hands, was an understatement. Or it might have been the request for coffee in my room.

In spite of the early hour, there were some people about the lobby. No doubt early departures for the rail station, or to some other destination.

"Careful there, miss."

I had been shifting the wrapped tins and cartons from one arm to the other, and looked up at the warning that was obviously meant for me as a hand went around my elbow as though to steady me, which I did not need.

He was of my same height, quite slender of build with a thin face and watchful grey eyes. Rather than business or travel attire he wore a tweed Norfolk jacket with a tweed vest, and herringbone trousers all in muted shades of brown and gray. Not unusual when in Scotland.

However, it was those watchful eyes beneath the rim of the deerstalker cap, that instinctively had me removing my elbow from his grasp and taking a step back. I did not care for anyone, in particular a man whom I did not know, presuming to "handle" me when I was quite capable of handling myself.

"Out to make some purchases? And with the weather quite amicable at the moment?" he commented, eyeing the bundle of packages in my arms. "Do you need some assistance?"

"No, thank you," I replied, turning away from him, a clear signal to anyone that the conversation was ended. "I am quite capable."

"Well then, I'll be on me way." He touched the bill of his cap.

What an odd encounter, I thought, as he moved toward the entrance to the hotel, without a similar offer to another woman he passed. I stepped to the front counter.

"Who was the gentleman who was just here in the tweed jacket and deerstalker cap?"

The manager, Mr. Ambrose by his nameplate at the counter, acknowledged me. "I thought that you must know him, miss. He seemed to be waiting for someone. Yerself, perhaps, as he seemed quite familiar."

"I've never seen him before. I would appreciate it if you would let me know if he returns."

"Is there anything wrong, Miss Forsythe?"

I shook my head. "No," I replied and thanked him, then turned toward the lift.

It wasn't anything specific, nothing I could put my finger on. It was a... feeling.

My friend, Templeton, who communicated regularly with the spirit world, would have laughed at that.

When I reached the lift I glanced once more to the front desk area, but didn't see the man I had encountered.

Brodie was up and about when I returned to the room, which was a generous description considering that he was bent forward at the waist, a hand pressed against the bandage on his side, beads of perspiration on his forehead.

There was a comment that immediately came to mind, something I'd heard or read, that the best way to convince a fool that he was wrong was to let him have his way.

As I watched Brodie move from bed to chair, then chair to table, leaning heavily on both as he went along, it did appear that Munro had decided to let him have his way rather than argue that he was not quite up to being out of bed yet.

"What are ye lookin' at?" Brodie demanded.

A *fool*, I almost said, but decided not to poke the bear, especially a wounded bear.

I retreated to the sitting room and proceeded to open containers and most particularly that flask of strong coffee. I poured two cups, letting the steaming fragrance fill the room, along with the scent of eggs with bacon and those cheese scones.

"Breakfast if you feel up to it," I announced, at which Munro joined me and scooped off a portion of eggs into the carton of scones since we were making do, much like being in the wild. Considering the look on Brodie's face, that didn't seem far off.

He made it to the doorway of the bedroom, leaning against the frame. I pushed back the urge to assist him. The fool had practically been running laps about the bedchamber. Let him navigate the sitting room as well, I thought.

I will admit I had a moment or two of guilt over that. Brodie had taken extraordinary care of me when I was injured. I would argue, however, that I did not go running about immediately after.

He eventually arrived at the sitting room table, expression drawn and quite pale.

"I've noticed that ye have a wicked side, Mikaela Forsythe." He grinned.

I exchanged a look with Munro. "Whatever do you mean?"

Munro made quite an effort at the food while Brodie ate only a small portion. Coffee courtesy of the hotel staff arrived, and he appeared somewhat revived.

I had refilled my own cup, and thought back over the brief conversation when Brodie and Munro had returned to the hotel.

There was something that had bothered me at the time, but it had slipped away in the urgency of cleaning and bandaging his bullet wounds, and silently assuring myself that he would survive.

"I've been thinking," I said over the rim of my coffee cup.

Brodie sat across from me at the table, leaning against the back of the overstuffed chair that Munro had pulled up for him, his eyes closed. Munro sat at the other. I heard the expected groan from Brodie.

That I had been "thinking of something" was a frequent topic of conversation in our inquiries, and had quite often contributed some worthwhile points.

"What have ye been thinkin'?" he replied. I heard the weariness in his voice and saw the pain on his face as he sat up and looked over at me.

"I suppose it is easy enough to acquire a revolver," I commented. "However, it's very likely that few possess one as they can be quite expensive, beyond your usual gentleman, a criminal now and then, and the local police."

That dark gaze narrowed.

"Outside a tavern in Old Town it would seem unlikely that it was a random encounter with a gentleman," I continued. "And under the circumstances that you've described it would seem that it was not a random attack by some street thief."

"What are ye sayin'?" Munro commented.

"It would seem that the odds are that it was someone else, someone who possibly knew Mr. McQueen would be meeting with you," I explained my thoughts in the matter.

"And someone who also had a revolver."

I caught the look that passed between Munro and Brodie. Munro made a sound that I was quite familiar with, one of those typically Scottish sounds that might mean anything. However in this particular instance along with the expression on his face, there was definitely surprise and anger.

"I did warn ye about her," Brodie told him which was not what I was expecting.

Warn Munro? What did he mean by that?

Eight

"I BEG YOUR PARDON?"

I didn't know whether to be insulted or to simply accept that the comment was made in a moment of delirium on Brodie's part. Although admittedly, he didn't appear to be feverish, in some fit of pain from the wound, or suffering from exhaustion.

Munro rose from his chair and proceeded to pace about the sitting room, or was that full retreat. For his part, I could have sworn there was a bit of humor in Brodie's dark gaze.

"I thought he should know what he's dealing with in the matter," Brodie said.

"He mentioned that ye have a way of expressing ideas that can be helpful from time to time," Munro explained.

From time to time.

How very diplomatic on Munro's part. However, in consideration of Brodie's injury this was very likely not the time for further discussion.

"He did say that ye can be most insistent in matters as well," Munro continued. "Which is an admirable quality, Miss Forsythe."

Admirable? Which sounded very much like an attempt to mollify me if I was inclined to point out certain facts.

"And I am inclined to agree with yer assessment of the situation. It would seem that the encounter was not through happenstance."

It was at this point that Munro glanced over at Brodie, cleared his throat, then proceeded to become quite fascinated with the remnants of coffee in his cup.

"The Agency frequently used Mr. McQueen in their information gathering. We should let them know of the situation," I commented, deciding that taking a different direction was probably the best course of action.

I stood then, everything decided. At least as far as I was concerned. I wanted to send off a telegram to London, and then I intended to go to Leith. At least I could do that and see what might be learned from Mick Tobin's widow, if she even still lived in Leith.

"Where are you off to now?" Brodie asked Munro.

"To find where Archie has taken himself off to after last night's scramble."

Scramble? That seemed to be a somewhat odd way of describing the circumstances, and definitely an understatement.

"Ye know that I don't like the man."

"We need someone connected into the people on the streets, and he's the best one I know for that. And he's usually forthright in his dealings, unlike someone else we both know who happens to now be dead."

That was certainly putting everything rather bluntly, I thought.

"But most important, it isna as if we have a lot of choices in the matter to find information about something that happened almost thirty years ago," Munro added and headed for the door.

"Ye are free to return to London any time," Brodie told him.

"Ha!" Munro replied. "With yerself shot to hell and gone and bloody well determined to carry on? Not likely." He slammed out of the room.

It was probably safe to say it wasn't the first argument

between them, nor the last. I headed for the door as well. I knew when best to not be there as the saying went.

"What about you?" Brodie said. "I know that look."

I could have pretended not to know what he was talking about, but that would have been a lie. And he would have known it to be.

I explained about the telegram, then quickly added, "Then I'm off to Leith to see if I might be able to learn something from Tobin's widow. That seems the best clue to follow at present."

"I'll need another shirt. Munro undoubtedly has one that I can wear, and my jacket," Brodie replied.

I looked at him incredulously. "You were injured only a few hours ago. You can barely walk. You are not going with me."

As I was saying...

The telegram had been sent to Alex Sinclair in London. I had gathered my carpetbag and umbrella against a change in the weather.

The original plan was to simply leave Brodie and be on my way to the tram depot.

However as I have learned plans have a way of going out the window along with the day's flotsam and garbage.

Speaking of... I glanced over at Brodie who looked much the worse for wear in the hack beside me.

The plan had been for me to walk the short distance to the tram platform at Haymarket where the cable tram left for Leith on the hour. However, Brodie changed that part of the plan.

"Ridiculous," I muttered my thoughts on the matter of his accompanying me, as if I hadn't proven myself most capable in the past of pursuing information on my own.

I had attempted to persuade him against going with me. I argued that I would be hard-pressed to attend his wounds if he should start bleeding again.

Somewhere along with that argument was a threat on my part, albeit an empty one, that I was tempted to put another hole in him for such foolishness. He simply proceeded to put on the shirt and jacket.

Bloody stubborn fool!

We arrived at the platform in good time to board the Number 10 tram that would take us to Leith. It was a moderate day with the sun breaking through clouds. Normally I would have chosen the upper deck of the car, however it was obvious that Brodie would never make the climb up the steps. We chose seats on the lower deck.

I had ridden the tram system previously on some matter or other for my aunt when in Edinburgh.

It was said that the city had gone to the cable-driven tram system as there were places along the route where the streets were quite steep and often required five or six horses to make the climb with the horse-drawn trams. The cable system was modeled after the one in San Francisco, California, and obviously more efficient than those drawn by a team of horses.

Modern inventions. What next I thought? Flying machines?

I looked over at Brodie as the tram rumbled along and swayed round curves in the street. He was quite pale, to be expected after being shot and loss of blood. His mouth was set in a line surrounded by that dark beard and there was a determined expression in those dark eyes.

I was tempted to say, "I told you so" but thought better of it.

It was not a great distance, and we reached the depot at Leith in under twenty minutes, including the time we were brought to a standstill by, of all things, a parade of elephants as part of a circus performance that was to be given. I thought Brodie might have apoplexy.

"I've ridden atop an elephant while on safari in Africa," I commented as we waited to resume our travel. "Fascinating creatures."

"Why am I not surprised?" Brodie mumbled between clenched teeth.

That ended further conversation regarding my travels and elephants.

When we arrived in Leith, I inquired about directions to Number 238 Leith Walk, the last known address for Mick Tobin according to the information Sholto McQueen was able to find. If that could be relied upon.

"Not a place those such as yerself should go, miss," the depot manager informed me. Then he took note of Brodie.

"Is yer husband all right? He looks a bit under the weather."

"Quite all right," I replied without bothering to correct the man as to the reference to "husband."

The address for Number 238 Leith Walk was a four-story tenement with shops on the ground floor, much like those found in London and Edinburgh.

It had a black slate roof with four-pane timber sash windows, and was built of light-colored sandstone with a doorway to a common stairway. There was a carved emblem over the doorway grown over with moss and grime.

A placard inside a wrought-iron frame on the wall inside that stairway contained the names of the tenants. The name, Tobin, was *not* among them.

"It cannot hurt to ask," I told Brodie as I read through the names once more.

I knocked at two doors but received no answer. An older woman answered at the third door. She had lived there for only a few years, but indicated the shopkeeper who owned the grocery store at the street level might know since she had lived there for many years and her father before her. Brodie accompanied me.

The woman by the name of Morna Adams appeared to be somewhat older than myself, but was most congenial as she took care of customers and chatted away about people who lived in the tenement.

"There was a young woman some years back," she commented. "I was just a chit, but I do remember me da saying as how sad it was to be a widow at such a young age. She moved into one of the flats with her father for a time. If I remember it right, she remarried a year or so later."

Thirty years ago, a young widow, and then remarried.

"Do you have any way of knowing where she might have gone after she was married. It's important that we find her."

She looked past me to Brodie. "Are ye all right then?" she asked.

I glanced over at Brodie and hoped that he hadn't started bleeding again. It was the sort of thing that might put someone off.

He nodded. "Well enough. We would appreciate it if ye could help with information."

She smiled and I could have sworn that was an invitation there, the sort that had nothing to do with shopping at the grocer's store.

"Me da might remember," she said then. "He doesn't get around so well, but he's sharp as a blade. We live just above." She indicated the flat over the store.

She called over her son who made deliveries for the store and left him in charge as we accompanied her up the stairs to their second-story flat. I glanced back more than once at Brodie. He seemed to be managing quite well in spite of the pain I knew he was in.

Her father looked up from the cage beside the window where he hand fed a canary as we entered the small flat.

"He's hard of hearing," Morna Adams explained as she went to the window and laid a hand on her father's arm. He looked up and smiled. In a rather loud voice, his daughter introduced us.

"Mr. Brodie and Miss Forsythe are looking for someone who lived here some time ago. I thought you might remember."

He nodded a greeting, gave the canary another bit of seed, then crossed the room, and took my hand in his.

We chatted, with Morna's assistance. Brodie then asked about a young woman with the last name of Tobin. His daughter explained that it would have been almost thirty years earlier, and the young woman was a widow who came to live with her father.

Warm brown eyes smiled at me as he nodded, but there was a sharpness there as well for Brodie. He was shorter than his daughter and wore a grocer's apron.

"It keeps his hand in the business and the mind sharp." Morna explained that he still worked at the age of eighty-seven.

"And he knows all of the customers by their first names, as well as the children." Then she warned, "He can be a bit flirty, but its harmless."

He greeted Brodie in that broad Scots Gaelic, and Brodie replied in the same as well. I realized that it was a test of sorts. My pattern of speech was obviously English, and it was a reminder that for some, particularly those who were older, there was a certain... caution toward those like myself.

As for Brodie, his response along with some other inquiry I wasn't familiar with, came naturally from those early years on the street. He patted Brodie's shoulder.

"I remember the girl," he replied. "She was young, not more than eighteen or nineteen years. Verra sad little thing, came from the city after the death of her husband." He nodded.

"She lived here for a time. Young Letty, so sad. Her father worked at the rubber mill. She had all that red hair and pretty blue eyes."

"Do ye remember where she might have gone?" Brodie asked.

"I remember that the young man she married was a docker at the port. Her father used to visit then went to live with them before he passed..." He paused, thinking back.

"On Pilrig off Leith Walk, it was," he continued.

"Do you remember her name after she married?" I asked. He was thoughtful again.

"Voltmer was the man's name. I remember her father said it was foreign. There's so many that come in through the ports, and he said that he had an accent."

A sharp memory indeed, I thought.

"Is there anything else you can tell us," I added. "Were there any children?"

He shook his head. "Not that I heard of. The father never mentioned, and then he moved as well."

We thanked him. He smiled again then accompanied us back to the shop with his daughter.

"We have apples on special," he said with a twinkle in his eyes. "The last of the season, and turnips for the cookpot."

Eighty-seven years old and still minding the store. I purchased a bag of apples, passing on the turnips as there was no place to prepare them even if I could cook. I could have sworn that Brodie laughed at that one, with no small amount of discomfort.

"Latha math dhut a bhean bhòidheach," he said in Gaelic in parting as he took my hand.

I looked over at Brodie as I collected my bag of apples, and we left the shop.

"He told ye 'good day, pretty lady'," he translated.

Pretty lady? Flirty indeed.

"No turnips today?" he asked.

There had been no record of marriage in the documents I had looked for, but that was not surprising. And apparently Sholto McQueen hadn't found any record either. People moved away, took on new names as this young woman had.

There might not even have been a record of her marriage to Mick Tobin, if it was even that. I had learned that it was not uncommon for two people to live together under their own birth names even when married, and when not married.

We now had a name, Voltmer on Pilrig at Leith Walk. If they were still there.

The obvious was to make further inquiries, however I was concerned about Brodie's condition.

"We can return another time," I suggested. And in that way that he had the uncanny ability to know exactly what I was thinking...

"No, we'll see what we can learn today."

"I thought that perhaps…"

He looked at me then as we stood on the pavement at the sidewalk. "I know and I appreciate the thought, but we need to do this now. If we can find the woman, she may remember something from when…" He paused. "From that night."

It wasn't so much the expression on his face, the pain of the wound obvious even as he refused to give into it. It was something in his voice, the way he said it that I understood— the need to know the truth about that night.

"We need to find a hack," I replied. He didn't argue with me.

Pilrig off Leith Walk was not far, a row of two-story tenements with businesses below on the street, and a line of cottages at the far end. Among the shops was a smoke shop, a milliner's shop, and a bakeshop.

The smoke shop seemed the most likely source for information for a man by the name of Voltmer, if he still lived in the area.

"Ask at the bakeshop. I'll ask the tobacconist," Brodie told me, and when I hesitated to leave him alone, he added, "I've had worse, lass, and not died from it. Go on with ye."

Worse.

It was, of course, pointless to argue with him. I would simply have to find someone to assist in picking him up off the pavement if he passed out.

The man at the bakeshop had lived in the area for several years. I described what I knew about a young woman by the name of Letty who had moved to Leith Walk some years past with her new husband, a man by the name of Voltmer. It was a bit like searching for a needle in a hay bundle.

However he did know of a woman, older of course, who came to his shop weekly for bread and cakes. She lived nearby although he didn't know the exact address or flat number.

I thanked him and purchased some meat and cheese scones. I then went to the tobacconist shop and found Brodie.

"The man at the bakeshop seems to remember someone who resembles Letty Tobin, but doesn't know her name."

He nodded. "Voltmer is known, he stops here for smokes. He lives in one of the cottages down the way, at Number 28."

It seems that we had found our needle in the hay bundle. But what would Voltmer or Letty be able to tell us.

The cottage at Number 28 was whitewashed with a timber-frame door and about the windows that faced out onto Leith Walk.

I was hopeful, for Brodie's sake, for what we might learn. At the same time I couldn't help but feel hesitation for whoever might answer the door.

Be careful what you wish for, I thought with a look over at Brodie as we waited for a response at the door. Delving into the past and digging up old memories, I knew, could be a double-edged sword.

He knocked a second time.

"Hold on!" a woman's voice came from within. Several moments passed, the door finally opened.

"Letty Voltmer?" Brodie asked. There was a hesitant nod.

"I would like to speak with ye about something that happened a long time ago."

Recalling the grocer's description of Letty Tobin with red hair and blue eyes, it seemed that we had found her, even though her hair was faded and there were lines about her eyes. No longer a girl, but an older woman, she set aside the laundry basket as Brodie mentioned Mick Tobin's name. I saw the caution in the expression on her face.

"We would be very grateful if you would be willing to speak with us," I added.

I wondered what she would remember, if anything; what she would tell us as I glimpsed the curiosity and the natural suspicion.

We shared the scones as we sat across the table from Letty Voltmer, née Tobin.

"That was so long ago, I suppose there's no harm answerin' yer questions," she began.

"Mick and me wasn't married then. He worked at the leather-works off the High Street."

"Did he mention anything about Bleekhouse Close and something that happened just before Christmas that year?" Brodie asked.

She offered more tea. Brodie made a cursory gesture, but I caught the faint shaking of his hand as I accepted more.

It was several moments more before Letty replied.

"He knew a woman there who worked at a tavern."

"The Tollbooth Tavern," Brodie replied.

She nodded. "She was a friend, or so he told me. She was on her own with a boy eight, maybe nine, years old at the time. She did sewing on the side to earn extra money. One of the things she made was men's coin purses; one of them things that folds together for coins and notes and such."

As she explained it, Mick would take the woman bits and pieces of leather the owner of the shop tossed away. Then, he would sell what she made at the marketplace and split the profit with her.

Letty took a long drink of tea as if thinking what to say next, or how to say it.

"He went to see her that night, just before Christmas, just as he had before... When he came to see me afterward, I knew something dreadful had happened."

I glanced over at Brodie. Was he prepared to hear what Letty might have to say? Would it make a difference?

"He said there was an awful scene," she continued. "Such as he'd never heard before, her screamin'. Then everything went quiet. And there was a man wot came out of the flat."

"What did he tell ye about the man?" Brodie asked.

She shook her head. "He wouldn't say, told me that it was best I didn't know. The only thing I could think was maybe he recognized the person."

"Did he go inside the flat at Bleekhouse Close?" Brodie asked. "Was there anything else he told you, something he saw inside perhaps?"

"He went inside after the man left, thinkin' maybe there was something he could do for the poor woman..." She shook her head. "She was hurt somethin' awful. He went to get help, but when he finally found the watch, the constables were there, and he overheard that she had died."

"And afterward?" I asked.

"It was after that we made plans to leave the city. He seemed in hurry to go. We weren't married. There wasna time, and then... Mick was gone. A robbery I was told." She looked over at me. "He never carried more than a few pence. A few pence for a young man's life!"

It was not uncommon. I knew that as well as Brodie. But for something like that to happen after Mick Tobin had encountered a man at Bleekhouse Close the night Màili Brodie was killed?

"I came here and lived with me father until I met Mr. Voltmer."

A look at Brodie and I knew his thoughts were the same as mine.

Was it possible that Mick Tobin had been killed because of what he saw that night?

"Is there anything else ye remember?" Brodie asked. "Something the woman might have said to Mick, that he told ye afterward?"

"He said that she spoke once about the boy and that she hoped to save enough for them to leave that place..." She hesitated again. "He knew there were men who paid her a visit from time to time, but it was all for her son, so they could leave." She looked over at Brodie.

"The boy would be about yer age now," she added, then suddenly stopped. "Ye did say yer name was Brodie?"

He nodded. "My apologies for any unpleasantness this has brought ye. I appreciate yer time."

Letty pressed a hand over her mouth. "Father in heaven! Yer him! The boy!"

Brodie stood with some effort, one hand pressed against his side inside the front of his jacket. He laid several coins on the table.

"Ye've been more than generous with yer time. I thank ye kindly."

I thanked her as well, then glanced over at him as we bid her goodbye.

He was deathly pale, but whether it was from the wound or what we'd learned I had no way of knowing.

It appeared that Mick Tobin had been innocently caught up in a dreadful situation the night Brodie's mother was badly beaten and then died. He had then planned to leave Edinburgh with Letty, only to be killed during a robbery a short time later.

What had he seen that night? What was it he refused to tell her? Was he killed in the midst of a robbery as she said, a common enough occurrence on the streets of the East End of London and apparently in Old Town Edinburgh as well?

Or was it something else?

Nine

IT WAS midafternoon by the time we returned to the Waverley.

I had hired a private hack rather than returning by way of the tram that we had taken earlier after seeing fresh blood on Brodie's shirt.

"Bloody Scot" had taken on an entirely new meaning as he slowly walked into the hotel on his own.

I kept a watchful eye on him and a hand on his arm. Which was ridiculous if he should go down since I had no way of assisting him back to his feet. In which case, I would need assistance from hotel staff which would then raise all sorts of questions, particularly in the matter of the blood on the front of his shirt.

I doubted they would look favorably on a person with bullet holes in him.

"Where the devil have ye been?" Munro had very obviously returned. He took one look at Brodie and made another comment under his breath.

"Ye look like the very devil himself."

"The bleeding has started again," I told him.

"Aye," Munro nodded. "Best get him up to the room."

"What were ye able to find out about last night?" Brodie

insisted as we walked to the lift, his hand pressed against the front of his jacket.

Munro shook his head. "Not here," he said with a look around at the other guests we passed.

When we reached our floor, he wrapped an arm around Brodie and handed me the key to his room. Once inside, he deposited him onto a chair at the table in the sitting room, then opened the front of Brodie's coat.

He made a comment, which by the sound of it, I was inclined to agree with.

"Leave off!" Brodie told him.

"It would serve ye right if I did," Munro replied, "however I doubt Miss Forsythe is prepared to explain a body in the hotel."

"I've had worse injuries," Brodie snapped at him.

"Aye, we both have. However if you lose any more blood, none of that matters. And ye won't be able to continue in yer search, now will ye?"

That was being rather blunt. However, it worked.

"What have ye left for bandages?" Munro asked me.

"More than enough."

Munro nodded. "Ye need more than fresh bandages," he told Brodie. "But in place of tying ye to the bed, ye need a physician. One who can provide treatment for the wound and perhaps stitch you back together. Although I'm tempted to leave ye as ye are."

Only Munro could have gotten away with telling him that. He looked over at me. I nodded, in complete agreement.

"I'll not go to hospital. Ye know as well that it would only raise questions about the way it happened. I'll not have the police brought into this."

Munro was in agreement as far as that went. "There's someone who can help," he told Brodie.

"MacNabb?" Brodie replied with a grimace of pain as Munro helped remove his jacket.

"Aye, MacNabb. I know yer feelings in the matter, but he knows those on the street. We don't, havin' been away a long time." He was eventually able to remove the jacket with my assistance.

"It's either that or I put ye on the next train to London, or let ye bleed out."

I glanced over at Brodie. Interesting choices, and I believed that Munro would carry out any one or all of them.

I especially appreciated the comment about putting him on the next express back to London. But I knew from the expression on Brodie's face, that was not even a consideration.

He nodded. I could have sworn there was a gleam of satisfaction in Munro's eyes.

"He's just below on the street," he told him. "I'll let him know that we need a physician, and to be discreet in the matter." He paused on his way to the door. "The man has a bit of a reputation here at the hotel and needs to be careful."

When he had gone, I removed my jacket and set about making more bandages from the remnants of the sheets from the night before. We were obviously going to need them.

"I told ye that this was not for ye," Brodie reminded me, that dark gaze watching as I went about the sitting room.

"I told ye that I didn't want ye to be part of it." And when I didn't immediately respond, "Mikaela?"

"I heard you, there is no need to shout."

"When will ye listen to me?"

Considering his boorish behavior, possibly never, I thought, but didn't say it. I do know when to pick my battles and now was not the time when the particular *boor* was in an exceptionally nasty temper. As I bent near to retrieve his jacket, he took hold of my hand.

"Ye can see now that ye need to go back to London. I don't want ye caught up in this. If anything was to happen..."

I was fairly certain what he was thinking. I saw it in that dark gaze, the past somehow repeating itself in some way?

He had never before expressed himself in such a manner. It

seemed that perhaps I mattered to him, at least just a little. He wasn't playing fair at all.

Damn bloody Scot!

I thought of several things I might have told him, most of them already said. I pulled my hand from his.

"We are going to need supper," I replied. "On the assumption that you're going to survive, of course." I gathered my bag.

There was nothing more to be done until Mr. MacNabb was able to return with a physician, and there were things I needed to attend to. He would be all right until I returned.

"Mikaela..."

"I won't be long," I told him then, and headed for the door.

Once I was out in the hallway, I let out the breath I had been holding.

What was that all about?

I didn't bother to examine it as I returned to the lobby of the hotel.

Coward, that little voice whispered.

I returned to my own room, found that my meager wardrobe had been returned sometime earlier from the hotel laundry, along with a new set of sheets.

I could only guess what the hotel staff must have thought about missing sheets.

I had been gone too long, I rationalized, and was about to return to the room across the hall when there was a knock at the door.

Munro had returned accompanied by a much shorter man in rough-cut street clothes in shades of brown and gray with a tweed cap. The notorious Archie MacNabb I presumed.

They were accompanied by a stout fellow with ruddy cheeks and disheveled hair as if he might have been roused from his bed in spite of the fact that it was early evening. He also carried a black leather case and reeked of alcohol. I looked questioningly at Munro.

He shook his head then went to his room across the way and entered accompanied by the two men. I followed, sincerely hoping they had not been seen or we might well have the hotel manager along with the police arriving because of their somewhat questionable appearances.

Brodie had moved from the chair to the settee. He still wore the bloodied shirt and a particularly dark expression.

"Archie MacNabb," Munro introduced the shorter man.

"Pleased to make your acquaintance, miss," the little man replied, and made what could only be considered a ridiculous, courtly bow in my direction.

"This," he made introductions of his companion, "is my good friend, Benjamin Frye. Mr. Munro indicated there is a need for his assistance," he commented as he stepped farther into the room and caught his first glimpse of Brodie.

"Old acquaintances, eh, young man. It seems that you haven't changed yer ways," MacNabb commented to Brodie.

"Nor yers," Brodie replied.

"Aye, it's been a while," MacNabb continued with what could only be described as a sly grin. "And now yer traveling with high company, I see. The lady might need protection. I can offer my services," he added, unexpectedly taking hold of my arm, his hand brushing the bodice of my shirtwaist.

The last was meant for Brodie's benefit, of course, and only succeeded in bringing him up off the settee with a furious expression as I retrieved my arm and took a step back.

"Get him out of here, or I'll finish what I should have done years ago," Brodie threatened.

Of the assorted street people I had met in partnership with him, Mr. MacNabb had to be one of the most outrageous, even disgusting.

Whatever their history, I thought Mr. MacNabb was treading a very slippery slope. Brodie was a good foot and a half taller and even in his condition I most certainly wouldn't have been one to cross him.

However Munro seemed to think he could be useful and proceeded to intervene.

"First things first," he told both men. "Before ye bleed all over the place, Brodie. There are more important matters!"

"No offense, miss," MacNabb grinned at me.

"I assure you, I do not need protection." I made it perfectly clear. "And if you touch me again, I will cut off your hand."

That set him back on his heels with a slightly amused expression. Munro nodded then warned him.

"I gave her the knife myself, and lessons as well. Ye've been told, Archie. Let's get on with this, and we'll talk after."

If I was concerned about Archie MacNabb, my concern was only sharpened by Benjamin Frye, who looked more the sort one might find in a stables administering to an injured horse.

"Are you affiliated with the university?" I inquired, curious about his qualifications.

The University of Edinburgh was very well known for their research and advances in medicine.

"University?" he replied with a slightly hazy look. "No, I'm a bit of a private practitioner, as needed from time to time."

And when sober? I thought, considering the fumes that filled the air about him as if he'd been soaked in gin.

Once the bandages were removed, he proceeded to examine the wound.

"You will need to wash your hands," I commented, thinking again that I wished that we had the services of Mr. Brimley, or failing that, a legitimate physician.

Benjamin Frye looked up at me from where he sat in front of Brodie. "I washed them this morning, miss, when I assisted in the birth of a child."

As recently as that?

Poor thing, I thought, and the immediate question came to mind— did mother and child survive?

I didn't say it, instead I retrieved the bottle of Old Lodge from the previous evening and thrust it at him.

He smiled. "I do appreciate it, miss..."

"It is a very effective *disinfectant*," I informed him. There was a muttered comment from Mr. MacNabb.

"Is she always like this?"

Munro nodded and replied loud enough for Mr. Frye to hear as well. "Aye, best not to cross her. She's also an excellent shot, I'm told."

Mr. Frye accepted the bottle of whisky, doused his hands with it, then took a substantial swallow.

"For medicinal purposes," he said with a grin.

"Get on with it," Brodie told him.

There was more poking about the wound, and I thought Brodie might come up off the settee.

"What of the bullet?" Mr. Frye inquired with a look up at Brodie, then Munro.

"It went through, if ye care to have a look," Munro replied.

"Ah, yes, exit wound. Most fortunate."

I was inclined to question what was fortunate or unfortunate under the present circumstances, but chose not to say anything.

"It will definitely require stitches," he announced, then sat back.

He took several instruments out of that black bag— one a rather large, nasty-looking needle and a spool of thread. He then took another drink of whisky.

"It helps steady me hand," he said with a wink.

I looked over at Brodie as the man handed him the bottle.

"A bit to dull the pain?" Frye commented.

Brodie took the bottle then set it aside. "I prefer to keep me head clear in the event ye fail to have a steady hand."

Mr. Frye nodded. "Suit yerself."

Brodie wrapped a hand over the back of the settee, his expression not one I would have challenged as Mr. Frye threaded a needle. He then took the bottle of whisky and with a look over at me, doused both needle and thread.

I was confident that Brodie was in safe hands with Munro standing over Mr. Frye, and stood to leave.

"We're going to need something to eat," I announced. "I'll make arrangements." I headed for the door.

In a way I pitied Mr. Frye if he should make a wrong stitch as it were, with two capable Scots, even if one of them was injured, to see the matter set right.

"I would accompany you, miss," Archie MacNabb commented. "However I'm not presently welcome at the Waverley due to past situations."

I didn't want to know, and didn't ask.

I'll admit that I felt like a coward not remaining while Mr. Frye attended Brodie's wound, it's just that... I didn't know what it was.

I wasn't squeamish at the sight of blood, for heaven's sake. I had most certainly been through such a difficulty myself, and had seen all manner of wounds in the past. It was just that...

It was Brodie, that little voice whispered.

"Oh, bloody hell!" I whispered as I left the room.

As I had previously, I put in the order for supper to be delivered to my room. The head waiter was accommodating, if most curious. I then went to the men's smoking room once again. It was still early enough of the evening and there were only a handful of guests. I approached the mahogany counter and made my request.

"I will take it with me," I informed him.

It took several moments as he assisted another guest, but he eventually retrieved a bottle and made note of my room number. At this rate, I was going to have a sizeable bill.

I returned to the second floor. Whatever I assumed that I might find, I was pleasantly surprised as I knocked and then entered the room.

A fire burned in the hearth and some order had been set to

the room, no doubt due to Munro's efforts. Mr. Frye was just finishing attending to Brodie's wounds and sat back with a satisfied grin on his face.

The only outward indication of the ordeal in Brodie's face was a sheen of sweat at his forehead that had dampened the hair that fell there.

"Ah, there you are," Mr. Frye announced. "Quite admirable work if I do say so myself. And more whisky! Excellent, my dear, as we've used all of what was left."

I set the bottle on the small table by the hearth, out of reach lest it immediately disappear. I looked at Brodie.

I had to admit, the stitches were all neatly lined up in a row, both wounds closed. Mr. Brimley couldn't have done better. Mr. Frye proceeded to apply salve to the wounds, a particular scent I was familiar with.

"Camphor?" I commented.

"Among other things," he replied. "Including extract from juniper berries, an old remedy my grandmother swore by. To guard against infections. She lived to be ninety-seven and patched many wounds in her time. The camphor is just to be certain."

In spite of his earlier manner, I found that I liked Mr. Frye whatever his calling might have been, and I had to agree he had a fine hand with a needle and thread.

"You know a bit about medicine?" he asked.

"From a similar situation," I explained.

He smiled. "Now, perhaps another wee dram," he suggested as he finished securing the bandages. "And I'll be on me way."

He poured himself a healthy portion and it disappeared in one swallow.

"As I said," he repeated. "I'll be on me way, now."

Munro paid him and then reminded him to leave by way of the service entrance at the back of the hotel.

After Mr. Frye had left, Brodie turned to MacNabb.

"Tell me what ye know," he said in a tone that warned it might be dangerous to refuse.

"And none of yer tricks or schemes. What do ye know about what happened to Sholto McQueen and the man who killed him?"

Whatever their history Brodie was willing to listen, but I suspected he also was not above tossing MacNabb out the window in spite of his condition. There was most definitely no love lost between the two.

"Ye'll not be threatening me, Brodie. Ye need me, and what I can learn for ye out on the street, aye? And by the looks of her," he gestured to me, "I'll wager there's good coin to be had in it fer me."

Brodie came out of the chair with amazing speed, considering his wounds, and seized MacNabb by the throat.

"Ye'll be paid what ye deserve and not a farthing more. And best to never threaten me again, Mr. MacNabb. Or I will make known to those who would be most interested about yer business ventures taking advantage of the dead to line yer own pockets.

"Wot do ye know about that?" MacNabb managed to squeak past Brodie's grasp at his throat.

"Enough to know that it has been a very lucrative enterprise for ye and those who work with ye these past years. Ye know well enough there are those who would be very interested to know, and there would be nothing Munro or anyone else would do to save ye.

"And if ye ever speak to Miss Forsythe again as ye did earlier, I will cut ye and let ye bleed out in the gutter where ye belong. Do we understand each other, Mr. MacNabb?"

I didn't know whether to believe what he was saying, or not. However, it was apparent that it was enough that Mr. MacNabb did.

"I meant no harm!" he squeaked again. "I canna breathe, and I canna help ye if I'm dead!"

Brodie finally released him, and he dropped to the floor like a sack of rocks. He slowly got to his feet, rubbing his throat.

I looked over at Brodie, as I feared that he might have opened his wounds again. When I would have gone to him, Munro motioned me back.

If Brodie had suffered any ill-effect, it was not there in the expression on his face or in that dark gaze.

"Now, about Sholto McQueen," he reminded MacNabb. "I'm told ye know everything that happens in the streets. What did he learn that got him killed? Who had he met with? And was the man there besides yerself? Did ye recognize him? And if ye lie, I'll use Munro's knife to cut the truth from ye, slowly."

"I bit of the drink, if ye please," MacNabb had the audacity to request. "Fer me parched throat."

Munro poured him a small amount and handed the glass to him. MacNabb's hand shook slightly. But it was impossible to know whether it was from genuine fear or lack of air moments earlier. Brodie sat back down across from him.

"Talk to me."

MacNabb rubbed his throat again. I was certain that he would have bruises.

"He was askin' round about a man named Meeks who was with the bloody peelers some time back." MacNabb emptied the glass. He held it out for more. Brodie shook his head.

"Who was he talking to?" he asked.

"Word on the street was that he had been with a man named Calhoun earlier, who left the police some years back on an injury and knew the man, Meeks, from before, when they served together. Sholto was supposed to meet with the fella again."

Brodie nodded. "What about the man who killed McQueen?"

MacNabb shook his head. "I never seen him before and with it bein' dark and all... Lucky as well fer yerself." He laughed, then stopped. "That he couldna see ye well enough or the outcome might have been different."

"What were ye doin' there?" Brodie demanded.

"I had some business with McQueen. And we had arranged to meet as usual. He sent word round to meet him there, and then..."

Ye know the rest of it. Now, I'll have to find me someone else to replace him."

And just like that, Sholto McQueen was dismissed. Not that he wasn't without his own questionable dealings according to Brodie, I thought, but it seemed such a pitiful, cold response for a man's life.

And then there was Mr. MacNabb, apparently an entrepreneur of the worst sort— grave robbing.

I shuddered at the thought. Not that I was particularly religious, and it reinforced my own thoughts about arrangements for my own ending. Dust-to-dust, no grave to rob not that it would be worth it to anyone.

I could only imagine what my friend Templeton would have said about his so-called "profession."

If what she believed was possible, that the soul went on, moving about in the afterlife as she claimed "*Wills*" had a tendency to do, I thought it safe to assume that Mr. MacNabb— disgusting little man that he was, might be in for quite a surprise from those on the other side for his activities. There were times I supposed, that justice was served in strange ways.

"What about the man, Calhoun?" Brodie asked. "Where does he live?"

"I don't know..." MacNabb replied.

Brodie slammed a fist down onto the table between them.

"Where?" he insisted. MacNabb held up a hand as if to protect himself from a blow.

"At some home for those who are retired from the police," he blurted out. "But I have no way of knowin' if that's correct, or if the man is still there as he supposedly moves about on the street and is hard to find."

"Could be Beecham's," Munro provided.

"That's all I was able to find out," MacNabb insisted. "I swear, on me mother's grave."

Possibly not the most appropriate thing to say, I thought,

considering what Brodie had just revealed about the man's criminal activities. Brodie poured another portion of whisky for him.

"Ye know the reason I'm here?"

"Aye." MacNabb took a swallow, his narrowed gaze fixed on Brodie. "I doubt ye'll find what yer lookin' for after all these years."

Brodie poured him another dram. "That is not for ye to say, and there are those still alive who might know what happened. I want to know what ye can find out about Officer Martin Graham."

"Such as?" MacNabb demanded.

"He was there that night, but the police are sayin' the files are not available. You know people still alive from then, including the police, those who may owe ye favors. I'd wager more than one is in yer back pocket. I want to know the reason there's no record available. At least none that anyone will provide."

"That can be dangerous."

"No more so than getting caught for robbing the graves of the rich."

When MacNabb would have grabbed for the bottle, Brodie pulled it out of reach.

"You'll be paid when ye provide the information, not before. And if ye say a word of the reason for yer inquiries, there will be no payment at all except... what I promised ye earlier."

"The years haven't cooled that temper of yers," MacNabb replied.

"Best ye remember that."

MacNabb set his empty glass on the table. "I'll get on with it then. I'll send word when I have the information."

Munro accompanied him to make certain he left the hotel unnoticed. Despicable little man.

"Would you do it?" I asked after they left. "Would you do what you threatened him with?"

Weariness lined Brodie's face as he sat back on the chair.

"It is only important that he believes it. And there are reasons that he does, and we will leave it at that."

Reasons.

There was a sound from the hallway outside the room. I glanced at the watch pinned to my shirtwaist. It was just past eight o'clock in the evening. It seemed that supper might have arrived. I stepped out of the room and found one of the hotel staff with a cart, looking somewhat bewildered.

"I was told to bring this to room two hundred twelve, miss?"

"Yes, thank you." I handed him six pence. "I'll take care of it from here."

I waited until he had returned to the lift and the floor below, then pushed the cart into Munro's suite.

Brodie still sat at the table, his head back on the chair, eyes closed. I thought he might have dozed off. God knows he had to be exhausted. His eyes slowly opened, and that dark gaze found me.

"I ordered supper brought up..." I explained. "You need to eat something."

God knows I hadn't felt like it at first, under similar circumstances. But that was undoubtedly due to the laudanum Mr. Brimley had given me.

"You sound like Miss Effie at the Public House near the office, always fussin' when she thinks that I don't eat enough."

He slowly stood. I crossed the room to give assistance should he need it. He shook his head.

"I'm not dead, lass. I can walk on me own. And I'm not bleedin' thanks to Mr. Frye."

I wasn't ready to give thanks for that just yet, considering the man hadn't been concerned about infection.

He managed admirably well, and slowly lowered himself into one of the chairs at the table.

I had ordered roast pheasant with the usual accompaniment of side dishes. He ate sparingly. Although, all things considered, I was impressed that he managed anything at all.

"Ye haven't made a comment about MacNabb," he said as he set his fork down beside the plate.

"That is not like ye."

I ignored that last part. "Do you trust him?"

"No, but I trust his greed. According to Munro things have not been profitable for him lately."

"Oh, fewer graves to rob?" I made no attempt to hide my disgust.

"And other things. He's a man of many talents from many years surviving on the streets."

Talents, seemed an odd way to describe thievery, blackmail, and grave robbing.

"How do you know him?" I asked, curious about the anger toward the man, other than the natural disgust for his crimes.

"When ye are fighting to survive, yer willing to do most anything." He took a long swallow of whisky.

Dear God, I thought! Had he and Munro been involved in some of MacNabb's enterprises.

"It's not wot ye think, lass. He made the connection for me and Munro to run numbers, along with some other lads. We were his '*employees*,' if you will, with promises that he would take care of us and pay us a portion of the fees."

He leaned back and closed his eyes again as if attempting to pull those memories back up all these years later. When he looked at me again, his expression was one I had never seen before— sadness and quite bleak.

"We ran mostly with a lad by the name of Alfie— no last name. None of us used them, or had them. On one of our runs, Alfie got himself tangled up with another street boss who wanted the money Alfie had collected." His fingers tightened around the glass, then slowly relaxed once more.

"He was cut up bad. We didna hear of it until we all came back in for the night where MacNabb had a place to collect the day's take. Alfie didn't return and the word on the street was that he was badly wounded at the house of a woman we knew."

I wanted him to stop, but it was as if he needed to tell me, for whatever reason. And so, I listened.

"We wanted to go and bring him in. MacNabb wouldna allow it, even made it so we couldna leave. He said that it was part of doin' business, and best keep to ourselves.

"Business," he repeated.

"Poor Alfie was found in the gutter in the old town the next day. He might have lived, with care." He took another swallow. "He bled to death, just so much garbage to be tossed out."

The threat Brodie had made, to leave MacNabb in the gutter, made sense. Pay back perhaps for things of the past. I wiped the sudden dampness from my cheek.

I never cried... But it was there— for Alfie, and Brodie and Munro, and all the other boys who were thrown away. I knew what that look was in his eyes— it was regret, and a promise if MacNabb should betray them.

I had no idea how he was still conscious in spite of having no laudanum; what both he and Munro had been through, loss of blood, and little sleep the night before.

"You need to get some rest," I said, struggling with my own emotions.

"Are ye goin' to pester me about it?" he commented with a small smile.

"Of course, foolish man." I then told him the thing that obviously mattered most.

"If you don't, you won't be able to continue. Up and at it, then. You can lean on me, I'll help you into the bedroom. Munro can sleep here. Come along."

I went and stood beside his chair and took hold of his arm opposite the side of his injuries. He slowly stood, leaning against me as I wrapped his arm about my shoulders.

"*Phlàigh!*" he muttered as we slowly made our way into the adjacent bedroom.

I hadn't heard that before, obviously in Gaelic, and probably didn't want to know. I decided to ignore it.

"You're quite welcome," I told him as we reached the bed and he dropped down on the edge.

I assisted in removing his boots and set them aside. I hesitated, then decided not to worry about his trousers.

A hand stopped me when I would have reached for the blankets to cover him as there was quite a chill in the room.

"I called ye a *pest*."

How wonderful, I thought. Here I was attempting to make certain the man might recover and he had called me a pest. However, in view of past situations that we'd shared, I supposed he was entitled to that. It could have been worse.

His fingers brushed my cheek. "Don't go."

Don't go?

The man had been trying to get rid of me ever since I arrived.

"Stay with me."

Just those three words, and tears threatened again. Bloody stubborn Scot!

I unbuttoned my skirt and stepped out of it, and removed my shirtwaist.

It wasn't the first time, but there was something different now — something in the way he pulled me against him as I slipped under the blankets, as if he was holding on as he wrapped himself around me.

I slipped my hand in his and drifted off to sleep.

Ten

MUNRO RETURNED SOMETIME LATER from escorting Mr. MacNabb from the hotel.

I heard him briefly as he moved about and half expected him to appear at the doorway to the bedroom.

He did not but apparently slept on the settee or perhaps the floor as that was where I found blankets when I rose early, dressed, and left the bedroom, Brodie still sleeping.

There was nothing in Munro's expression or by word, at my having shared the room and bed with Brodie. He merely nodded.

"There's hot coffee, and I spoke with the man downstairs about breakfast. He was most perplexed."

I could imagine, although I was convinced it was a service that should be provided without question, if requested.

"Mr. MacNabb?" I inquired, pouring myself a cup and then savoring that strong brew.

"Off on his business," he replied. "And assured that if he double crosses us, he will prefer what Brodie threatened over what I will do to him."

I reminded myself that this was not the Dark Ages— that whole *"drawn and quartered"* period with heads left on a pike at the gate.

This was the modern age with a new century just around the corner and marvelous new inventions every day. Although having met the man, I was inclined to agree that the threats were warranted.

Munro glanced past me at a sound at the bedroom door as Brodie emerged, shirtless, bare of foot, with his trousers on of course and bandages that were mercifully dry with no signs of more bleeding. However, it that made him look like a Christmas goose all trussed up for a feast.

With just a quick glance at the dark gaze and the way it held mine, I went no further with that thought. Best keep to the matter at hand, which was the next steps in our inquiries.

If he was discomforted in any way, he hid it quite well as he crossed the room, albeit a mite slowly, and Munro handed him a cup of coffee.

"Yer goin' to need another shirt. I've only one left," Munro commented. "I would send the others to launder but hotel staff might be a bit put off by all the blood. Do ye have any left?"

This with good humor, morbid good humor, I might add.

"Enough," Brodie replied, draining the cup, and holding it out for more. "MacNabb?" he then asked.

"We'll see what he is able to come up with. I did impress him that when ye were through with him, I would finish it," Munro replied.

I had little to no sympathy for the man, but I wouldn't have wanted to have either Brodie or Munro as enemies.

We ate bread and jam, along with eggs, and a rasher of several pieces of bacon.

Munro had eaten, provided Brodie his last shirt, and then set off for Beechum House, the home for the injured and poor, in hopes of finding the man, Calhoun, who might have information about Constable Meeks.

Brodie had slowly pulled on the clean shirt, and his boots.

"What are ye about?" he asked as I rose from the table and that last bit of coffee, and went to the door.

"I'm going to change clothes and make my notes. Then I want to go to Carnegie Street."

"Constable Graham's widow?"

I nodded. "If she is still there, she may be able to provide something that might be useful."

He nodded. "We'll go together."

I had changed into a clean shirtwaist, finished dressing, and pinned up my hair. I stood in front of the chalkboard as I added a new note with Calhoun's name.

"I like it down."

I turned to find Brodie standing in the doorway.

"Yer hair," he added.

It had been well enough down this morning when I wakened, having somehow come undone during the night. I suspected those long fingers of his might be responsible.

There was a moment, perhaps one of shared memory of the past night, or other thoughts as I dusted chalk dust from my hands.

"Best get at it, if you're certain that you're up to this," I commented, stepping past those thoughts as I gathered my jacket and umbrella, and met him at the door.

"Aye, well enough," he replied with a gentle tug at a wayward strand of hair that was forever escaping my best efforts to restrain it.

The tenements along Carnegie Street were in the Georgian style, three or four stories of sandstone masonry common about the city. We made inquiries and were directed to Number 24 which was in less dire condition than some of the other tenements the South Side.

We let our driver go after he informed us that he made a return circle at midday if we were in need of a driver. With a sideways look at Brodie, I was certain of it in spite of his best efforts to show no effect from his wounds.

The Number 24 was etched into a stone above the entrance to the last tenement on the east side. The building appeared to be well kept as opposed to the others and there was even a late-blooming pot of flowers at the top step at the entrance. An effort perhaps by someone, to make the building seem not quite so austere.

"I'll inquire about Mrs. Graham if you wish to stay here," I told Brodie as a lad of about six or seven years charged by with a stick and ball in hand, no doubt for a game on the street as I had seen others play on our ride across from the Waverley.

"That's me grandmother's name!" the lad boasted with a toothsome grin. He looked at us with curiosity.

Or I should say that he looked at Brodie and the substantial bruise on one side of his face from the encounter at the White Hart Tavern. The color had come up quite nicely— somewhere between blue and purple, but not yet the green or yellow as I had seen on others in our inquiries.

"What exactly is yer name?" Brodie asked him, going down on bent knees so that he was at eye level with the boy.

"Marty Graham, after me grandfather," the boy boasted.

Brodie and I exchanged a look.

"Does yer family live here?" Brodie asked.

Young Martin nodded. "Me Grandmother at Number 24-B — I know me letters," he boasted with a smile.

"Who else lives with you?" I asked.

"Me mother, and Gran. There," he pointed overhead to the second-floor row of windows.

"Me mother can see from the window and calls down when it's time fer supper."

"Are they home now?" Brodie asked.

"Me mother is there. Gran went to market."

Brodie shook his hand and thanked him, and he was swallowed up by a group of boys about his same age as they set off.

It seemed that we had found the Graham residence, even after all these years. The question was, what would young Martin's grandmother be willing to tell us or even remember?

We found the flat at Number 24-B and I knocked. The door

was eventually opened by a woman perhaps my age or somewhat older, considering how long it had been since that night so long ago. Sarah Graham looked out at us with more than a little curiosity.

She was initially hesitant, as well I could imagine once Brodie introduced himself and me as well. On a matter to be discussed with her mother.

"I don't know what she can help ye with..."

"It's in the matter of Constable Martin Graham, from several years ago," Brodie explained in that way I had seen a dozen times; taking care with his words, his manner gentle and caring.

She explained that her mother would be back soon and offered us tea.

I saw the questions in the expression on her face as she set out tea and biscuits, a touching gesture as I looked around at the meager but well-kept furnishings in the room that also contained the kitchen and a firebox for coal, with articles of clothing on the table along with thread, buttons, and scissors.

She sewed garments for the milliner on the street next over while her mother— Martin Graham's widow, cleaned businesses at the High Street.

Two women and a young boy, apparently alone in the world, yet there was a pride in her words.

"And me boy. He means the world to me. I work here so that I can be home when he comes from his lessons. He's going to have an education. Perhaps be a bookkeeper." She beamed with pride. "He's good with his numbers."

We had accepted a second cup of tea when there was a sound from the landing outside the flat. Sarah went to open the door and took several bags of food from the woman who entered the apartment— Elsie Graham who was once married to Constable Graham.

Sarah set the bags on the table near the kitchen, then made the introductions.

"They came to ask ye about Father, and when he was with the police."

I saw the surprise on Elsie Graham's face, then the way it changed and the sadness there.

"He was a good man," she vehemently told us. "No matter what ye might have heard or they might have told ye."

I explained that was exactly the reason we were there as no one was willing to even acknowledge that he had been with the Edinburgh Constables.

"Ain't that the way of it though," she replied, anger in her voice. "Even after all these years, they still refuse to give him credit where credit was due." She looked from me to Brodie.

"My husband was a good man. He worked hard... he paid for this flat so that we would always have a place to live. It's not fancy like what yer most likely used to, but it's ours. They can't take that away! Even with their lies."

"That's what I want to speak with ye about," Brodie told her. "About a night that was just before Christmas, a ... murder that yer husband was called out on at Bleekhouse Close.

"It was almost thirty years ago," he continued. "A long time, I know but I was hoping he might have said something about it. The woman was quite young and worked at a local tavern, and there was a boy..."

I watched as he explained, the emotions that suddenly came and then just as suddenly disappeared behind the mask of the police investigator he had once been.

"The murder was particularly brutal, and she was left to die. If ye could remember anything..."

"I remember," she said in a quiet voice.

Brodie looked over at me, then at Elsie. "Are ye certain?"

She nodded. "I'm certain. Ye don't forget the ones that yer man brings home with him, the ones that he canna forget. And then he was gone so soon afterward. What reason do ye want to know?"

I watched Brodie as that professional mask disappeared. "The woman was my mother."

Elsie stared at him. "It was as he feared; a young boy left to his own on the streets. He woke up nights, dreamin' about it; about how young she was." She nodded.

"I'll tell ye what I know, though there's not much to it. He didna like to speak of it."

Sarah Graham put on another pot of tea as her mother told us what she remembered.

Constable Martin Graham was a respected officer on his shift with Constable Meeks. They were called to Bleekhouse Close that night, a violent quarrel and screams between a man and woman they were told. When they arrived, the man was gone, and the woman was dead. A pretty thing, and there was a child the woman who collected the rents told them.

The woman knew of a young man who came regular, but this was different. Her sense of it was that this was someone else. The man and woman quarreled then everything went quiet.

The two constables looked for the child, hoping to spare the boy returning home to the empty flat, but weren't able to find him.

"When he went to make his report; he was told to state that it was just another death in the slums. But there was something about the way they told him, like it was an order. So he did as he was told but he didn't much care for it.

"There were more than enough accusations of bad goings on against the police back then over one thing or another. But that brush painted all of 'em to his way of thinkin'."

Elsie then told us about the night her husband died.

"Said it was during a robbery, that he got caught in the middle of it, and a man with a knife went at him." She shook her head. "Not my Martin. He knew the streets and the people in them. He'd grown up not far from here. The man they said wot did it was what Marty called a part-time thief, mostly food and maybe a warm coat just to survive."

The man, known on the streets for being not quite right, disappeared afterward. His body was later found in a horse barn at the Haymarket. Elsie was told that he'd gotten drunk nearby and stumbled into the barn where his neck was broke in the bottom of a stall where he tried to sleep for the night.

Sarah had gone out to find her son as Elsie continued.

"Lyin' bastards," she said, cheeks bright with anger. "I knew the man, pathetic as he was, he couldn't have kilt my Martin on any day of the month."

"Did you question what they told you?" I asked.

She shook her head. "You didn't question them, not if I wanted to keep what was left of my family safe. And then there is this place," she added.

"The flat was paid for, in full, and there was the monthly stipend that we depended on. If it wasna for Sarah and the boy, I'd go far away. But I canna leave. Not now at least."

She leaned forward and covered Brodie's hand with her own.

"My husband was a good man. If he could have, he would have saved yer mother."

She stood then and went into the adjoining room. She returned with a photograph. It was old, of the sort taken before more recent developments in photography. She handed it to Brodie.

It was the type of early photograph known as a daguerreotype. I recognized the look of it from early photographs my aunt had in the library at Sussex Square of her father, of her as a much younger woman, and photographs of my sister and myself.

"My Martin," she said with obvious pride. "On the day he first made constable."

He had been a very handsome young man, and so very proud I thought, not more than twenty or twenty-five years old. And then all of that apparently changed in the years that followed with the things he saw and the crimes he was called on, including the murder of Brodie's mother.

"Is there anything else that he might have told ye?" Brodie

asked. "Something that one of the other tenants might have said that night, or the woman who collected the rents."

She shook her head. "Not that he said. But he knew folks were uneasy in that part of the Old Town. People talk, and they were gossiping about other murders that had happened before and in the same way, the poor woman beaten to death. He wanted to find who had done such a thing."

"Blackmail," Brodie said as we finally found a driver for the return to the hotel, and then explained when I looked over at him.

"The flat paid for, and a monthly stipend. Ye may call it whatever ye wish, but it's blackmail. Her silence in exchange for the roof over her family's head."

"The police don't have a charitable fund for constables in need?"

He shook his head. "They are on their own. I know from experience. Perhaps someday. It would be only right for such a thing when a man is willing to risk his life to protect others. But no, and blackmail is the only word for it."

I thought of Elsie Graham. For whatever reason, she had been provided for after the death of her husband, but according to Brodie no such fund or provision existed.

"What about the 'others' that Constable Graham mentioned to Elsie?" I realized how painful this might be, but I wanted very much to know his thoughts. "Do you think there might have been other women...?"

He stared out the opening of the hack. "Aye, it's possible," he finally replied.

"It might be important to see what might be found in the newspaper archive at the Scotsman," I replied. When he didn't immediately reply, I looked over at him.

That dark gaze was fixed on something beyond the hack that I suspected only he could see— the past perhaps, painful memories.

Then, unexpectedly, he replied. "Aye, it could be useful."

I realized that he had been listening all along.

"I want to go back to the Scotsman after we see if Munro has returned. I might be able to find something."

We made the rest of the ride back to the Waverley in silence.

When we arrived, a short stout figure stepped out of the shadows at the entrance and waved furiously at us. It seemed that Mr. MacNabb had returned.

"Check for messages at the front desk," Brodie told me. "I'll see what information he has."

When I would have protested, considering his condition, he asked again for me to check for messages; possibly from Munro as he apparently had not returned.

"I don't like the man," I announced.

"Neither do I, but it's not necessary to like him to get information."

I watched as he approached MacNabb. They crossed the street toward the Public House.

There were no messages from Munro. He had obviously not returned after setting off to find information about the man, Calhoun, who supposedly might know about Constable Meeks who had been with Constable Graham the night Màili Brodie was murdered.

I waited for Brodie in the guest concierge. The expression on his face said a great deal.

"What was he able to tell you?" I asked as it was obvious that he wasn't at all pleased. He shook his head as he joined me in the concierge room.

"The people he knows supposedly don't know anything about files being unavailable."

"Do you believe him?"

"I believe he spoke with someone regarding the response ye were given..." He paused. "Aye, I believe him. He was verra cautious in the way of a man who knows he may have come upon something that is dangerous. I sent him off to inquire about the man who killed Sholto McQueen."

"He's a man of many connections," I replied. And not exactly in a good way, I thought, but didn't say.

"Could it be dangerous for him?"

Brodie looked up at me then. "Don't tell me that yer worried for the man after yer encounter with him?"

Worried was not how I would have put it. The man did seem quite capable of taking care of himself.

"Not exactly, disgusting little man that he is. I suppose that I wouldn't wish him any harm. I was hoping he might be able to provide information that could be helpful to you."

"He is disgusting," Brodie admitted with a hint of that old smile, then surprised me. "It means a great deal to me, Mikaela, that ye are here. I want ye to know that."

I was taken back. It was not like him to say what he was thinking, particularly when it came to his personal feelings, that penchant for keeping everything inside, closed off.

"Even though you were most determined to send me back to London?"

"Aye."

"I'll remind you if you should forget."

"I'm certain that ye will."

"I've been thinking..." I said then, something that had stayed with me on the ride back from Carnegie Street. Those dark brows arched over that dark gaze.

"Why am I not surprised?"

"You shouldn't be. You should know me well enough by now."

"Aye. What have ye been thinking?"

"There might have been other murders that were similar." I had chosen the words carefully, so not to cause him more pain over his mother's death.

"Other murders?" he replied. I nodded.

"It seems that it was something that bothered Constable Graham at the time; enough that he mentioned it to his wife."

He nodded. "I'll send off a telegram to Alex in London. They need to know about McQueen, and he might be able to learn something about the files that are not available. Although that could be a difficult matter. From experience, I know there are those here in Edinburgh who consider inquiries from London to be interference."

"Hmmm, politics?" I suggested.

"There is somewhat of an irony in the term— United Kingdom. There are those who would prefer to be under their own laws and their own government. Not one almost five hundred miles away," Brodie admitted.

"Old feelings that die hard? Not unlike the American colonies over a hundred and fifty years ago who refused to be under the rule of a king two thousand miles away?" I suggested.

"Perhaps. But for now, it could be helpful to have their assistance once more."

History and politics in the modern world— change.

I thought of a parade I had seen just the past year, in May in London to celebrate Queen Victoria's birthday. The Queen had been seen in her royal carriage with Bertie, the Prince of Wales, dressed in her usual black mourning gown and veil.

The Royal Horse guard had been resplendent in their uniforms mounted astride their horses with the Queen's personal guard and those in their military finest, along with representatives from throughout the empire. However, it was the sight of the Scottish guard that had caught my attention among all the red uniforms, polished black boots, and black-dyed bear hide hats of the guard.

The Scots wore traditional plaids that had once been banned, with sporrans, smartly cut jackets, sabers, and the pipes.

It gave me goosebumps as they passed by, the pipes that were also once banned as England sought to crush rebellion over a hundred years earlier, being played once more.

It might have been my association with Brodie that made me more aware of those men in the parade, somber, even defiant, and I was reminded of something.

I had once heard that the more things changed the more they stayed the same.

There was no need to return to my room, except perhaps to add to my notes on the chalkboard. That could wait.

For now it was more important to see what might be found in those newspaper archives, and what it might mean if I found what Constable Graham had spoken of decades earlier.

I returned to the hotel entrance and had the doorman wave down a driver for the ride to the Scotsman as Brodie went to the concierge office to send that telegram off to Alex Sinclair.

Eleven

I SIGNED in at the Scotsman after I arrived and went up to the floor where they kept their archive. I put in the request for editions of the newspaper six months prior to the date Brodie's mother was murdered. That seemed as good of a place as any to start.

As before, reading through the section with reports of crime incidents, was slow and painstaking.

I took a chance and narrowed it down by looking for the names of the constables who had responded to the incidents, specifically Constable Graham and Constable Meeks.

Hours later, just after the clerk had reminded me of closing time for the office, I found two separate incidents of women who were assaulted and then killed in Old Town. One at Tollcross on September 11th, and the second one at Cowgate on October 24th that same year. Both were called murders of women of "low class."

There was an accompanying article in the issue about the apparent rise in crime against women of their class in that second issue of the daily.

The clerk appeared in the small alcove where I had been going through those back issues and reminded me once more that it was time for the office to close.

I quickly wrote down the information from the second crime report that included the name of the victim— Katherine Eldridge, along with the details of that article in my notebook, then returned the issues to him.

Was it possible that Elsie Graham's husband was correct, that there had been other similar murders?

There certainly seemed to be a possibility. There were striking similarities in what little information there was, to additional murders that were referred to as a dispute over money.

I thanked the clerk and then left the newspaper office, waved down a cab, and gave the driver the name of the hotel.

I looked up when the driver made a hard turn at a corner that threw me against the side of the hack. I braced myself as the driver picked up speed.

The street and passing buildings that flashed by were not at all familiar to the ones I had traveled twice before to the Scotsman. There was another sharp turn.

I called out to the driver to stop, but there was no response. I called out again and demanded that he stop. Something was wrong and my thoughts raced.

I tried once more and once again there was no response.

What the devil was the driver trying to do?

Other thoughts crowded— it now seemed that I had easily found a driver in late afternoon traffic. Perhaps too easily? And now this wild, even dangerous ride through streets away from the Scotsman, and the hotel?

I tried once more to get his attention. Nothing as the hack barreled down another darkened street absent any passing streetlamps.

I had to do something. I was not about to be a victim to robbery or...

The hack lurched around another corner. The fear was there but I refused to give into it. Then, came the anger.

I had not survived other mishaps, some moments on my

travels that would have been considered dangerous, or being shot to either end up in a wreck, robbed, or worse.

The hack was the sort, much like a hansom cab, with a gate that closed over, left open.

I could jump, but I was not in favor of a broken neck. Neither was I in favor of hanging on until we reached our destination, wherever that might.

It took several attempts, between being tossed about and bracing myself against the wall of the hack, but I finally retrieved the revolver that Brodie insisted I carry from my travel bag.

I didn't want to kill anyone, but a desperate situation called for desperate measures. With any luck I would get the driver's attention and force him to stop. I braced myself against the side of the hack, managed to aim at the canopy overhead, and fired. The sound was deafening, and the inside of the hack filled with smoke.

The pace of the hack immediately slowed, and I was thrown forward against the gate. Then it suddenly stopped.

I scrambled to right myself, the revolver still in my hand as the hack tilted slightly. I fully expected to see the driver's face at the opening. Instead I heard a string of curses, then the sound of someone running that quickly disappeared.

I opened the gate and stepped down from the hack, the horse snorting and stomping. I was much of the same opinion.

The driver was gone, and except for the horse that was quite lathered from our mad dash about the city, it appeared that I was alone. I attempted to calm him, but he sidled, spooked, and then bolted, the hack careening wildly behind him down the darkened street.

Now, I was most certainly alone.

Had it been an attempt at robbery? Some other crime that I had read about earlier? Or something else?

I looked down the darkened street. There was only a single streetlamp at the far end and my sense of direction was turned around.

Had the driver made three turns after leaving the Scotsman, or more?

"*When lost retrace your steps.*"

I had learned that when traversing foreign places, and retraced to the corner at the other end then continued on, my hand tight about the grip of the revolver if I should encounter anyone else.

I reached the next corner, the street filled with tall buildings on both sides. They were not the usual tenements with shops on the street, occasional lights gleaming through the misty night, but what appeared to be warehouses and a factory building with a stack that disappeared into the night sky overhead.

I turned at the next corner and quickly continued on, glancing cautiously about for anyone who might have followed me.

How far had I come? Was it even in the right direction?

The street rose at the next corner and a familiar sight suddenly loomed out of the darkness, the towering walls of Edinburgh Castle lit up with hundreds of gleaming lights.

I quickened my pace again, almost running toward the castle. I was almost certain that the Scotsman offices were the next street over. I turned, the streets now lit up with streetlamps, the newspaper office, along with traffic on the street, just ahead.

There were shouts over the noise on the street, I thought I heard my name. I was suddenly grabbed about the shoulders and very nearly taken off my feet.

My first instinct was to fight. I tried to raise my hand with the revolver. A hand clamped over my wrist, stopping me.

"I've got ye, lass!"

There was only one person who called me that.

I am not one to overreact... usually. However, seeing that dark gaze, the obvious worry in the expression on his face, and the strength of his hand around mine, I seriously considered overreacting.

"What are you doing here?" The moment I said it, I realized how ridiculous that must have sounded to him.

"I thought I'd lost ye, lass."

I thought it as well, but didn't say it. Instead, "Just an unexpected ride about the city."

There was a softly muttered curse as Munro joined us.

"Ye are all right?"

I nodded.

He exchanged a look with Brodie. "Best to get off the street," he cautioned.

"Can ye describe the man?" Brodie asked as he poured me another dram.

"I didn't pay attention when he arrived at the newspaper office, and it was too dark when we finally stopped, and he ran off."

"I can well imagine," Munro commented, "a woman shooting at him. Must have been a terrifying experience for him."

I ignored that.

"I have no idea where he was going, only that it was in a part of the city with warehouses and a factory."

"Aye." Just that one comment from Brodie, that dark gaze watching me.

"What were you doing there?" I asked again. "How did you know that something had happened?"

"When ye didn't return, I set off for the newspaper office. The office was closed. The clerk inside saw ye leave."

"The hack was stolen," Munro added. "The owner was struck from behind. We arrived just after."

The remnants of supper, brought from the Public House across the street, were on the table in the sitting room in Munro's suite.

I had been too upset to eat, trying to understand what the night's events might mean beyond the usual street crime as Brodie called it. Two drams of 'Old Lodge' had calmed me.

However, whether it was the whisky, my run through the streets, or questions with no answers, I was quite drowsy.

Brodie took the empty glass from me, then took my hand. "Enough, fer tonight." He pulled me to my feet.

"I'll be across the way, if ye need me," he told Munro.

And just like that, Brodie accompanied me to my own room. Nothing was said, nothing asked. He was there and it seemed the most natural thing in the world.

He set the lock at the sitting room door then led me into the adjoining bedroom. One-by-one, he pulled the pins from my hair as if he had done it a thousand times, until my hair fell loose about my shoulders.

He then unbuttoned the skirt and my shirtwaist, those strong hands gentle yet reassuring as once again, nothing was said or asked, then eased me down onto the bed.

I heard sounds that I had come to know in the past, as he set aside his revolver, a handful of coins that jangled onto the bedside table, the sound of his boots on the floor. Then the dip of the bed as he pulled the blanket over both of us, the solid warmth of his body wrapped around mine.

How was it possible that I needed this? That I needed him? The assurance of his warmth against me, his hand over mine on the coverlet, when I had never needed anyone?

Somewhere in the midst of sleep that crowded in, I asked, "Are you all right?"

"Well enough, lass."

"The bandages..."

"They will keep until the morning."

I drifted, but there was something else— something important I needed to tell him.

"I found something at the newspaper office..." Although at the moment it slipped away.

"That will keep as well."

I was sore and would undoubtedly have bruises from my unexpected ride across the city the previous evening. However, there was a curious thing that set in after such an encounter— I wanted very badly to find the person responsible and provide them with a few well-placed bruises of their own.

Brodie, of course, pointed out the foolishness of those thoughts as I stood before the chalkboard in my sitting room and added notes about what we'd learned the day before in our visit with Elsie Graham— most interesting, along with the information that I'd found in the archive at the Scotsman.

Katherine Eldridge, age twenty-three years, seamstress, of #14 Thistle Street, found dead, September 11, 1860, at Tollcross. Injuries about the head and torso, no known witnesses.

Bettie Dowd, age twenty-seven years, prostitute, found dead October 24, 1860, at Cowgate. Injuries about the head and torso, no known witnesses.

Brodie's expression was thoughtful.

"What are you thinking?" I asked. The strangeness of that question from me had him looking over at me.

He was still a bit haggard but there had been no additional bleeding of the bullet wounds when I changed the bandages.

I had to admit that, aside from the swath of bedsheet bound around him, he was a very stirring sight with that light dusting of dark hair at his chest as I very slowly secured the wrap, "fussed with it a bit" as I tucked in the ends, until he grumbled at me, "Enough! Leave off! Quit yer fussin' about."

Indeed.

Now however, I really did want to know what he was thinking. I had discovered in the past that he had a remarkable mind for details and with his experience with the MP, not to mention the streets where he grew up as a lad, he had a unique perspective that I admired and was usually spot on.

"There are always witnesses," he commented now, studying my notes. "It's a matter of finding them and persuading them to tell what they know."

"I can imagine how you might do that."

He shook his head. "But after thirty years— as we've already learned, people leave, they die, and who would remember a prostitute, the seamstress, or a young woman who worked at a tavern."

"What are you saying?"

"I'm saying that perhaps it's a fool's errand."

"It's not a fool's errand. It's important, and now with what we've learned..."

"And after what happened last night... That could have ended badly."

"But it didn't and all the more reason that we have to continue."

He came away from the table and the remnants of scones and coffee. Those hands closed gently on my shoulders.

"If anything had happened to ye..."

"But it didn't," I pointed out. "And all the more reason that we cannot stop now." I caught that stubborn angle of his chin.

"You may return if you wish, but I will not," I announced. "Naturally it would be easier if you remained, but I understand if you chose to quit looking. After all, you've been injured. I really do understand."

"If I quit?" he repeated.

"I would hope that Munro would remain. He knows the streets and certain people..."

"If I quit?" he repeated, a sharpness in the words this time. His hands tightened on my shoulders.

"I know what yer doin'."

"I beg your pardon?" I asked.

That dark gaze sharpened along with the words. "Ye have a devilish way about ye," said the *"pot."*

"What is the next step?" I asked, since we were past that discussion.

"Munro is off to find MacNabb. At present, even though I don't like the man, he's the best source for word on the street about what happened last night.

"I want to send another telegram off to Alex in London about those files that are 'unavailable' from the police." He pointed to the chalkboard.

"He may also be able to pry information out of them about those two ladies; information not written in the newspaper. Sir Avery's influence carries a lot of weight."

"What about paying a visit to Beechum House?" I suggested. "It could be helpful to find Mr. Calhoun and learn what he knows about Constable Meeks."

He made a sound. "Yer like a dog with a bone. Ye don't let go."

"No." I smiled. "I don't."

There was that sound again. He shook his head. "Ye are a rare one, Mikaela Forsythe."

~

Brodie sent off his telegram while I gathered my notebook, sent my few clothes off to the laundry along with his and those he'd borrowed from Munro. I then met him in the hotel foyer and had the doorman summon a hack for our cross-city ride to Beechum House.

There was a brief conversation between Brodie and the doorman. When a hack arrived, the doorman nodded that he recognized the driver, as one of their regular drivers that assisted hotel guests.

I wondered if either the doorman or the driver were aware that Brodie then carefully closed the front of his jacket over the revolver at his waist, out of sight but not out of reach.

According to the information we had from MacNabb, the man we were looking for by the name of Calhoun was known to live at Beechum House now and again, and supposedly knew Constable Meeks at one time.

We rode the length of Princes Street from the hotel into Old Town, then traversed a series of streets past tenements and shops, the spires of St. Giles Church poking through the gray gloom that hung over the city. Beechum House, was at the end of an annex very near the church, a charity that the church sponsored.

It was said that the church was founded in the 12th century before becoming Protestant during the Scottish Reformation. It had once held the status of cathedral and supposedly still supported different faiths, including Catholic.

I glanced over at Brodie as we left the carriage at the corner and walked past that centuries' old church that had been torn down once, then rebuilt, those spires as much a part of Edinburgh as the castle.

His expression changed as we passed the church and I thought that I caught something he said, low, almost indistinct.

"You speak Latin?" I asked with more than a little surprise.

"Only a few words she taught me. It's fer her."

I realized that he spoke of his mother.

We crossed the annex and walked toward a multi-story drab and dreary Georgian building with two-story wings at each side, and windows looking out like so many sad eyes on the street below.

"This place was here when I was a lad. The east wing is a hospital," Brodie explained. "Although I would prefer Mr. Brimley's care.

"The main part of Beechum is for residents, the poor with no other place to go and those such as Calhoun, as well as the west wing. They're provided rooms through the church charity." He gave me a long look.

"It's not an easy place to see. I understand if ye'd rather not go inside."

Our past inquiries had taken us into many places. Not only here but in Paris as well, for a past client. I wasn't put off by a hospital or poorhouse.

"Not at all," I assured him. "You'll need someone to make notes, and I might have a question or two for Mr. Calhoun, if you should forget," I replied.

The expression on his face softened. "Most wouldna come near a place like this. Yer to stay close."

Of course.

We entered the foyer of the central part of Beechum House and made our inquiry regarding Mr. Calhoun and a request to see him.

We were asked to wait.

Edwin Calhoun, who had once been a constable with the Edinburg Police and knew both Constables Graham and Meeks, eventually appeared.

He was painfully thin and walked with a noticeable limp. The clothes that hung on his body were an odd assortment of street fare that I had seen countless times, with a gentleman's frock coat worn over— no doubt from the charity bin, along with shoes that appeared to be too large for his feet. A knapsack hung over one shoulder and there was a top hat, caved in at one side and undoubtedly from the charity bin as well.

The attendant who let Mr. Calhoun know we were there to see him then went about his way.

"Who the devil might ye be?" Calhoun demanded somewhat less courteous than I might have expected.

"It's in the matter of someone you knew some time ago when you were with the Edinburgh Police," Brodie explained. "Alvin Meeks who was a constable at the time."

The man's gaze narrowed as if in confusion, "A name I havena heard in a while," he replied. He then looked about as if concerned that someone might overhear. He waved Brodie closer.

"I was just about to set out." He indicated for us to follow him with another look back over his shoulder, then set off.

We followed him out onto the street where he continued without stopping. When he reached St. Giles Church, he turned and headed across the street without looking to see if we had followed.

I wondered if we were on a fool's errand?

We continued to follow him, down one of the wynds that

were quite common, to a door with a narrow window beside badly smudged with grime and soot. A tavern sat across the way, already open for business. Calhoun knocked at the door.

It abruptly opened on a ruddy-faced, heavy-set woman. "Wot yer got today, Mr. Calhoun? And who might these people be? Not the bloody peelers, I hope."

At a glance past into the equally narrow establishment, I realized it was a second's shop with various items displayed about— clothes and odd bric-a-brac and what appeared to be a customer, a woman with a young child.

Calhoun assured her that we weren't with the police. The woman frowned, with a look over both of us. I noticed that her expression changed to one that could only be described as keen interest at Brodie.

"It's crowded this mornin'," she announced in a different tone. "If yer lookin' fer somethin'."

"Thank ye, kindly. We'll wait out here," Brodie replied.

In a very short time, Calhoun reappeared, the knapsack noticeably empty at his shoulder as he pocketed a handful of coins. Without a word he shuffled past the shop to the opposite end of the passageway.

Brodie hesitated.

"What is it?"

"These places are an opportunity for pickpockets and thieves. Do ye want me to take ye back to the street?"

"I want to find out what he knows, if anything, about Meeks."

"Aye, ye'll stay close and let me handle any encounter."

I nodded in spite of his injuries, and slipped my hand into the pocket of my skirt, my fingers brushing the smooth metal of the revolver.

We emerged at a street that backed up to the building with the second's shop, Calhoun only a few paces ahead. Brodie glanced about. He nodded and took hold of my arm as we continued across the street as well as Calhoun waited in front of a coffeehouse.

"A good strong bit of coffee to clear me head?" he said with a look up at Brodie as we arrived. It was the first he had acknowledged Brodie since we left Beechum House.

"I'll stand ye a cup," Brodie replied. "And breakfast as well for some information."

Calhoun nodded and stepped inside.

Food was ordered and brought to the table, along with hot black coffee. Still no questions were asked in that way I had seen Brodie with others. He poured Calhoun more coffee, then set aside the pot that had been left on the table as the man pushed back his plate. I had to admit I had never seen anyone consume so much food.

"Wot's she to do with this?" Calhoun asked, aiming a look in my direction.

"She's with me," Brodie replied. "That is all ye need to know. Now, tell us what ye know about Constable Meeks."

Calhoun hesitated and for a moment I thought he might refuse to tell us anything.

"I knew Meeks, all right. He was a good man. We walked the streets together for a while."

"This is about the time he worked with Constable Graham," Brodie replied. "Before Graham was killed while on the watch."

"Aye, sad that was. First Graham, then Meeks."

"It was written in census records that his death was a suicide," Brodie said then. "What do ye know about that?"

"Wot might yer interest be all these years later?" Calhoun demanded.

"In the *interest* of a death both Graham and Meeks were called out on. In particular, the case of a young woman murdered at Bleekhouse Close a good many years ago. Then Graham died a short time later— only a matter of days afterward while on duty. There is a possibility that Constable Graham's death might have been murder as well."

I looked over at Brodie with more than a little surprise. There were most certainly very suspicious circumstances surrounding Constable Graham's death shortly after that of Màili Brodie. Then the additional deaths afterward, and Elsie Graham's comment that she knew the murder at Bleekhouse Close bothered her husband, but he hadn't explained the reason.

Calhoun sat back in his chair, his gaze narrowed on Brodie. "A dead constable. Most doona give it another thought. Wot is yer interest in Graham or Meeks?" he asked again.

"A man hears things out on the street with the man he partners, and from other places. Ye might have heard something that could be important."

"Ye sound like a man with some experience in these things," Calhoun commented.

Brodie nodded. "Aye, some."

"Yer not from Edinburgh or any of the districts."

"Not for a long time."

"Wot would interest ye, thirty years after?"

It was several moments before Brodie replied. "The woman at Bleekhouse Close was my mother."

"And ye want to find those responsible." Calhoun shook his head. "A long time. Ye would have been but a lad." He sat in that chair for the longest time, and I wondered if the conversation was at an end. He held out his cup and Brodie poured more coffee.

"There are things ye see, things ye hear, and things that stay with ye..." He shrugged. "Meeks might have said somethin' about that."

"What *might* he have said?" Brodie asked.

Calhoun leaned in close once more and spoke in a quiet voice. "He worrit about the way Graham died. He was always lookin' over his own shoulder when we were out and about."

"Go on," Brodie told him.

"As if he thought the same might happen to him. I asked him about it," Calhoun replied. "He didn't say anything right away. But we came across a situation, another death that scared the man. It was then he said that there was another man there that night at Bleekhouse Close. Someone he saw, but kept it to himself at the time."

Possibly Mick Tobin, I thought? Brodie nodded, his thoughts no doubt the same.

"What did he say about the man?"

"That's the thing." Calhoun looked around, appeared to look carefully at each of the other patrons, then apparently satisfied that there was no one about who showed any interest in our conversation.

"He said the man wore the uniform."

It took me a moment for that to register.

"Did he say who it was?" Brodie asked.

Calhoun shook his head. "He didn't see the man, and Graham never said who it was."

"When did he tell you this?"

"Not long after we were put together to walk Princes Street near the castle. He said that it could be worth his life if anyone knew."

It took Brodie several moments, then, "What did he tell you about the murder at Bleekhouse Close?"

"He said that it bothered Graham after them other murders, that it was the same in each case, the women beaten to death, that he didn't believe it was a coincidence.

"Makes me think of them murders of them women in London where the police still have no clue who kilt them," he added.

I knew he spoke of the Whitechapel murders that had filled the dailies in London for almost two years. The murders had set the entire city on edge. Everything had eventually returned to normal, whatever that might be, as there had been no new murders, even though the murderer had never been caught.

There were all sorts of rumors and gossip, of course, one suggestion that it might even be someone connected to the royal family, and they were determined to protect whoever it was, hence no one caught, no one arrested. And there was always a new scandal of rumor for their gossiping.

"What else did he tell you?" Brodie then asked.

"He said that Graham had tried to pull the reports on the other two murders; I thought the man was bloody daft. But he said there was no record to be found." He looked sharply at Brodie.

"If ye have the experience I think ye do, then ye know maybe one record goes missin'— perhaps misfiled, or on someone's desk. But not two, as well as the one at Bleekhouse Close. And then Graham was kilt supposedly in that robbery only days after," he added.

"It got to Meeks. Some of the lads said he just wasn't right in the head after losing his partner. He never said nothin' about what he was goin' to do, just turned in his papers, and left.

"The watch captain transferred me to another district rather than puttin' me with another man," he continued. "But I heard about Meeks just the same in that way that we know what goes on with others that wear the uniform.

"The word put out was that he kilt himself," he continued. "The lads at the precinct said how it was such a terrible tragedy. But to my way of thinkin' with wot he told me, and Graham kilt durin' a *robbery*?" Calhoun shook his head. "Graham was too good a man to have somethin' like that happen.

"I don't believe in coincidences, and I don't believe Meeks kilt himself, if ye get my meanin'."

"What about yerself, after Meeks death?" Brodie replied.

"I stayed on for two more years, then went out on an injury, livin' at the charity house since." Calhoun stood then, eased onto that leg that carried a limp, and secured the knapsack over his shoulder once more.

"As I said, I don't believe in coincidences."

We stood as well. Brodie reached out and took the man's hand. I caught a brief glimpse of the pound notes he passed to him.

"I thank ye for yer time. Will ye be all right?" Brodie asked.

Calhoun grinned. "Aye. I know all the good places to hide from the peelers, an advantage of havin' once been one of 'em."

"Do you believe him?" I asked as we departed and walked toward the busy intersection of streets as Calhoun disappeared in the opposite direction.

"He knew details. That is where ye find the truth." Then he added, "Aye, I believe him."

We returned to the hotel. Brodie immediately went to the concierge office to see if there was any word from Alex in London.

He returned just as Munro arrived.

"Were you able to find MacNabb?'

Munro nodded. "Aye."

A look that passed between them. To his credit, Brodie nodded. "Ye can tell us both."

"At first the word on the streets was that it was a possible attempt at robbery," Munro replied. I sensed there was a great deal more.

"What else?" Brodie demanded.

Munro looked over at me. "A man was found stabbed to death near the sawmill. He was seen earlier of the evening at the yards where the coachmen keep their horses."

And had then somehow appeared at the Scotsman and relieved the driver there of his rig and team. Another *coincidence*?

"Aye," Brodie nodded.

We used the lift to the second floor. I had notes that I wanted to add to the chalkboard. I had no idea where this was taking us, only that it seemed the more we learned, the less we knew, or thought we knew, about who might have killed Brodie's mother.

Munro went to his room.

My hand was on the lever of the door to my room. I suddenly stopped.

"What is it?" Brodie asked.

He looked at the door and immediately saw what I had seen. Marks were gouged into the doorframe next to the lock, pieces of wood splinters on the carpet below. The door had been forced open.

Brodie pulled the revolver from the waist of his pants and called out to Munro.

"Stay here," he told me as he pressed the lever and the door opened.

I waited for several moments, and then entered after them.

Twelve

THE SITTING room had been completely turned out.

There was broken china and glass from our supper the night before, drawers had been pulled from the writing desk, a rather poor rendering of a hunt scene had been pried from the wall, and the chalkboard stood askew.

The bedroom had fared no better. A water pitcher on the bedside table had been tossed aside and shattered, the wall still wet where it had been hastily thrown. Bed linens torn from the bed, the feather mattress cut to shreds, feathers scattered everywhere.

"Someone was lookin' for somethin'," Munro commented. He looked over at me. "Ye seem to have caught someone's attention, miss."

"Aye," Brodie frowned. "The question is what were they looking for?"

A vague memory stirred, something I had dismissed at the time.

"There was a man..."

Brodie looked over at me. "What man?"

"Here at the hotel. I ran into him when I returned with breakfast from the Public House as the hotel restaurant was not yet open."

"Can ye describe the man?"

I thought back to the encounter. "He was thin, very near my height. He wore a tweed Norfolk jacket, trousers, and a deer-stalker cap. He asked if I needed assistance."

"Ye spoke with him?"

"Very briefly. He asked if I needed assistance. I told him that I did not, and he left. He didn't seem any different from the other guests who were departing for the early train."

There was something else. "His eyes..."

"What about them?"

"There was no emotion in them, no surprise at the encounter..." I looked at Brodie, those dark eyes where I'd seen anger, frustration, the way they softened.

"They were cold," seemed the best way to describe them. "And I had the strangest feeling."

"A feeling?"

"You would call it instinct," I replied.

"What did yer instinct tell ye?"

"For just a moment, I had the feeling... I wanted to get away from him. It was probably nothing."

"Perhaps."

Or perhaps not. I saw it in the expression on his face. He righted the chalkboard.

"What about yer notebook with everything we've learned since ye arrived?"

"I had it with me when we left this morning."

His eyes narrowed as he read what I had written on the chalk-board. The names of Graham and Meeks were there, but I hadn't added others yet— Elsie Graham, Archie MacNabb, or Mr. Calhoun.

Nor had I the chance to enter the information I'd found about the other women who were killed.

"Gather whatever ye can find," he told me then. "Don't touch anything else. Leave it as it is," he told me with a glance over at Munro.

"We're leavin'?" Munro asked.

Brodie nodded. "There is always the possibility that whoever did this will be back." He looked at me then. "It's also possible they know about the notes ye keep in yer notebook."

They?

"What are you saying?" There was obviously something he hadn't told me.

"I'll tell ye later, after yer away from here."

"Ye have a place in mind?" Munro asked.

"Aye."

There wasn't much of anything to gather as he called it. I had sent the only other clothes I had brought with me to the hotel laundry, and they had not yet been returned.

I did find the tin of salve Mr. Frye had left for Brodie's wounds and put it in my bag. As for fresh bandages, I went into the bedroom and would have stripped off the bed linens. Brodie stopped me.

"Leave it."

Out of caution, we didn't leave by the front entrance of the hotel, but by the back service entrance where Mr. MacNabb and Mr. Frye had left the night before. We then walked to the adjacent street. Brodie waved down a hack and assisted me inside.

"Find MacNabb," he told Munro before departing. "Find out what he knows about this."

Munro nodded.

"I want anything he can learn on the street. Then, let me know."

"Where will I find ye?"

A look passed between them. I was usually quite good at reading those looks. This one told me nothing other than it was something they both knew.

"Aye," Munro said then.

"Watch yer back, my friend," Brodie told him in parting then stepped into the hack.

I eventually discovered what that silent message was as Brodie directed the driver a circuitous route that eventually took us into Old Town.

There, off the main street in Canongate, we left the hack and walked that last distance to a medieval two-story building made of sandstone block with timber frame windows.

It was an old medieval church that had somehow survived the past few hundred years.

Several of the windows were lit up, including two at the street level, one conspicuously with a red lantern.

Before I could ask the obvious, Brodie seized me by the arm and escorted me to the corner and around to the back of the building where there was a set of stone steps that led up to a landing in the back alley. Another red light glowed over the back entrance. In the event someone lost their way?

"Is this what I think it is?" I whispered as he rang a service bell at that back entrance.

"A safe place," Brodie replied as a woman opened the door, which raised the question about the meaning of "safe."

She was dressed in a gown that I would have bet my last farthing was a Worth creation— my sister raved about the designs that were elegant and very expensive.

It was in a shade of deep burgundy with black lace over the bodice and accentuated the woman's tiny waist.

"Brodie," she greeted him with a familiar smile. "A pleasure as always."

Her smile seemed to say a great deal more.

"Miss Antoinette," the woman identified herself.

And a first name. I was fascinated.

"Your usual room?" The woman's gaze slid over me.

He nodded.

"You know the way."

I was quickly escorted past and into what could only be described as a lavishly furnished sitting room where several "guests" and their hostesses reclined on settees, in various states of undress, and coupling beneath a timber-framed and buttressed ceiling that had no doubt witnessed other "ceremonies" in the past. I did attempt to keep my composure.

I am not usually given to surprise, having seen my share of things in my travels, not to mention in the inquiries Brodie and I made on behalf of clients. That was the only word that came to mind, along with a good number of questions.

However my questions would have to wait as I was firmly and quickly led to the stairs, then up that winding staircase to the top, and into the room at the back. The door closed behind us, and the lock clicked into place.

I turned to find Brodie leaning back against the door, a different expression on his face. There were several things that came to mind that included any number of questions.

He came away from the door. "There's a common room for necessities at the end of the hall, and a cook who provides meals for... the ladies and guests. And before ye say anything— yes, I know the woman who answered the door and I've been here before, but it's not what ye be thinkin'. It's in the matter of a business arrangement."

"Of course," I replied. "Business." I did attempted to contain my laughter.

"That's not my meanin'. It's in the matter of an arrangement with Sir Avery."

Sir Avery and the Agency.

That explained a great deal, if I was inclined to believe him. In any event, this was apparently where Brodie had been staying before my arrival in Edinburgh. A church that had been appropriated as a brothel. Most interesting.

"I've used the room before when I've made inquiries on behalf of the Agency," he added to clarify.

"Do continue," I told him.

He swore. "The location in this part of the city makes it easy for me to come and go without being noticed. I don't use the services."

"Of course not."

There was another curse. "I wouldna have brought ye here, except for what happened at the Waverley. Ye couldn't very well remain there."

I had noticed in the past that his accent thickened when he was most serious, or trying to make a point, or cursing.

"I understand. Really I do. A church, the perfect location for nefarious activities."

"Nef...?" He attempted to repeat what I'd said. "What the devil is that supposed to mean?"

"Clandestine, secretive," I translated. "Covert, which is French for something covered." If I was one to believe in such things, I did wonder what God might think of it all.

That dark gaze narrowed. "Covered up. I would expect that of the French."

"So says the Scot who has just dragged me into a brothel where he is on a first-name basis with the Madame," I replied. "Antoinette I believe it is."

I set my travel bag on a high-backed over-stuffed chair that might have been found in my own front parlor. I caught him watching me as I reached inside it.

"Mikaela...!"

There was a warning tone in his voice. I saw the wary expression on his face as I retrieved my notebook.

How interesting. Apparently he thought I might retrieve the revolver instead.

"I must admit that no one will think to look for us here..."

There was another curse. He went to the door.

"I'll see what there is for supper. I know how you can be when you havena eaten in a while. Lock the door behind me." He hesitated as I walked to the door.

It was there, something else he would have said. Perhaps the request not to shoot him when he returned?

I set the lock after he left, and turned back to the room.

It was minimally furnished almost stark, with two chairs, a small table between, a second table possibly for meals or games, and the bed. Tucked in under the rafters I couldn't help but wonder who might have once occupied the room centuries earlier. However, it did seem as if it might have been appropriated for the "business" of the establishment and by what I had seen downstairs, furnishings— other than the bed, were not a priority.

I set my notebook onto the larger of the two tables. The few clothes that I had brought with me and was able to retrieve before leaving the hotel, I hung in the small alcove closet with a satin curtain drawn over.

I had to admit, that in all my adventures, I had never stayed in a brothel. I thought of Brodie, and his attempt to explain our hostess's familiarity. It would have been too easy to be upset about the possible meaning of their relationship whatever it might or might not be.

The truth was that in spite of certain feelings on my part, I had no claim on Angus Brodie. We were business associates, partners in the inquiries we made on behalf of clients.

The fact that he stirred those feelings— if I was to be perfectly honest I couldn't deny that as my great aunt put it, he most definitely made my toes curl. In spite of that, I had no claim on him. His personal life was his own.

So here we were, business partners, nothing more, and certainly with no obligation to the other. I was here to assist him finding the truth about his mother's murder. It didn't mean anything more.

"*Of course,*" that little voice inside me whispered.

"Oh, do be quiet," I said to the room.

Supper, when Brodie returned, was a plate with curried lamb, an abundance of small potatoes, a baguette of French bread with a delicious crust while fluffy on the inside, and a decanter of wine.

I was impressed. Behind the facade of that gloomy medieval exterior of the house and the red lantern at the ground-floor window, it appeared that Madame Antoinette conducted a very lucrative enterprise.

We ate in what I would have described as companionable

silence. Afterward, I retrieved my notebook and pen, and proceeded to enter notes from our visit with Elsie Graham and my return to the Scotsman with what I had learned there, and a brief note about the attack and death of Sholto McQueen.

"I have the salve Mr. Frye left for the wounds. You will need fresh bandages," I commented without looking up. "Perhaps Madame has something she can provide."

"Mikaela..."

There was a knock at the door before he could finish the thought. He rose, answered it, and then let in a slip of a girl in a maid's uniform. She retrieved the dishes from the table.

"We will need fresh cloth for bandages if there is something that can be provided," I suggested.

The girl looked wide-eyed from me to Brodie. "Of course, miss. I'm certain something can be found."

Much to my surprise, she curtsied. I could only imagine where the next few years might find her— understudy perhaps to Madame or one of the other "ladies" I had seen downstairs. Not a hopeful prospect, but then who was I to criticize, sitting in the room at the back on the top floor of a brothel.

She returned shortly with what appeared to be an abundance of linen bandages, along with linen towels, a small salver of fragrant soap, and a pitcher of water.

"For the lady, compliments of Madame Antoinette." She set everything out, then went to the firebox and lit the fire.

"There's water in the copper pot, as well," she added as she came back to the table where I sat.

"Beggin yer pardon, miss. Are you a real Lady?"

That took me back just a bit, not what I might have expected. It seemed that someone— I looked over at Brodie, might have said something to someone. For whatever reason, perhaps other than to emphasize that I was not there to "work", as it were.

I set my pen down. A real lady, whatever that might mean. I smiled at that, considering how I was dressed in my split skirt, shirtwaist that was in need of laundering, and the boots I wore that were far more functional than fashionable.

"I ain't... haven't," she corrected herself, "never met a real Lady before. And ye can write as well?"

I caught the look on Brodie's face. A warning to behave myself?

"I will be honest," I replied. "I'm not certain what a real Lady is." I thought of my aunt and my sister. "It's more than the clothes one wears. I think it must come from inside the person; how they treat another person, their kindness and care. I think that is what makes a Lady."

"Like yerself, willing to speak with such as me and not turn a blind eye?"

I looked over, that dark gaze watching me.

"Yes."

She smiled. "Yer a Lady all right. Is there anything else ye need, miss?"

I thanked her, strangely affected by the conversation.

"That will be all. Thank ye, Lily," Brodie told her and handed her a coin.

"Oh, no. I cannot accept that. Madame pays me well enough and ye are her guest."

"The girl seems quite taken with ye," he commented when Lily had gone.

I looked up.

"But then ye do have a way with most people, shadowy criminals, low sorts, and stray dogs."

There was undoubtedly a compliment in there somewhere.

"It was good of her to bring the bandages," I pointed out.

"But hardly necessary," he replied.

"You wouldn't want to bring on infection," I pointed out in the aftermath of that backhanded compliment.

Shadowy criminals, low sorts, and dogs? I wondered where he fit in there. He made a sound, one that I had heard before.

"Rotting away with infection and pustulant wounds doesn't seem like a good prospect," I commented.

"Pustulent...? What the devil is that?" he demanded.

"It's not good, according to Mr. Brimley."

"And ye won't let it rest until ye have yer way."

I hid my smile beneath my hand as I kept to my notes. Who said that a stubborn Scot wasn't capable of learning?

I was fairly certain I heard a curse. I looked up to find him peeling off his jacket, then attempting to remove his jumper.

"Jesus, Mary, Joseph!" filled the air as he struggled to pull the wool jumper over his head, the pain it caused quite obvious in the expression on his face.

I set my pen aside and retrieved the salve Mr. Frye had given me for his wounds.

"Before you do yourself more harm..." I commented as I crossed the room.

I brushed his hands aside and assisted in removing the jumper. Having been previously wounded at my shoulder, I sympathized... to a point.

"Sit," I told him, indicating the nearby chair.

"Yer a bossy creature."

"The only way to get things done at times," I replied. "Something most men I've encountered are familiar with."

I untied the wrap over the bandages, exposing lean muscles across his ribs, flat stomach, and that ribbon of dark hair that disappeared below his belt.

Jesus, Mary, Joseph, indeed! I thought with appreciation that most certainly wasn't getting the task done.

I carefully removed the square patch of linen over the first wound, and felt that dark gaze on me.

"Ye've a gentle hand in spite of a sharp tongue."

"More than you deserve." I opened the tin with the salve and applied it to the narrow strip of the wound neatly tucked together with those stitches.

"Turn," I told him, much like a military commander issuing

orders to his troops. I then spread salve on the second wound low on his back.

"Madame Antoinette seems quite well-prepared for any occasion," I commented regarding the linen the girl had provided.

"It comes with the work, I suppose," he replied. "An occasional dispute between guests."

"Hold this in place," I told him, pressing a fresh bandage over the wound in back as I pressed one over the first wound, then proceeded to wrap a length of linen around his ribs to hold both in place, reaching around to tie it off.

Much like cinching a horse, I thought. He grunted. I had obviously "cinched" him a bit tight. That dark gaze was watching me.

"I'm not a client of Madame Gerard," he finally said, still watching me. As if he had been giving the matter considerable thought.

"When I said it was the business of the Agency, I spoke the truth."

I tied off the bandage and gave it an extra tug.

"I didn't ask," I pointed out.

"But I'm sayin' it because I need ye to believe me... It's important that ye believe me."

That dark gaze met mine in that way when he was being very serious. Oddly enough, I did believe him, simply because in that moment I saw something else. I saw someone who was strong and good, in spite of the horror of that early loss and all those years on the streets as a boy and then a man, hardened by what he must have seen and done.

I didn't say it in so many words. I laid my hand against his cheek, his beard soft at my fingertips.

"However, if you were to go downstairs in the middle of the night, I might be tempted to use the revolver you gave me," I told him.

He took my hand in his and kissed the palm. "A reminder of the foolishness in giving a weapon to a woman."

The easy banter that we'd discovered in the past was there, but there was something different in it, something different in him. He held on to my hand.

"I'm forgiven then for bringin' ye to a brothel?"

"I will let you know about that," I replied. A smile appeared at one corner of his mouth.

Brodie added more coal to the fire in the firebox as the night cold set in. There was only that glow that now provided light in the room.

It was late, somewhere in the middle of the night, as he sat in one of the chairs before the fire, staring into the flames.

Munro had arrived earlier with a light knock at the door. Words were briefly exchanged through the opening, then he left to find a bed somewhere else.

"He was able to find MacNabb. There was no word as yet about the situation at the Waverley."

No word, very few clues, only hazy memories all these years later, and information in those newspaper archives that was a coincidence?

We needed more.

"We need a map of the city," I said then. "A way to lay out everything we know with locations. There has to be something that we haven't come up with yet."

"A map."

I heard the doubt in his voice.

"You know the streets and places from a long time ago," I pointed out. "However, things change, the city with its reform efforts to clean up the poor areas do away with other places.

"There might be something on a map that shows the old areas before all that reform and rebuilding that would tell us something." I pointed from the bed that he insisted I take earlier while he retreated to the chair.

It seemed an odd juxtaposition, considering that we had occupied the same bed in the past, and as recently as the night before.

Who would have thought there was something very near chivalry in a very modern man who was more accustomed to chasing down criminals and low sorts.

"It wouldna seem right," he had said at the time with a gesture to the door and the rest of the "establishment." He had looked at me with that smile.

"Ye bein' a *Lady,* and all.

"Aye, a map," he said now bringing me back to my suggestion. "I'll see what can be found in the mornin'. Is there anythin' else?"

"Motive, means, and opportunity," I replied those oft repeated words that he had brought up time and again in our previous inquiries.

"We need a list of each possibility." I looked over at him, my chin propped on my hand and had a moment— the firelight surrounding him, dark longish hair that curled at his neck, that chest even with bandages wrapped about.

Hmmm, I thought as my toes curled beneath the blankets.

"Lists," he repeated.

"You must admit that it's been helpful in the past," I pointed out. "Although I do wish I had my chalkboard."

"Goodnight, Miss Forsythe."

"Goodnight, Mr. Brodie."

Thirteen

I HAD SLEPT LATE. Past any sound as Brodie dressed then left, the *"church"* unusually quiet.

However, as I finally roused, well after ten o'clock, I supposed that was the nature of the place— late nights and then late mornings after the guests had departed.

Quite intriguing, I thought, as I dressed and pinned up my hair, and discovered that I was starving.

I had no idea what the rules were for the morning after the night before, but went in search of food. A biscuit and jam would do, and hopefully coffee. Yes, definitely coffee.

I caught the scent of it as I descended the stairs, and followed it to what had obviously once been a dining hall— possibly for monks— where several pairs of eyes looked up at me with obvious curiosity and a few smirks.

"What might her Ladyship want this morning?" one of the ladies commented.

I was too ravenous to deal with smirks or snide remarks just yet. I headed for the silver carafe and bone china, with a silver salver of scones, biscuits, with slices of ham, and wondered what the going rate was for the ladies' services, considering there were such elegant and abundant breakfast offerings.

"I never seen a real Lady before," one of the other ladies commented.

The coffee was strong and fortifying. I took two of the scones.

"I hear they carry a knife to keep unwanted advances away," one of them commented.

"I sometimes carry a knife," I replied. "Courtesy of a friend, but I prefer the revolver. So much more efficient at a distance, and knives can be extremely messy. Whom do I owe for the scones and coffee?"

You could have heard a pin drop as the ladies about the table stared at me.

"A revolver?" one of them finally managed to say with a look somewhere between curiosity and disbelief.

"I keep it in the pocket of my skirt," I replied, which immediately drew glances toward said pocket, even though I had left the weapon in my travel bag in that room at the top of the stairs.

"Have ye ever used it?" Another question from a young woman with red hair that was obviously not her real hair color.

"I've only needed to use it once." I thought of that earlier situation then remembered that more recent ride across the city.

"Twice," I corrected myself and then sipped more coffee. "Most effective in both instances. Would any of you ladies care for more coffee?" I asked.

"Food is already taken care of by the gentleman," another replied to my earlier question.

"I can see where ye might use a revolver," another comment. "To keep the women off yer man."

My man? There was a round of laughter.

"Here ye are! I looked for ye in yer room."

Lily, dear girl, with a rolled bundle under her arm. "Mr. Brodie said as how ye wanted this."

It was a map!

Wherever Brodie had taken himself off to, which I discovered had included Munro, he had remembered about the map.

I grabbed two more scones, one for myself and one for Lily, and motioned toward the stairs.

"I never seen a map before," Lily exclaimed as we entered the bedroom at the top of those stairs.

I noticed the curious gaze that swept the room.

"Bring it to the table," I told her as I set the scones aside.

"The mapmaker's shop was just two streets over," Lily continued to explain. "Imagine that, a shop full of maps that people pay for."

I smiled at her. Imagine that, I thought, as I staked out the curled corners of the map on the table.

"I thought Mr. Brodie mighta wanted to give ye something a bit fancier," she said then, peering over my shoulder.

"It's perfect," I told her, scanning the different parts of Edinburgh laid out on the thick paper with the cartographer's date in the lower right corner catching my eye— *City of Edinburgh, 1857.*

That would have been before recent changes in the city, and very near when Màili Brodie was killed.

Perfect, I thought, and hoped that it might tell us something when I had plotted out events that had taken place.

"He also said to purchase this for ye." She handed me a fountain pen in a wood case. "I was able to find it at the print shop. He said ye might need it as well."

She looked past me to the table where my notebook was spread out with notes I'd made earlier.

"He said that ye write books? I've never met anyone that did that. I can barely write me name."

Brodie told her that?

"I've written about travels I've made."

"He said that ye've been to China and Egypt! I canna imagine the things ye've seen. I never been anywhere else, but I would like to go."

"How old are you?" I asked.

"Almost fourteen years."

I gave her a long look.

"I will be in a year," she added.

Thirteen years, small and slender for her age. But curious.

I thought of my protagonist in the books, Emma Fortescue. I had written her to be adventuresome, curious, and determined. A bit older than Lily to be certain, but just as eager to take on the world.

"Then you should do what you can to make it happen," I replied. "There are a great many places beyond Edinburgh or London for that matter." I handed her a half crown.

"For the '*Lily travel fund*.'" I told her. "You need to put it in the bank and then add more when you can."

And when I can, I thought. A worthwhile enterprise if ever there was one, a young girl with hopes and dreams.

She flung her arms around me and hugged tight. "I'll get one of the girls to help me, that makes regular trips to the bank." She whirled around then on her way to the door.

Emma Fortescue indeed, I thought. Meet Lily, new world explorer.

I spent the next couple of hours leaning over the table, mapping out locations regarding information we already had. I finally stood back, looking down at the map then at my notes so that I hadn't missed anything that might be important:

September 11, 1860: Katherine Eldridge, of Albany Street, Seamstress, age twenty-three years, beaten to death, body found at Tollcross Street;

October 24, 1860; Bettie Dowd, prostitute, age twenty-seven years, beaten to death, body found at Cowgate;

December 20, 1860; Màili Brodie, tavern server, age twenty-eight years, beaten to death, body found at Bleekhouse Close, Canongate;

December 29, 1860; Martin A. Graham, Police Constable, Age thirty-two years, dead in the course of a robbery;

January 17, 1861; Michael Tobin, aka Mick Tobin, leatherworker, Age nineteen years, beaten to death, body found at South Bridge;

April 20, 1861; Alvin Meeks, Police Constable, Age thirty-seven years, death by suicide, body found at Canongate.

Each one had lived south of the castle in the Old Town, with the exception of Katherine Eldridge who had lived on Albany Street at the time of her death.

I located Albany Street on the map. It was north of the castle, in the area now known as New Town. In fact, it was the only mark I'd made in New Town on the map.

What did that mean? That Katherine Eldridge was found dead in a part of the city other than near her home?

Was that near where she had worked, or had been visiting an acquaintance or gentleman friend at the time?

Were there others?

If so, did it mean anything other than the crimes committed in any large city like Edinburgh or London, and reported on the crime sheets in the dailies?

It was near midday when Brodie returned. His expression, usually unreadable when he was out and about, a holdover from his days with the MP in London, clearly indicated frustration as he returned to our current domicile.

"Were you able to find Mr. MacNabb?"

"Aye," he replied, removing his neck scarf as the morning had arrived with frost on the window and a sky overhead that suggested we might be in for a dusting of snow.

His comment reminded me of his opinion of MacNabb. Still, a source was a source. It was merely a matter of deciphering what the man was telling us, and of course there was Brodie's threat as leverage. I certainly wouldn't have wanted to cross him in any way if I were MacNabb. The man seemed to be of the same opinion. So far.

"Yer encounter in the cab is being called a simple case of

attempted robbery at present. The police made a report of it after they were contacted by the clerk at the Scotsman."

Robbery.

"If it was simple robbery what reason would the man have continued very near across the city?" I asked. "I would think it would be simple enough to drive a short distance, do the deed, and then disappear."

He poured himself coffee from the remnants in the pot that Lily had brought earlier as I added to my notes. He made a familiar sound of disgust as it was obviously cold with mostly the dregs at the bottom that now filled his cup.

"Have ye seen Munro?" he asked.

"No, he hasn't returned. I hope there hasn't been a difficulty."

"He can handle himself," Brodie assured me. He glanced at my notebook, open on the table and map of the city spread before it.

"Ye've been busy."

I nodded. "Thank you for the pen and the map."

"I know how ye are with yer lists. I thought it might help."

Other women could keep their flowers and jewelry, those usual tokens of a man's regard. I wouldn't have traded my chalk-board at the office on the Strand or the map for a cluster of freesia or begonias.

"I've marked the map with every location of the incidents that we know about," I explained as I turned the map so that he could study it, as I pointed out each one in turn.

"And I've noted the dates of each one at each location. I thought it might be helpful to see it all laid out."

He nodded, frowned as he downed the last of cold coffee, that dark gaze fastened on the map.

"You're far more familiar with Edinburgh than I am," I added. "But you can see that all the murders were clustered in Old Town, except for this one." I indicated the location where Katherine Eldridge's body was found.

I watched for any reaction. Except for the mark at Bleekhouse

Close there was none, that former MP's expression void of any emotion. Only at that one location was there a brief moment where his expression changed as he touched the map with a finger.

"The location where she was found might not mean anything," I continued. "Although she was killed in the same manner which seems a bit unusual."

He looked up his gaze meeting mine. "Ye did all this, just this mornin'?"

"It isn't as if there were a great many other things to do. I wasn't of a mind to join the ladies in their 'daily activities.' I suspect they might have objected to that. Although, we did share breakfast."

"Why am I not surprised?"

"I was quite hungry. Lily made the suggestion, and it was delicious. The coffee was strong and hot, and we had a lively conversation."

"I can only imagine," he commented. "Ye seem to get on well with the young girl."

"She reminds me of me, when I was younger of course— curious, not at all intimidated, and eager for adventures. I felt a kindred spirit."

"Kindred spirit?" he repeated and made that familiar sound. "I suppose ye'd like to help her; like the Mudger or the hound?"

"Perhaps."

"God help the rest of us with more than one of ye out there loose in the world."

"Breakfast *was* several hours ago," I proceeded to point out, and feeling the confines of my somewhat unusual accommodation.

"And I have completed this with the information we have. However..."

I couldn't very well assist him if I was forced to stay there. There were things to be done, more questions to be answered.

"According to Lily there is a coffeehouse very near," I suggested. "And clearly no one would think to look for me here."

"That was the idea," he replied, then shook his head. "If I was to order ye to stay until this is resolved, ye would go out and about anyway."

"Two hands and two heads are better than one," I replied. "And you must admit that you are quite impressed with my map."

"Ach! Bring yer bloody notebook and the map. It's better to know what yer about than to have you going off on yer own. Unless I were to tie you to the bedposts."

Something that the patrons indulged in perhaps? Hmmm. Interesting.

We left the same as we had arrived the night before, by way of the back alley. The only person we encountered was the coal man as he made a delivery.

On the street, there were those who went about their day, including two women we passed, one with a basket over her arm perhaps on her way to market, the other at the street corner with an infant in her arms and two children beside her, waiting to step off the curb.

Their clothes were mended, the children dressed in oversized coats that might have come from a second's store, one with a hole in the toe of his shoe, the little girl wearing a tattered scarf.

I had seen poverty before in the faces of people including children, in the East End of London and on my travels. But this was different, somehow more personal, something that took hold and wouldn't let go.

Perhaps it was because this was where Brodie had lived as a boy, on his own after his mother was murdered, then living as best he could, perhaps like other children I had seen scavenging through garbage that was tossed out. Or others who participated in whatever might earn a few coins so that they could survive to struggle all over again the next day, and the next— stealing, running numbers.

It was only natural that I thought of Lily, serving as a lady's maid in a brothel.

What were her chances, I thought, in a world where a young

girl, like the one standing on that street corner, was already at a disadvantage, and might well end up like Màili Brodie or Bettie Dowd?

The day was sharp and overcast, the coffeeshop with bow windows fogged over from the cold outside.

Brodie was in the habit of taking a table far to the back when at a Public House, his way of "*keepin' an eye on those who came and went*", as he put it.

I wondered if that was a characteristic of all who served with the police, a natural instinct from the days spent living on the street as a boy, or possibly both.

The coffee was hot and more than strong... strong enough to stand a spoon in it, as my friend Templeton had once said.

The potpie with a thick crust was the fare of the day. It was hot as well and smelled of leeks and potatoes with chunks of meat we were assured was beef no more than a few days old from a local butcher shop, and kept on ice.

"Tell me about what it was like here when you were a boy," I asked as the meat pie was served.

That gaze met mine. "Ye've seen the East End of London. It wasn't so different than that. But no opportunity."

I listened as he explained what he remembered— the cold nights not unlike the ones last night, often with snow in the winter months.

"It was not unlike the way it is for the Mudger."

Mr. Cavendish who occupied the alcove just below the office on the Strand.

"It made the bones ache when ye couldna find a place to get out of the wind and rain. I couldna go back afterward..."

I knew that he spoke of that night, when everything changed for him.

"I lived for a while with my grandmother, or so I was told she was my grandmother, until she tried to sell me."

At my startled expression, he explained. "She was old and not very well. She had an offer for my services at the mill. To my way of thinkin' I was better off on my own. I left her what coins I had, and set off to make my way best that I could.

"There are other places where young boys and girls can make a small pittance for work at night. Not unlike Madame's."

My fork clattered down onto my place, horrified by the thought of a young boy forced to do such things in order to survive.

"I didna go to those places," he said then. "What few things my mother taught me, I knew such things were a sin. And, she had given me this."

He reached into his pocket and retrieved what appeared to be a bronze coin on a chain. But hardly a coin as he held out his hand. It was a medallion. I recognized the image on the medallion.

"St. Christopher, the patron saint of lost souls, to guide and protect."

"She believed that it would protect me," he explained. "She gave it to me that night... I've always carried it."

Neither of us said anything for several moments. He eventually tucked the medallion away.

"To answer yer question, I see some changes... some of the old buildings have been taken down, but there are still many things that havena changed."

The way he had looked at those two children and the woman with the infant in her arms as we passed by, I knew he was thinking of them, and something learned at school in France stirred my memory.

I looked over at him *"Plus ça change, plus c'est la même chose.* The more things change the more they stay the same."

"So it seems."

"If you were still a police inspector, what would you see in the marks on the map?" I then asked.

He was quite thoughtful for some time. "They were clustered in the poor part of the city, as ye noticed. Except for the one. And ye've already told me that the reports in the dailies described their deaths as the same."

"Would they have simply been random?" I asked. I did so like the workings of his mind— clear, incisive, the experience he brought to it even under the most dreadful circumstances.

"It's always possible, but in my experience, such an attack is meant to be quickly done, then the suspect leaves, usually with a blade. It is quiet and efficient. The sort of attack as ye've found with the others wouldn't have been quiet, or quickly done."

I saw the look that darkened in his eyes. Was he remembering that night so long ago? He looked away as if that would clear the memory, then looked back at me.

"It might, I say it might suggest a pattern."

The woman who served meals had returned. The meat pie had been quite delicious. I really did want to have a piece of the blackberry pie, and... I had more questions.

Brodie ordered the pie for me. I waited until she had gone.

"If not quickly and quietly, as you say, then for what reason? Why take the risk of perhaps being caught if someone should come along and hear something?"

His gaze met mine and for a moment I saw the pain that he had carried all this time, then it was hidden once more, and the police detective remained.

"It is for the thrill of it, of having someone weaker under their hand, hearing them beg for it to stop until it finally does."

The woman returned and set the plate before me with that slice of blackberry pie. I pushed it away.

"How do you do this...?" I whispered, my throat tight at what he had described, knowing that was very near what his mother had suffered.

"How do ye do it, lass? Why did ye come on that train and then refuse to leave?"

The answer for me was simple. "I wanted to help you."

He had the pie wrapped and put into a paper bag so that I could take it with me. He was certain that I would want it later.

"I want to return to the Registry Office," I said as we returned to the street. "I want to see if I can find more information about Katherine Eldridge."

There was no argument, no insistence that I return to where we'd spent the night. Neither was he about to let me go alone.

"I'll go with ye," he replied.

The records search was somewhat easier this time. I had an address where Katherine Eldridge had lived at the time she was killed. It was merely a matter of looking at the earlier census.

Records revealed that in 1851, a man by the name of Harold Eldridge lived at the address at #14 Thistle Street. His occupation was listed as stonemason, married with two children, a son and a daughter.

"I found it," I announced. Brodie came to stand over me as I pointed out the entry in the official census.

"The Eldridge name is shown again at that same address for the next census in 1861, for Thomas Eldridge, possibly the son who was shown earlier?" And just a year after Katherine Eldridge was found dead at Tollcross.

"Occupation is stone mason. He appears that he took the same trade as his father." Not unusual.

I then opened the census for 1871 that showed Thomas Eldridge had married at some point in the previous decade and then had two children. They were still shown living at Thistle Street, in the 1881 census.

"It might be worth it to see if they still live there. If so, it's possible they might remember something from when Katherine was killed."

Brodie nodded. "Possibly. It's always a delicate matter, speaking with people about something like this. And it's possible as well, that Thomas Eldridge doesna know anything or may choose not to speak of it."

Still, he agreed that it was worth seeing if Thomas Eldridge still lived at that address on Thistle Street.

We left the Registry Office and stepped out into a heavy rain, the sort that set streets awash. Most people simply deployed their umbrellas or waited out the latest downpour under an awning or step into a shop, then continued on their way afterward.

Brodie was eventually able to wave down a driver. I stepped out from the recessed entrance of the Registry Office, my notebook with the information and address for Thomas Eldridge tucked safely out of the rain in my travel bag.

Thistle Street was north of Princes Street, a cluster of small houses at the far end across from St. Andrews Church. Number fourteen was the third house, a small stone and timber cottage. A light shone from one of the windows that faced onto the street.

Brodie had the driver let us off at the church, where it appeared that people were gathered for late afternoon service.

"Afternoon service?" I commented with some surprise at the sight of people slowly entering the chapel.

"They serve several faiths," Brodie commented as he took hold of my arm. "Including Catholic as well as Anglican, Islam, and others."

St. Andrews had gone through many changes over the past one hundred years, including the Disruption of 1843. My aunt had spoken of it. She was a young woman at the time.

More than a dozen ministers had walked out of the church over resentment of the Civil Courts infringing on the Church of Scotland to serve the people of other faiths. While St. Andrews was primarily a Presbyterian church, it apparently still served people of the Catholic faith as well as others in spite of the actions of the courts.

We stepped between hacks and coaches, and crossed Thistle Street, Brodie's hand firm on my arm as rain on the street washed over my boots.

The cottage at Number 14 was like the other half dozen that lined the street, except for the stone walkway from the street, sandstone bricks neatly laid out. The mark of Mr. Eldridge's profession perhaps?

We stepped up to the door and Brodie knocked.

The door was eventually opened by an older handsome

woman, an apron tied over a woolen gown. The smell of supper drifted through the door opening as she wiped her hands on the apron, a curious expression in her gray eyes.

"If yer here about the work at the church," she began with a nod across the street, "ye need to speak with Mr. Eldridge."

Brodie explained that we were not from the church, although we did want to speak with him if he was about.

"He's here, but hasn't been able to finish the work on accounta the weather."

He introduced us both, and explained, "It's in the matter of Katherine Eldridge from some years back."

"After all these years?"

"We have questions that he might be able to answer," I added, having found in the past that a woman often responded more easily to another woman.

She nodded and held the door for us to enter the small parlor.

"He's in the shop in back. I'll tell him ye wish to speak with him."

While we waited, I noticed two photographs on the wall in the parlor. One was of an older man and woman with two young children. The other was a studio portrait of a young woman. Katherine Eldridge perhaps?

The man appeared followed by the woman. Brodie made the introductions once more. We had found Thomas Eldridge, Katherine's brother.

"What brings ye here about Katherine?" Thomas asked, wiping his hands from his work in the shop with a cloth behind him.

"We would like to ask ye some questions about what happened," Brodie began.

"For what reason?"

"It's possible that her death might be related to other deaths at the time," Brodie explained. "Anything you might be able to tell us, might help in finding who was responsible."

"After all these years...? What is yer interest in this?" Thomas Eldridge demanded.

I looked over at Brodie and wondered what he would say, how much he would tell him.

"Two other women were murdered in the same manner, within months of yer sister's death..."

Thomas Eldridge's expression was like stone, any emotion hidden behind silence, and I was certain he would refuse to speak of it. I looked over at Brodie. He realized it as well, understood it from years of experience with victims and families, and his own experience as well.

"One of them was my mother," he said in a quiet voice that made me ache inside.

Three women who had died in the same way, all within months of each other. A shared tragedy? Was it also a coincidence, or something more?

Thomas Eldridge nodded, and his expression softened. "I donna know wot I can tell ye after all these years, except that my sister was a fine, God-fearin' young woman. We were only a year apart, and she was especially close with our father."

His mouth worked and he glanced away, old memories that were suddenly new and raw again.

"It was in the newspaper. They said that she was found at Tollcross and that it was obviously in the matter of..." He suddenly stopped, his wife coming up behind him and laying a hand on his arm.

"They said that she was a prostitute and that it appeared that she was most likely killed by a man she had been with." His expression hardened once more but there were tears there.

"She would not have done such a thing. She didn't need to. She lived here and had a good position as a seamstress."

It was heartbreaking to listen to, but once it began, he wanted to tell us all of it. There was no man, according to her brother. Katherine was betrothed to a fine young man who worked for Northern Railway.

They planned to marry the following spring. He was on a northern run with the railroad when it had happened.

"She lay there in the police morgue for three days while we searched and asked those who knew her. There was nothing, and I finally went there.

"It's not something that ye ever forget, seein' someone ye love treated that way. And I believe to this day that it killed our father. He was never the same afterward and gone less than a year later."

I glanced over at Brodie and could only imagine what it had been like for him as a child to see something that horrible.

"Was there a report made?" Brodie asked. "Were ye given any information from them?"

Thomas shook his head again. "There was only the dailies and the article in it, the only way we knew what had happened. You said there were two other women, died the same way very near the same time."

"Was there a reason she would have been at Tollcross?"

Again, Thomas Eldridge shook his head. "She usually left work at five o'clock. The ride from Princes Street to here was short. She was usually home in less than thirty minutes unless she went by the market to purchase something our mother needed for supper."

"Where did she work?" I asked.

"Sloan and McNamara, haberdasher and women's clothing. She was verra particular and careful with her work. They told our father they never had a seamstress or tailor who was so precise in their work." He was thoughtful.

"Ye said there was another woman."

"The third was a woman on her way home from work as well," Brodie replied and left it at that. He didn't mention that Bettie Dowd was also shown to be a prostitute according to the newspaper archive. It served no purpose.

"And yer mother as well," Eldridge said, shaking his head.

Brodie nodded.

We thanked him for being willing to speak with us. He took hold of Brodie's shoulder as we were leaving.

"I know that it's been a long time, but I would know if ye find out who did this..." The rest of it went unspoken, but I sensed he hadn't said it merely to know once and for all who had killed his sister.

"Aye," Brodie replied.

The sun slanted across the tops of the cottages beneath the layer of clouds, the last light of day falling briefly across the wet street and those who departed St. Andrews Church.

It was just a glimpse, the sort of thing caught just at the edge of one's vision— a man in a tweed Norfolk jacket with a deerstalker hat. When I stopped and turned he was gone.

"What is it," Brodie asked.

What was it? Had I seen anything at all? Or was it just the passing glance of one of those who had attended late afternoon service?

"For just a moment I thought I saw the man I encountered at the Waverley."

"Where?"

"Just outside the church."

That dark gaze swept across the street to the entrance where electric lights had just come on at the church.

"Yer certain?"

It had only been a glimpse. I could have been mistaken with so many others about, leaving the church.

But I was certain I had seen the man once more.

Fourteen

WHAT WAS it that connected three murders from almost thirty years ago? Then, the deaths of two police constables, the death of a man, and Sholto McQueen. And now the driver from the night I was abducted.

Thomas Eldridge, Elizabeth's brother had defended his sister's reputation and refused to believe that she had been the victim of prostitution as had been written in the daily after her body was found.

Mick Tobin, the young friend, who had helped sell the hand-made leather wallets that Màili Brodie made, to help support herself and her son— mysteriously dead less than a month later. The young girl he had married left to mourn the loss of the young man she had loved and hoped to build a life with.

Constables Graham and Meeks who were there the night that Màili Brodie's body was found, her death assumed to be from prostitution, a child left orphaned. Constable Graham reportedly killed during a robbery he came upon shortly after her murder. Constable Meeks dead sometime later in what was called a suicide.

Bettie Dowd, a known prostitute, discovered dead, months earlier, along with the death of Elizabeth Eldridge.

Nine deaths, if one included the death of Elizabeth Eldridge's father in the months after the loss of his daughter.

Was it random? A coincidence.

Former Constable Calhoun insisted that he didn't believe that Constable Meeks had taken his own life... He didn't believe in coincidences.

Was it a former constable's instinct?

I looked over at Brodie as we eventually found a hack and rode back across Princes Street, the frown on his face was there in the light from a streetlamp as we passed by.

I had learned a great deal about the way his thoughts worked, in our partnership, those quiet moments where he seemed to go off to some other place.

What was he thinking now? About his mother's murder? The other deaths? Calhoun's certainty that Meek's death wasn't a suicide as had been put out to the newspapers?

And my own encounters since arriving in Edinburgh, along with Sholto's murder where Brodie was wounded?

Whatever his thoughts, I certainly had my own questions.

"How are the schedules and the areas they work determined for police constables?"

The question brought Brodie back from wherever his thoughts had taken him. I wanted very much to know, however from past experience that would have to wait.

"Most constables work seven days a week, with five days their own time after a length of service," he replied, obviously from his own experience with the MP of London.

"And the areas that they walk?"

"That would depend on their rank and experience. Some areas have higher numbers of crime and the most experienced are usually given a rotation in those areas. In those instances a newer man would be paired with a more experienced one."

"Then they don't get to choose the areas they walk," I concluded.

"That would depend."

I looked over at him. "On what?"

"Influence, favors, their reputation on the streets, and with the people that might make the Deputy Chief Constable appear favorably to his superiors."

"Who might those be?"

He didn't reply immediately, but not for lack of knowing. I saw it in the expression on his face, as if he considered whether or not to tell me.

"The Deputy Chief Constable would answer to the Chief Constable."

"And who would the Chief Constable answer too?"

"That would be the High Commissioner of Police."

"Influence and reputation," I replied, those age-old qualities had toppled kings and empires throughout history, and more recent history.

I thought of rumors I had heard about the man sitting beside me along with a passing conversation with my aunt when I first requested Brodie to look into the disappearance of my sister. That there had been some sort of dust up when he was with the MP of London.

He had left afterward and opened his own establishment for making private inquiries, a private investigator, as it were.

"Something about someone in a very high position with the Metropolitan Police caught in a bribery scandal that apparently raised questions about several other high-placed officials."

And it was Brodie, she had gone on to explain, who had exposed it. Rather than remain among those who were caught red-handed as the investigation continued, he chose to leave the MP. And then there was our own case that had exposed spies among the highest positions in British government.

A man of integrity, a man I could trust.

"What are ye thinking?" he asked.

I smiled to myself. He might make his comments when I came up with an idea or thought, but there was no one else I knew who really wanted to know, who valued what I had to say. At least not any other man I knew.

"What if it is all connected? The murders from thirty years ago, Constables Graham and Meeks, Mick Tobin? Three other persons who were there that night.

"Records that are 'sealed.' For what reason? What would be in those records that might tell us more?" I was on a roll, as Brodie would say, but needed to make some sense of it all.

"And what about these latest incidents? You arrive in Scotland and start asking questions. Now Sholto McQueen is dead, and you've been badly injured. What reason? Another coincidence? Some random encounter on the street?

"I don't believe in them. Most certainly Thomas Eldridge doesn't believe in them. And neither do you," I added, though it hardly needed saying.

We had left Princes Street and now rode into Old Town. Brodie signaled for the driver to stop outside of a tavern, and we left the hack. With a look about I recognized buildings from earlier that day and realized that we were not far from Madame Antoinette's place of business.

"No, I don't believe in them," he replied.

He looked about as well, and I realized he was looking for any indication that we might have been followed.

I had seen no one, but he had far more experience in these things. He took my hand and pulled my arm through his.

To any casual observer we undoubtedly seemed like any other man and woman out for a walk, in spite of the weather. The tavern, I realized, added to that impression as he escorted me inside.

It was the same as any tavern about Edinburgh or London for that matter— crowded with those after leaving work for the day, others who made a tavern a pastime, and two women who moved among them setting down tankards of ale and glasses of whisky.

We passed through seemingly unnoticed except for a wink from one of the women and a brief nod from Brodie. We slowly made our way through those who had gathered, then we left by way of the back of the tavern.

We slipped into the shadows, then silently waited. No one emerged after us, and we continued along the wynd to the end, cut through a narrow passage then turned in the direction of Madame's establishment.

His left hand was firm on my arm. As we passed under the single streetlamp along the street I caught sight of the revolver in his right hand.

We entered the church the same as the night before, and as before I was struck again by the novelty of it all. I had previously seen the private suites at a men's club, but I had never been in a whorehouse, bordello, brothel, or whatever one wished to call it. Although it seemed that my good friend, Theodora Templeton, might have had some experience in that area. As a guest, of course.

"*Fascinating!*" was how she described it at the time. "*In some of the higher class 'houses' in Paris, the ladies have regular clients, and some are even allowed to choose who they... spend an evening with. They wear costumes, live very well, and often are put up in their own residence. One is a very well-known actress at the theater!*"

It had been a most interesting conversation and I could only wonder what my friend's thoughts might be to know of my foray into the oldest profession known to man, metaphorically speaking, of course, situated in an old church.

I proceeded up the stairs to our room while Brodie went to see if Munro had returned. He was to go to the Waverley and send a telegram to London to Sir Avery at the Agency.

I studied the map Brodie had Lily purchase for me, locations marked of the deaths we knew about with the pen she had also purchased.

Not a coincidence? And not random?

Had there been other murders?

And if not random or coincidence, were they deliberate? A series of murders, seemingly nothing more than the usual crimes found in a poor part of a large city. Except for Elizabeth Eldridge, who didn't live or work in Old Town, a polite, respectable young woman who was planning to be married.

Brodie let himself into the room with the key that Madame had provided. I was vaguely aware as he moved about the room. He came to stand beside me.

"What do you know about the case of the women who were murdered in Whitechapel?" I asked.

The papers had been filled with nothing else for months after the second body was found horribly mutilated, then the third, and two more, with a great deal of opinion about who might have done it.

At first the murders were explained as random, isolated incidents in an area of the East End of London where crime was rampant. However, as the next woman was found, then another with frightening similarity with internal organs surgically removed, there had been speculation of who might have done it.

Was the murderer in fact someone with surgical skill? A physician perhaps, or someone else with knowledge of a woman's anatomy? What reason was there for something so cruel and heinous?

Or was it the work of a client, the women apparently all known prostitutes?

"The Whitechapel murders were after I had left," Brodie replied now.

"You know people who were still with the MP. You must have had thoughts about the sort of person who might have done such a thing."

He nodded. "Aye. There were those who had their thoughts in the matter as well. A handful of arrests were made, the usual sort known on the streets who frequented those areas."

I heard something else in his voice. "You don't believe that the person has been caught."

"Let us just say that none of those who were brought in had the ability or the skill to have committed those murders."

"And yet the word was put out to the newspapers that the police were confident they had found the man," I pointed out.

"To stop the fear and the gossipmongers," he replied.

"And the person responsible?"

"He's clever and careful, and highly skilled."

"You believe that he will kill again."

His response was interrupted by a knock at the door. But he didn't need to answer. I saw it in that dark gaze.

He opened the door for Lily who entered with a tray of food for supper. She smiled in greeting.

"Cook is serving late supper for some guests who will be arriving later on. She sent up roast meat, vegetables, and cakes." She set the tray on the table. "And I've brought more bandages if ye need them."

Brodie thanked her which caused the girl to blush.

"If needs be, I can have yer clothes washed and cleaned," she told me. "I send out the other ladies' clothes regular. Madame Antoinette is fussy about that. She says that nothin' puts off a gentleman like a woman wearin' soiled clothes and not bein' washed herself."

I looked at Brodie with some amusement as he seemed to have suddenly become extremely interested in a thread on his jacket. The man was a constant surprise.

I was reminded that my wardrobe since arriving was somewhat limited and thanked her.

When she had gone, I removed the linen cloth from the service tray and discovered that I was starving.

From working with Brodie, I was aware that the things I saw here— food that was remarkably fine, and the ladies well-dressed, were not what was usually found in brothels.

Prostitution was illegal, but then so was the importation of opium, and the kidnapping of young boys who then found themselves serving as part of a crew aboard a ship bound for some distant port, very likely never to return.

Mr. Cavendish, who lived on the street below Brodie's office, once said of thieving and robbery— where there was a will there was a way, and where there was a customer there was obviously someone to provide what he wanted. The house mistress, Madame Antoinette, seemed to fill a very lively and lucrative need.

I was starving while Brodie sat across from me and barely touched his food.

"Are the wounds bothering?" I asked.

He had given no indication earlier, but then that was not his way. I suspected that he could be bleeding from a dozen wounds before he might admit that he was in a bit of discomfort, the stoic Scot and all.

"I've been thinking..." I commented. "For whatever reason," I had my thoughts in the matter, "the police have not been of any assistance in this. I refuse to accept that the files are 'sealed', or not 'available'. Perhaps Sir Avery might be able to assist as he appears to have a great deal of authority in certain matters."

I looked up from my cake to find that dark gaze narrowed on me.

"It is frightening how ye think, more like a man," he commented, then added, "perhaps. I've had the same thought."

I took that as a compliment. "Merely from studying people and learning their ways and mannerisms for my novels," I replied. "What of Munro?" I asked, curious, since I had not seen him since earlier in the morning.

"He was to send a telegram off to London, and tend to some other things that might be useful. I'm to meet him in a while."

I had finished the cake, quite delicious. "I'll go with you."

There was so much we didn't yet know, and anything that Sir Avery might provide could be extremely useful.

"No," Brodie replied.

When I would have objected, he provided very sound reasons that I was not to be included.

"Yer safe enough here. Out on the street, ye have a way of drawing attention. We saw that today at St. Andrews. And there's already been one attempt to abduct ye."

"Which I was able to escape," I pointed out.

He reached across the table and took my hand. "I need ye to do as I ask."

He had said as much before in the cases we investigated with some apparent old-fashioned need to protect me, which was quite ironic considering how I'd lived my life. So far.

This was different. There was something in his voice, that stopped me and my objections. And I realized that what I had sensed might be true, though he had not said as much.

"You do believe that it's all connected. It wasn't random or coincidence. The murders were connected, and these latest ones..."

He simply repeated what he had already told me. "I need you to stay here. That is the way ye can help me now."

Naturally, I wanted to argue the matter. It went against the grain to be set aside, but I did see his point. Plainly put, if something were to happen, again, with everything that had already happened, I might be a liability. Plainly speaking, I would be in the way. And with so many unknowns, as well as who was behind this, I was forced to accept it.

I didn't much care for it, but I did understand. However, if he patted my hand, much like patting a child or favorite dog on the head, I might be inclined to tell him exactly what I thought of it. He didn't.

"Sir Avery may be able to provide information on this," he shared.

I couldn't help but feel like Rupert, the hound, being tossed a bone. It was then, as if perfectly timed, that it seemed the first of the evening's "guests" had arrived with a boisterous shout heard all the way to the top floor.

"Very well," I eventually replied.

That dark gaze narrowed. "Why do I have the feeling I might regret this?"

"I have no idea what you're talking about," I replied, although I did.

"Aye," he said with obvious suspicion as he checked his revolver, returned it to the waist of his trousers, then reached for his jacket and neck scarf.

It wasn't the first time Brodie had taken the position of the overbearing authority in our partnership. We very definitely needed to have a conversation about it. However, now was very clearly not the time.

I knew him well enough to know that I needed to pick the right time and place.

"Ye'll keep the door locked," he said as he went to the door.

I nodded. "Unless of course I get bored, or I'm needed downstairs." One last pithy comment in my favor.

"God help any man fool enough to try that."

And he was gone.

I dutifully locked the door, then turned back to my map and notes. It was going to be a very long evening.

I spent the next couple of hours going back over everything we'd learned, filling in places where I'd only made a brief entry, expanding it out much like an outline of one of my novels.

Then, I paced the room, came back to the map and studied it once more, attempting to see what it revealed.

Three women, then three more deaths within a very short time, our inquiries, and now two more were dead. I looked at the watch pinned to my shirtwaist. It was only a few minutes past twelve o'clock midnight.

The rest of the establishment had livened considerably after Brodie left. I heard laughter, a somewhat colorful conversation that drifted from the floor just below. A patron obviously chose to bypass the supper that Madame had planned in favor of a room on the second floor, by the conversation I heard, and the company of two, not one, companions for the next several hours.

I ventured out onto the landing to escape the confines of the room, ignoring Brodie's parting instructions to stay behind locked door.

I caught a glimpse of Lily as she and two other servants

appeared then quickly disappeared at the main floor below on some errand or another— a tray with decanter and two glasses, followed by an older maid with several items tucked under her arm, one of which resembled a riding quirt.

Most revealing. I had never realized how much work was required to operate such an enterprise or the process it entailed.

It was well after midnight when I returned to the room, questions churning through my head.

What information was Sir Avery able to provide? Something? Anything?

I instinctively knew there was undoubtedly a great deal more that Brodie hadn't told me about the past months, in that stoic way of his, when some "matter" as he described it, had taken him from the office on the Strand and I had taken myself back to my townhouse and my latest installment in Emma Fortescue's adventures.

I was aware the "matter" he was making was his own inquiries about that had to do with Sir Avery and the Agency. And that, only because of Mr. Cavendish's observations. If not for that, I wouldn't have known where he was between our inquiries on behalf of clients.

As the hour grew later, I wondered if Brodie and Munro had set off to pursue a piece of information they'd received. Something dangerous?

"Bloody stubborn Scot," I muttered. "And not in any condition to go chasing down potential murderers." I should have gone with him, I thought, or in the very least followed him.

I was, after all, a rather good shot...

The frantic knock at the door, brought me back from my thoughts. It came again.

Good heavens! What if it was one of Madame's clients, having stumbled his way up the stairs, and was now quite intent as the knocking came again.

I was not of the thought of adding a new vocation to my name as I slipped the revolver into my pocket and went to the door. Not that I was not of a mind to shoot anyone, only to persuade them that they'd made a mistake and kindly move on.

That persistent knock at the door came again. Oh, for heaven's sake, I thought, intent on sending away whoever was on the other side of the door. Short of that I was also quite accomplished in several self-defense maneuvers.

I jerked the door open...

"Lily!" I exclaimed with surprise. "What is it?"

Her expression said far more than she was able to explain at the moment. She looked quite terrified.

When she was finally able to tell me, no explanation was necessary as smoke billowed up from the floors below and filled the landing. It was very obvious what was the matter.

The church was afire!

Fifteen

I'D HAD some experience with a fire in the past; not an experience I wished to repeat or recommend for anyone. But here we were, and the situation rapidly became most serious.

There were shouts from the main floor as we both went out onto the landing, and saw those below fleeing in all manner of undress, or no dress at all.

"We have to go, miss!" Lily headed back toward the stairs. I grabbed her arm as a thick wall of flames and smoke churned toward us. The stairs were soon engulfed.

"There has to be another way out," I told her over the sound of the fire as it consumed those ancient timbers. "The window." I pulled her back into the room as I went to the opposite side of the room, then stopped as I caught sight of flames through the glass.

"I know another way," Lily announced. "We have to go back to the stairs."

The stairs? A glance back over my shoulder at the outside wall of the room convinced me that we'd never make it to the alleyway below before we were burned to cinders.

"What about the others?"

"Most were out already when I came back."

She came back to warn me... I nodded.

Ever practical— Brodie would have cursed if he were here— I grabbed my bag and thrust my notebook and the map inside. I then followed Lily from the room and farther up the steps where they ended just under the roof trusses.

"Can ye climb?" she asked.

My gaze followed hers up into those rafters.

"I heard that the roof leaked fierce when she bought the church," she added. "She had to have repairs made. The workers installed a hatch so they could work up there. I've used it before to leave when everything quiets down of a night. Madame locks the doors in case some of the guests try to leave without settlin' up what they owe."

I looked at her. She really was a girl after my own heart. Then, with a look up at those rafters, I nodded.

"Lead the way."

She dragged a bench over to the wall where the stairs ended, then climbed atop. She reached overhead and pulled herself up onto the first cross beam, agile as a monkey.

"The next one is a bit higher," she called down as I hiked my skirt up and secured the hem at my waist so that it wouldn't tangle about my legs.

My travel bag presented another issue, but I refused to leave it behind. I hitched it over my shoulder, then my skirt secured out of the way, I stepped up onto the bench and reached for that beam overhead as smoke swarmed after us.

I thought again of that "monkey" as Lily continued to climb, then seemed to disappear into the darkness.

"Three more, miss," she called back to me as I felt my way, hoisted myself up and cursed that I had grown so tall.

The final beam had been built at an angle and I discovered that long arms were not a hindrance as I firmly grasped the beam and pulled myself up.

The next part of our journey brought me up to the cross timber just below the roof where Lily had perched.

I couldn't see her smile, but I heard it, as if we were off on some grand adventure.

"All we have to do is open the hatch and climb out."

After our climb through the rafters it was quite easily done. I heard a scraping sound then felt cold night air. It was a brief reprieve as the smoke now found an outlet sucked up through the rafters where we had been only moments before, following us onto the roof.

The smoke blinded and stung at my eyes. A slender hand closed around mine.

"This way," Lily shouted over the roar of the fire and pulled me with her.

Past the opening at the hatch, the air cleared, and I could see the direction we were headed— a building beside the church.

Lily led as we negotiated our way across the church roof to that adjacent building, as the church behind us was engulfed in flames. We reached the edge and Lily grinned back at me.

"It's not far."

I reached the edge beside her as she scrambled over the edge, dangled, then let herself drop to the roof of the next building.

Not far, I quickly realized was according to one's perspective. However, my perspective at the moment was that I had the fire at my back, and a "not far" drop before me.

I levered myself over the edge, held on briefly, then dropped no more than a foot or so onto the roof. Not far indeed. I appreciated my extra height.

Lily had climbed into this building through an upper-story window, and I followed. I thought of anyone who might be living there but it seemed to be empty. For the best, I thought as the fire from the church glowed through the window and would undoubtedly follow.

We ran down the stairs and into the chaos on the street that included Madame Antoinette's ladies and clientele, along with those on the street from the tavern across the way amid the arrival of the first fire wagon as the church lit up the night sky.

I needed to find Brodie.

Lily screamed as the fire roared behind us, and then the thought was gone. I turned, thinking her in some danger only to have a cloth thrown over my head. Strong arms wrapped around me.

I fought those arms and tried to pull the cloth from my face, the bag lost in the scuffle. I fought and kicked as I was bound and lifted, carried some distance apart, then thrown into some sort of wagon.

My first thought was for Lily. I had heard her scream. What had happened? Was she all right?

I heard something that might have been a curse as the wagon lurched and then rumbled, picking up speed as I was rolled against the side.

Lily! It had to be. My next thought— where were we being taken and by whom?

We didn't have long to wait as the wagon turned, continued a short distance, then suddenly came to a halt.

"Bring them!" I heard through the suffocating cloth over my head that I now realized was a cloth sack that muffled the voices and any surrounding sounds that might have told me where we were.

I was dragged from the wagon then hoisted over a bony shoulder, the air momentarily knocked out of me. I heard a sound that might have been a door scraping over stones, and I felt a sudden coldness in my bound hands, different from the night cold on the streets.

It seemed that I was jostled and shifted a dozen times as I was carried for some time. Then I heard the sound of voices. I tried to listen for accents or any sound that might tell me who these men were.

It was all smothered by the sack over my head as I was dropped onto a stone floor. I heard a muffled sound and another curse. It seemed that Lily had joined me.

"Bastards!" she screamed.

Their answer was the slamming of a heavy door and a bolt thrown at the lock.

"Are you all right?" I asked when it seemed they had gone.

"Right enough, if I had a knife in me hand," Lily replied.

"Where are you?" I asked at the same time I attempted to breathe, the sack smothering over my face.

I felt a nudge on my shoulder. "Right here."

She leaned into me, and I realized she was indeed beside me.

"How can you breathe with that over yer head?" she asked.

"Not very well..."

"Lean toward me," she told me. "I might be able to grab it with my teeth."

It took three attempts as I leaned toward the sound of her voice, then felt her shoulder against mine. She tugged, cursed, then tugged again as she was able to pull the smothering sack from my head.

The rush of air was almost intoxicating, stale and damp as it was. And there was the feeble glow from a lantern on the floor of what appeared to be a storeroom.

Had it been left behind? Or was there some other reason for it?

"They didn't put a sack on your head?" I exclaimed with a look at her.

"One of 'em said it didn't matter. And they were in a bit of a hurry."

Didn't matter? That sounded quite ominous. And then they were off to do... what? To return shortly... And then what?

It was that part of it that had me concerned as I looked around at our surroundings as best I could see from the lantern. The chamber appeared to be for storage as there were shelves along the wall.

"I'm sorry, Miss Forsythe," Lily apologized.

"For what?"

"That I didn't see 'em in time to warn ye."

I should have been the one apologizing. I didn't believe for a minute that this was some random abduction. A slip of a girl in a maid's costume, and myself dressed quite common? And those two men who just happened to be in the street outside the church?

Not bloody likely, I thought.

It wasn't random. Whoever those men were might very well have something to do with the questions Brodie and I had been asking.

Were they responsible for the fire?

Lily had said that Madame locked the church up tight to make certain customers paid for the night's entertainment as it were. How much easier was it to have everyone out of the church and on the street, to find who they were looking for and then disappear?

If that was the case, there was also the very likely possibility that they were also murderers, and wouldn't hesitate to kill again to keep whatever secrets they were hiding.

"We have to find a way out of here, before they come back," I told Lily.

Easier said than done, of course, considering we were both bound with rope.

However, never underestimate a clever girl who climbed the rafters of a church with ease and then jumped from rooftops.

"Turn yer back toward me," Lily replied.

I squirmed about on the stone floor as I understood her meaning. Her fingers brushed mine as she set about working the knot. It was painstaking work, but it eventually loosened.

Lily made a triumphant sound as she threw the rope off.

"Your turn," I announced as I retrieved the knife I carried in the inside of my boot and sliced through the rope.

"I need to remember to carry one like that," she exclaimed when she saw the knife.

She kicked the rope away then went to the door as I looked around in the meager light from the lantern. She tried the door, but it held firm.

I had lost my bag during the struggle in the street outside the church, however I still had the revolver Brodie had given me in my pocket.

I suppose it was too much to hope for, but it was worth an attempt.

"Stand away," I told her and took aim at the bolt that secured the door. There was a flash and the dull sound of the bullet striking metal, but little else as the bolt held firm.

It appeared that there was only one other possibility— wait for the men who had abducted us to return, then...

It wasn't as if I would hesitate to use the revolver again. I had used it before, however there was Lily to consider, and the fact that there were now only two bullets left.

She had been peering out the narrow opening that might have once been a small window with an iron grate across it beside the door. She seized the lantern and held it up, shining that faint light out that small opening.

"I know where we are," she announced in a tone that was not encouraging. She set the lantern back down.

"The vaults."

I wasn't all reassured by that, and hadn't a clue what she was talking about.

"Vaults?" I asked.

She frowned. It wasn't encouraging as I thought of vaults I was familiar with, the sort in banks or at my aunt's estate at Sussex Square, the sort where money or other valuables were kept, and usually quite impenetrable once that metal door was closed.

"Poor people used to live down here, when they couldn't afford any other place," she explained. "They're below the city, like an underground town. There were businesses here, and a lot of crime, some said. That's the reason the city closed them down and moved the people out. But there was still those that came back as they had no other place to go."

She made another face. "Some folk say the vaults is haunted, by them wot came down here and disappeared or died from the fevers."

Wonderful, I thought. As we were meant to disappear as well?

I didn't believe in ghosts, although I respected others who did. Everyone was entitled to their own thoughts on the matter. And I was determined not to become one.

I had no way of knowing who the people were who had abducted us, but I could make a fairly good guess.

I thought it safe to assume that it may very well have to do with the reason Brodie was in Edinburgh raising questions about thirty-year-old murders that some people apparently didn't want raised.

"We have to find a way out," I announced, convinced that when those men returned, they would put an end to the questions on behalf of whoever was behind this.

"You said that people lived down here at one time. There must be other rooms." I was always at my best when there was something to be done.

"Bring the lantern," I told her as I headed for the door at the back of the chamber.

"Ye mean to go there? Deeper inside the place?" Lily exclaimed.

"We may be able to find something to pry that door open, or another way out. It's either that or stay here with the ghosts," I added.

She was immediately behind me, a hand on my shoulder as I led the way.

It was a very good thing that I didn't suffer from a fear of small rooms or tight dark passageways.

I was forced to duck several times as we explored, Lily holding on to me. The farther we explored the more fetid the air became, and more than once I felt something brush against my boot then skitter way.

I couldn't help but think that it was much like exploring some ancient tomb in the places I had traveled.

We found three additional rooms and what appeared to have once been a work room with a loom and a cobbler's bench.

There were tools that might be useful. I put them into my other pocket. We also found some of the more recent inhabitants scurrying about as the light spilled into the room, and a second lantern.

It still had oil in it from whomever had been the previous inhabitants. It did seem as if they had left quickly, leaving tools of their trade behind.

I found a piece of fabric still at the loom and used it to light the second lantern.

"They say a lot of people were forced to move because of the fevers and plague," Lily added with a slow look around.

"Did '*they*' also say how to get out of here?" I asked.

"I don't think so..." She stopped and looked at me. "We will be able to get out, won't we?"

"Of course," I replied, more because she needed to hear it. "I have no intention of staying down here. We simply need to find a way out."

Before those men returned, I thought, however didn't say it. But Lily was an intelligent girl. There was every chance she had already thought of that.

Escaping was easier said than done as we inspected the workroom and found another door.

"Where do you think this leads?" Lily asked.

"Possibly another way out as this was their place of business." I thought it very likely with those cobbler's tools and the loom. It was the first hopeful sign since we'd arrived.

I had to believe that we might be running out of time. While it was possible we might just be left down here to eventually starve to death or end up meals for the rats, it was also very possible those men would return very soon to make certain the matter was done.

"Check the door," I told her. "Look for anything loose, crumbling mortar, and check the lock. If it's badly rusted it might give way. I'll look for a key." Although by the look at the haphazard debris about that covered everything and those tools left behind, that seemed unlikely. Anyone who had left in such a hurry and leaving valuable tools behind very likely wouldn't have thought to leave a key about.

The lock, a stout iron piece, held fast. My luck at finding a key, admittedly thin, proved fruitless among the debris, rat droppings, and remnants left by the weaver and cobbler.

"This stone is loose," Lily announced with a look over her shoulder at me. I was immediately beside her.

The stone was among those on the wall on both sides that framed the doorway. Either from time, the elements in that decaying place, or possibly a workman who was in a hurry, the mortar between two of the stones had crumbled, part of it missing altogether.

The stacked stones that formed the wall were each eight to ten inches high and at least that amount wide. The mortar between the stones that had deteriorated and crumbled was on the floor at our feet.

I grabbed the cobbler's awl and hammer and began chiseling. As the mortar crumbled Lily scraped it out of the way, and I continued to chisel. I then hammered and chiseled at the sides of the stone.

Lily grabbed the metal shoe stand from the cobbler's bench and began digging crumbled mortar from both sides.

"It moved," she suddenly announced. "The stone moved."

I tried to wedge my fingers between the stone and the one above, to get some leverage.

"Let me try," Lily said, her fingers slenderer as she slipped them between the stones and was eventually able to move it.

She continued to move it back and forth, just that small sliver of space, but it was enough for me to get the other end of the hammer between and work the stone out of place next to that doorframe.

Lily wedged the shoe stand into the narrow opening between,

and inch by inch was able to lever the stone out of place until I was able to get both hands around it. I pulled it out of that niche that it had undoubtedly occupied for the past hundred years or more.

I stepped back as it dropped to the floor of the shop. We both stared at it for a moment. Her hands were cut from the shoe stand while my knuckles were scraped raw from working the stone from its place.

I grabbed the lantern and held it up to the opening we had created in the wall in an attempt to see what was beyond that opening. It appeared to be a passageway from what I could see, and it also appeared to be empty. For now.

Was it the same one we'd entered at that storage vault? Or did it lead somewhere else?

"We need to get out of here," I said, voicing my frustration.

The light at the lantern had begun to wane. If we were going to do something it had to be now. At a glance, it was obvious that there no way I could squeeze through that narrow opening.

"Let me try," Lily said. "It can't be any different than climbing out of the church or dropping down from a roof."

She did have a point and it was very likely the only chance we might have. If not, when those men returned…

I scraped more crumbled mortar out of the opening to give her as much room as possible as she dragged a wood chair over from the cobbler's bench to the opening.

She was small and slender. But was she small enough to be able to move through that opening without becoming wedged? And what then?

One step at a time, I reminded myself, and gave her a hand up as she climbed atop the chair, her expression most determined.

She thrust both arms through the opening, appeared to grab hold of the other side of the wall, then slowly inched her way through.

She stopped more than once and I was afraid she might have become stuck, then she moved on until her legs were all that remained on my side of the opening. Another few wiggles and she briefly disappeared only to pop up, looking back at me through the opening with a foolish grin on her face.

She was dirty, smudged, and bruised, but she had managed to crawl through that wall.

"Take the lantern," I told her as I handed it through and hoped there was enough fuel left for her to find her way out of our "tomb".

"There's a number over the door," she said, holding up the lantern.

"Is there any other door nearby, perhaps the one to the room where we were taken?"

She disappeared then quickly returned.

"It's just down the way. I'm certain it's the one."

It had been a fairly short distance from that wagon until we were carried into that room. I hoped that she was right.

"You will have to go back that way. I'm certain that it's the shortest distance out of here, however you must be careful. That will surely be the way they will return as well."

She nodded, her eyes wide. I then handed her the revolver through the opening.

"Take this with you."

"Miss...?"

I heard the hesitation in her voice, and ignored it.

"You'll need a steady hand," I told her. "Then, all you have to do is pull back the trigger, aim, and fire if you encounter anyone in the passage."

"I don't know if I can..." She protested. "I never shot anyone before."

"A girl brave enough to climb out of a burning building?" I replied. "I assure you that you can when your life depends upon it."

"I don't want to leave you," she protested in a voice that quivered slightly.

"I'll be all right. I have the hammer and a few other things I can use if necessary. You must find Mr. Brodie. He was to return to the church." However *when* was the question. Would she be able to find him in time?

I couldn't think about that now.

"Go now, before those men return."

She nodded.

I swallowed past the sudden tightness in my throat, and watched until the light from her lantern faded completely, the passage once more plunged into darkness.

I hoped that I wasn't sending her off right into those men's hands.

With the little light as remained from the other lantern, I chiseled away at the stone above the opening we'd created.

It was slow work as the mortar was still intact here, made all the more difficult as the light at the lantern flickered and I wondered how long Lily had been gone, then silently cursed that I had not checked my watch before she left.

However, a glance at it now revealed a cracked lens, no doubt from being tossed into that wagon. The hands had stopped just after midnight.

The lantern flickered again, and I looked about what had obviously been a cobbler's shop for another one that might have been left behind but there was none.

I thought briefly of attempting to find another way out. However if Lily was successful in escaping and if she was able to find Brodie, they would look for me here.

If... There were so many *ifs*.

The flame at the lantern flickered again.

I used the last of the light to gather anything that might be used for a weapon close at hand, along with the hammer, awl, and knife Munro had given me.

The wick of the lantern sputtered then went out completely. The vault was eerily silent as a tomb.

I was now completely alone, with Lily's ghosts.

Sixteen

BRODIE LOOKED DOWN at the sealed envelope Alex Sinclair had just handed him as they stood at the concierge office at the Waverley Hotel. He exchanged a look with Munro.

"When did ye arrive?" Brodie asked the younger man.

"On the express earlier this evening. Sir Avery said it was most urgent. He said that no one else must see it, and wanted it hand delivered to you. He said that there were others to consider..."

"Urgent..." Brodie repeated. *Others to consider?*

He'd expected a telegram after Munro had sent information to Alex regarding Calhoun. But an urgent message in response?

The muscles at his neck tightened in that way that told him something had happened, something contained in that envelope.

"He said that it was important that I get it to you right away..." Alex Sinclair added with a look at him, then a glance over at Munro.

Brodie slipped a finger under the wax seal over the flap of the envelope and opened it, then took out the unmarked piece of stationery with Sir Avery's signature at the bottom.

He read it, then once more to be certain he hadn't misread the information there. He handed it to Munro.

"He did say that no one else was to see it..." Alex Sinclair reminded him, glanced at the two men, then obviously decided to say nothing more of it.

Brodie and Munro exchanged a look when both had read the *"urgent message"* intended only for Brodie.

"It would seem there are some things Sir Avery neglected to mention to ye," Munro commented.

"So it would seem," Brodie replied, then asked Alex, "How long ago was this known?"

"I was told not to discuss..."

"How long?" Brodie demanded in a tone meant to convey that he would have an answer, and now.

"A few days, I believe," Alex replied, obviously uncomfortable. "Possibly longer. There are others... who were working on this from the inside."

Others working *"inside"*, as he and Munro were on the street, and Mikaela... And Sir Avery knew far more and had withheld that information.

For what reason? A witness he wanted? Someone who might know something from thirty years ago?

They had found that person— Calhoun. Only to now learn that the people in London had long suspected someone else had been there that night. They'd been watching and waiting, and he had given them the perfect opportunity.

It was a bitter taste that they had been used to get information that supported what Sir Avery and others had long suspected— murder and other things.

But it was more than that; a complete disregard for the lives they had put in danger. Was it any different from the man they were out to trap?

"What do you want to do?" Munro asked.

It was a hard lesson, one that he'd been forced to learn before about who could be trusted, and those who couldn't. His next thought, ironically, was one from the bible that he remembered from a long time ago— *"an eye for an eye."* It was a problem that he would take care of.

That would come later, he thought.

"Miss Forsythe?" Munro asked.

Brodie nodded. "She needs to be warned." And kept safe, the thought that immediately came after.

He thrust the letter into his jacket pocket as he headed for the door of the office.

"I say...! Mr. Brodie!" Alex called after them. "I was told that you were to wait here until the others that Sir Avery has sent arrive."

Brodie paused at the door. That had been in the letter as well, agents on their way on that special train from London to carry out the last of Avery's instructions.

It was on the tip of his tongue to tell Alex exactly what Sir Avery could do with that in no uncertain terms. But it would have served no purpose.

The truth was that he liked Alex Sinclair, even if he was naïve, and far better suited to his calculating machines and other inventions. He hadn't a clue that he'd been used in this as well.

"Ye need to remember there are few people in this world that ye can trust," he told him. "The others will use ye," he added with a flinch of pain that had nothing to do with the wounds on his side.

"Keep those ye trust close." He thought of Mikaela, the strangeness of the circumstances that had brought her into his life, and one of the few people that he did he trust. With good reason. She was brave, strong, and true, even at risk to herself. And Munro, who had shared the worst with him.

"And keep those ye canna trust even closer." He saw the confusion in Alex's eyes.

"I don't understand..." Alex stammered.

"Ye will," Brodie replied as he followed Munro to the street.

There was no driver at the hotel that time of the night.

They set out on foot, the imposing edifice of the castle looming up on that hill behind them as they left Princes Street and moved deeper into the old part of the city.

At a tavern, they found a driver dozing as he waited for a late-night fare. Brodie woke him as they stepped into the coach, and gave him the location of the church.

"Church?" the man asked. "This time o' the night?"

"Double the fare in half the time," Brodie replied.

He saw the glow at the skyline before the driver turned down the street at the end from the church. He was out the door of the coach before it came to a stop, Munro tossing coins to the driver.

Several wagons of the fire brigade filled the street, along with people from the nearby tenements, the tavern across the way, and the church, including the ladies who resided there. And their customers.

As a lad he had heard stories about the great fire decades earlier that had burned through a huge part of Old Town in spite of the efforts of those who fought it. With scarce water and no equipment, volunteers were able to do little more than watch as the fire ran along the rooftops and engulfed a good portion of the old district.

In the years since, there had been changes to the ability to fight fires that were a constant threat due to the poverty, poor living conditions, or from fires built at the streets just to keep warm on a cold night. There was now a city fire brigade, and wagons with uniformed men to fight those fires.

Among the wagons were two horse-drawn pumper wagons that shot powerful streams of water and had prevented the fire from spreading beyond the church and the smaller building at the side of it.

Among those on the street, he finally saw Madame Antoinette comforting one of her ladies, both of them smudged with soot and wearing whatever they had escaped with.

She looked up as Brodie made his way through the tangle of hoses, equipment, and people on the street.

"Are ye all right?" he asked. "And yer ladies?"

She nodded, then before he could ask, "It all happened so quick, there was so little time..."

"Wot are ye sayin'?" he demanded.

"Yer friend and the girl... I haven't seen them."

Brodie felt a hand on his arm. It was Munro. He threw off that hand and was about to set off on his own search...

He refused to believe that Mikaela hadn't gotten out.

"Wait!" his friend shouted after him.

"Wot!" Then he looked past Munro to the girl who pushed her way toward them.

Like the others, her clothes were smudged and torn, her hair tangled, tears bright in her eyes. It was the girl, Lily, who Mikaela had taken to.

"Mr. Brodie!"

"Is she alive?"

The girl nodded. "When I left her."

"What are ye talkin' about, girl?" Munro demanded.

"We managed to get out on the roof when the fire started, but they were waiting for us."

"Who was waiting?"

She shook her head. "Men on the street. They tied both of us up and put us in a wagon. She helped me escape, and said I was to find ye."

"Where?" Brodie demanded.

"The vaults... I didna want to leave her, but she said that she could manage... if they came back."

"How long ago?" he asked.

"It took me some time to get back here, and I been waitin' for ye to come back... The fire brigade had already arrived... must be near two hours."

Brodie swore. Two hours!

Anything might have happened in that amount of time. The men who took them might have returned. She might already be dead...

"The vaults?" He knew of them, knew those who had lived in them, a long time ago.

"There's dozens of 'em," Munro added.

"I know where she is. I memorized the number," Lily told them. "The entrance is at Blair Street, Number 28, at the cobbler's shop."

Munro nodded. They knew Blair Street from the old days as lads.

The girl pulled something from the pocket of her apron and handed to Brodie.

It was the revolver he had given Mikaela.

He took it and handed it to Munro.

Wide-eyed, Lily asked, "What are ye goin' to do?"

"I'm goin' to find her."

Seventeen

THE VAULTS

I HAD no way of knowing how long Lily had been gone as I sat back against the wall in the cobbler's shop.

Even if my watch hadn't been broken when we were abducted, it would have been impossible to see the time in the dark.

I listened, and the sounds came— vague scratchings amid the refuse and discarded leather as the other inhabitants moved about — rats no doubt and other creatures that inhabited such places after the people were no longer there.

I could hear them, but I couldn't see them.

It would have been so simple to give into the fear; the questions that filled my thoughts. The *what if*...

Had Lily managed to get away? Was she able to find Brodie? When would the men who'd brought us there return? What would happen then?

My hand brushed the blade of the knife, reassuring even in the darkness. And beside it the cobbler's hammer and awl. All of them extremely useful weapons... if one could see to use them.

There were other weapons, the things I'd learned while on my travels abroad after one particular encounter with an older woman who became a good friend and introduced me to the ancient art of self-defense.

Even now, or perhaps especially now, with no other distractions and the unknown of the dark, I could see her face in my mind, the mass of wayward silver curls atop her head, her slender figure that one would hardly think capable of fighting off a man, and the silent ferocity of what she had learned and then insisted that I learn as well.

"A woman alone is merely a target, my dear. My husband taught me that. A man among our staff who was from China, taught him how to protect himself bare-handed. And he in turn taught me. I have sought the best instruction since then on my travels, and now I share it with you."

Her name was Abigail Wentworth and along with other experiences in my rather unique and odd life, I learned the value and wisdom of friendship, and things to be learned.

Before that, it had never occurred to me that I might be able to overpower a man. I learned quickly, fascinated by the ancient discipline and learned all that I could before returning to England.

How long ago was that? Four years? Five? Longer? Before my adventures in Crete, and before Brodie.

Had Lily been able to find him? Would he come? Or would he be too late for whatever our captors had planned?

The fear would have been so easy, sitting there in the dark with the ghosts of the past and other things scrabbling and skittering about me. Instead, I sat up straight and crossed my legs on the floor.

I cleared my thoughts and pulled up the things I had learned from memory. It had been so deeply ingrained through hours of training that it had become instinct— how to clear my thoughts, control my breathing, letting my senses expand into the darkness, reaching out, then slowly breathing in, breathing out. Aware of every movement about me, then gathering that strength.

Of course, there was no way to know how long I sat there

when there were new sounds— voices, the brief exchange of conversation, footsteps, the sound of that other door scraping at the stones as it was opened followed by curses to find that Lily and I were gone!

I slowly stood, the hammer in one hand, the knife in the other. I breathed in, then out, and listened.

I glimpsed the beam of light from the opening at the back of the cobbler's shop, from the direction Lily and I had followed as we had made our way through the passage.

It wasn't from a lantern but the sort of beam from a handheld light, the kind the police carried on the watch, and the man who held that light gradually approached closer. Then, a second beam of light appeared just behind the first one.

"They've got to be here. There's no others way out," one said to the other as they reached the doorway, and those twin beams of light penetrated the darkness then moved along the walls, searching.

Now able to see once more, after hours in the dark, I moved from the door in the wall, and slowly made my way around the end of the cobbler's bench.

If I could make it to the doorway they'd just emerged from, I might be able to escape back to that storage vault where Lily and I were first taken.

And there was always the off chance that they hadn't bothered to lock that door behind them when they returned and discovered us gone.

I had been in difficult situations before, but not trapped into such a small space with no other way out. They continued to pass those beams across the walls, slowly, methodically searching.

I took a step then another, and continued to make my way toward the doorway as they came farther in the shop, the backlight from those twin beams revealing my captors— the first man in a dark overcoat, one behind with those gaunt features, a tweed Norfolk jacket, and deerstalker cap!

It was the same man I had encountered at the Waverley, and

had seen again outside St. Andrews Church! And the other man wore a long coat, open over what appeared to be the tunic of a uniform!

My thoughts flashed back to that other encounter outside the Registry Office as the rain poured down and I had made a mad dash for a cab; the collision with a man, his hand firm, almost painful, on my arm, that brief exchange and then he was gone, and that odd insignia I found on the sidewalk afterward.

No chance encounter of strangers in a hurry to get out of the weather; not an accidental exchange.

The man was with the police, that overcoat meant to disguise his uniform. He had obviously been following me!

To stop me? From what? Discovering the truth about the murders? What was in those hidden reports from the murders thirty years ago? A secret that was worth so many lives? What secret?

I thought of Lily and the ladies at Madame Antoinette's house, and the fire. Another accident?

It hardly seemed likely. And what of the lives of those whom we'd spoken with? I thought then of three women whose lives were tragically ended and apparently linked... Brodie's mother, a woman I had never met, perhaps glimpsed in the man he had become.

He'd not spoken of whether or not he favored her. Did she perhaps have those same dark eyes...?

The conversation of the two men brought me back to the moment, as they moved closer and pushed a crate then the spinner's loom out of their path, those beams from their handheld lights searching the shadows... searching for me. Very near.

"Remember, when we find them, there's to be no trace of any of this, nothing that can point the blame back to him."

They were obviously speaking of whoever was behind this, and now the murder of Sholto McQueen and the driver of the coach the night I was abducted. And others? How many more?

I was only a few feet from the door that opened out into the passage. As that first light steadily crawled closer I stepped from behind the cobbler's bench and made a dash for the door.

"Stop her!" I heard the shout behind me. I then felt the fist in my hair.

I was spun around and would have gone down but there were moments my height was an advantage, along with that earlier training. I was face-to-face with the uniformed constable and swung the hammer.

As we struggled, it was a glancing blow to the side of the head that momentarily staggered him back. I took advantage as he staggered back and swept his feet from under him. His hold on my hair suddenly loosened then freed me as he fell to the floor.

There was a curse and a powerful hand on my shoulder as I was grabbed by the man in that tweed jacket, and anger gave way to rage.

Brodie had spoken of it in the past, that moment where instinct might be all that was left.

It was there now. I saw my death in that ice-cold gaze and knew that I was nothing more than an inconvenience, an order to be carried out, with no trace left behind. The blow caught me on my cheek, and it was as if light burst inside my head.

I still had the hammer in my hand, but my fingers wouldn't obey the command to lift it up to defend myself. Then it was gone. Seized by the man in that Norfolk jacket?

As that burst of light disappeared I used what was left— my hands and clawed at the man's face, then far closer than I would have liked as he held on to me, I thrust my elbow into that soft spot high at his ribs. He grunted in surprise, then there was a curse.

Breathe in, breathe out, I told myself. The rage was there as I fought to bring my knee up.

The room erupted as if a cannon had been fired and those hands that had grabbed at me only seconds before immediately loosened, and I dropped to the floor.

I screamed and cursed, and fought my way back to my feet

amid shouts that I didn't understand. Then it came again— my name, the sound of it both urgent and fierce in a thick Scots accent.

"It's over, lass...!" And I was being shaken to get my attention.

Lass? There was only one person who had ever called me that.

Brodie pulled me to my feet, a revolver in his other hand. He didn't immediately look at me as he kept his attention on the man in that Deerstalker cap a few feet away with a bloodstain on the shoulder of his jacket.

Munro was there as well and moved past me. There was a grunt of what could only be described as pain, then silence.

Munro returned and took Brodie's place.

"That one won't be hurtin' anyone again anytime soon," he told Brodie.

"Enjoyed that, did ye?" Brodie asked. "He's still alive, aye? We'll need the man's information about the one behind all this."

Munro nodded, however with obvious regret.

"He'll live, and the information he can give is the only reason. I could never abide hurtin' a woman. But he'll think he's been kicked in the head by a horse when he finally wakes up." He looked at me then, shook his head, and smiled.

"And ye as well, I think, miss, by the looks of yer cheek."

Very likely I thought as both my cheek and head throbbed.

"But ye seem to have given as good as ye got," he added.

I thought a revolver a much more expedient and less painful way of settling a situation— for the person holding the weapon, not the one in front of it. I looked at the man in the Deerstalker cap and thought once more of all those he and his people had harmed.

As I had learned while working with Brodie, there was most often far more beneath the surface of a crime. It was like a web of deceit and lies that spread into so many lives.

And now? Who wanted me as well as others dead? Who was behind it?

The answer wasn't there, not then of course, as I gave into Munro's manner of settling things.

I drew back my arm and landed a fist on Deerstalker's face. There was an audible crunch, and his hand immediately went to his nose as he staggered back against the wall.

Brodie gently restrained me.

"Do ye feel better now?" he asked with that combination of concern and what might have been amusement.

"Immensely," I replied as I rubbed my now bruised hand, then asked, "Lily?"

Brodie nodded. "Safe and fared somewhat better than yerself by the looks of ye."

There was something in his voice that I had heard recently. As if there was something else he would have said, then decided against it.

He was to be commended. I was not of a mind to be reprimanded for involving myself. After all, it had been his idea for me to stay at the "*church*." Out of harm's way.

That was going to be a most interesting conversation when we got around to it.

Eighteen

OLD LODGE

THERE WAS, of course, an enormous scandal over the events that we had uncovered.

I say "we", as none of it would have finally come to light if not for Brodie's delving into the past and his determination to have answers for his mother's murder.

Not the least was the exposure of those missing police reports and the name of the man who had signed them, and had then very carefully arranged for them to disappear. They were found at his private residence.

A man by the name of William Burns, the "other" man, who was there the night that Brodie's mother was murdered, seen by Constable Graham, and the same man very likely responsible for those other identical murders.

All these years later, Sergeant William Burns rose through the ranks of the Edinburgh Police to the position of High Commissioner— a man with secrets that included the murder of Constable Graham who might have identified him that night years before.

As for the young man who was there that night, Mick Tobin; he became the other victim, a friend of a young woman who was simply trying to survive the poverty and provide for her son.

It was possible that Bettie Dowd, a known prostitute, had been another victim of a night spent with Sergeant Burns. It was also possible that the seamstress, Elizabeth Eldridge might have been caught up in such things, but I personally thought it unlikely.

According to her brother she made a decent wage as a seamstress and was planning to be married. I refused to believe that she would have been persuaded into that oldest profession— prostitution.

The person her brother had described very likely had found herself in the wrong place at the wrong time returning home from work, and became a victim of William Burns through no act or fault of her own.

She would have resisted, and then... The circumstances of her death, identical to those of Bettie Dowd and Màili Brodie, had laid a trap for Burns that he could not have anticipated even all these years later. Then, as Brodie began making his inquiries about his mother's death all those weeks before, the High Commissioner's murderous past threatened to unravel the career he had built.

As Brodie had said more than once, there was always the one thing in a crime that revealed an important clue, if one was willing to look for it. The tragic deaths most certainly had provided important clues, along with others even years after their own deaths.

Not the least was information Mr. Calhoun had provided when we met with him— of that brief time that he had walked the streets with Constable Meeks after Graham was supposedly killed in that robbery, and Graham had spoken of what he and no one else had seen that— the other man who was there.

Then, Meeks' supposed suicide. Calhoun hadn't believed it. It appeared that Meeks was another victim, even though a handful of years later, in Commissioner Burn's attempt to hide his brutal past.

That career was not only now ended, but very likely his life as well. Fitting justice, I thought. However, it would not bring back the people who were lost in all this.

There had been more to all this, I learned. Wasn't there always, when it came to hiding one's misdeeds, secrets, even murder.

I got up slowly from my bed, the wood of the floor cold on my bare feet, then made my way to the stone hearth and stirred the embers. I tossed in several small pieces of wood as well as dried moss, flames quickly appearing.

I added a larger piece of wood, then went to the windows at the far wall and threw back the heavy drapes that hung over the window casement.

Frost had gathered again on the windows and on the ground beyond the lodge.

I had been here the past two weeks after leaving Edinburgh. Brodie had insisted and I had not objected. I was bruised, battered, and needed time to sort everything through everything we'd learned, and those things that continued to be revealed.

I insisted that Brodie stay as well, to give his wounds more time to heal. He had stayed at the gamekeeper's cabin that Munro usually occupied when he attended to things at the distillery and the property at Old Lodge for my aunt.

He had arrived with word from Edinburgh, and the two of them had closed themselves away in the cabin for hours. Whatever they had discussed, Brodie's expression when they eventually emerged, had been grim but resolute.

He had then left. I overheard a brief exchange with Munro. He was returning to London to take care of "some matters" there. There was no further explanation.

I was not fooled. Munro had been left to see to my protection, along with Mr. and Mrs. Hutton who lived at Old Lodge and took care of the animals and saw to the shipments of whisky that were sent out to Edinburgh and other towns and cities, including London.

I knew them well as they had been at the estate since my aunt first brought my sister and I here after the deaths of our parents.

It was a place to heal after the loss and the place where my aunt first said that I looked as if I had sprouted from a thicket, my hair all wild upon returning from one of those early adventures about the forest that surrounded Old Lodge and the countryside beyond.

I dressed now as I saw the hounds set loose by Mr. Hutton, and thought of Rupert the hound and Mr. Cavendish at the office on the Strand in London.

Brodie intended to look in on them when his "business" was concluded with Sir Avery, and then he was to return. But I wasn't certain about that.

This particular case had been difficult, and I had noticed a change in him with answers he had wanted for all those years and finally... resolution. Although, as I knew only too well, even when resolved, there were things that a person always carried with them.

I fully expected to see the man from the village arriving in his cart with the latest mail that included a message from Brodie, explaining that he had been detained by one thing or another and wouldn't be returning.

I put another piece of wood onto the fire and then dressed in clothes from my last visit that had been retrieved from the trunk at the foot of the bed, as I was not one to go dragging endless baggage from one place to another as others might.

I thought of Lily and those incredible, desperate hours we had spent in the Vaults. Such a brave, remarkable young person. I was particularly fond of her.

I supposed that near death experiences had a way of doing that. Still, I would have been fooling everyone including myself if I didn't admit that I saw a bit of myself in the girl.

She was presently assisting Madame Antoinette relocate her business establishment. Then, I fully intended to offer her the opportunity for an education. My aunt would like her very much.

Munro had informed me that Madame had found another

abandoned church as she liked the irony of her ladies conducting business in a place that had once been a place for sinners.

Undaunted by the fire, that had apparently been deliberately set and destroyed everything including that medieval church, she was determined to open for business before the new year. The more I learned about the woman the more I liked her.

Mrs. Hutton greeted me as I entered the kitchen where she was taking a pan of *plen brid*, translated from broad Scot as "plain bread" as she called it, with that dark crust on top and bottom that I had loved to smear with butter and honey as a child. And still did.

She cut off a portion, put it onto a plate, and handed it to me, with a quick inspection of my face.

"Aye, the green has started to fade to yellow," she commented on my bruises that had started to gradually go away.

"No worse than when ye took a header off one of the goats, aye?"

I smiled at the memory, and agreed. "No worse."

There was also fresh coffee that Mr. Hutton insisted upon when he returned from feeding the animals.

I missed Brodie, which was somewhat surprising. I had never missed anyone other than perhaps my aunt or my sister when I was traveling about. It was a new experience for me.

However, I was grateful for the time alone— mostly at Old Lodge. Munro had kept to himself after he had arrived, spending most of his time at the distillery that was nearby, then returning in the evening for supper, before taking himself off to his cabin.

Of an evening, Mr. and Mrs. Hutton retired to their own house that adjoined the lodge, after sitting for a while before the fire at the big house, pipe smoke curling about Mr. Hutton's head as he read the daily that was brought from the village while Mrs. Hutton knitted or mended in companionable silence. And I...

I read from among the countless books that my aunt had collected since her own childhood. I had even begun my next novel, ironically an adventure about secrets, murder, and conspiracy involving Miss Emma Fortescue.

I had wrapped myself in a fur-lined coat as the days were suddenly shorter and the temperatures were colder, and headed out on one of my walks that usually took me past the pastures where woolly sheep still grazed on what they could find, while Highland cows— those great shaggy beasts with an appropriately grumpy Scottish attitude— roamed the other pasture.

And then there was the line of pine trees at the edge of the forest that had seen me on many an adventure as a child.

Now, I wore woven wool pants under the jacket with boots, and set off on an adventure of several hours that took me along a trail I had traversed countless times in the past. I eventually reached the point that overlooked the loch where it was said a great monster lived in those murky depths.

Mr. Hutton knew the story from his boyhood and had claimed, with a wink, that it was all true.

I had never seen this monster, of course, but it had filled my imagination with all sorts of things, and no doubt accounted for my thirst for adventure later in my life as well as the novels I wrote.

I started back along the path and realized it was quite late in the afternoon. But I had to stop and discuss my day's adventure with the Highland cows and their half-grown calves that had gathered about and stared back at me with curiosity.

They were mostly rust-colored, streamers of that long shaggy coat that protected them in the coldest of winter, hanging over their faces. I scratched the face of one, the coat bristly in places, soft in others, and thought of a man with a dark beard.

Not that I missed him, I told myself. It was simply the conversation that I missed with a good argument every now and again... and I did so enjoy the inquiry cases we took on.

"The damned beasts are known to bite, not to mention their horns. They can be a bit cantankerous."

Speaking of ... I turned at that voice and the way the Scot's accent wrapped around that very important observation of High-land cows.

"You are, of course, a man of some authority on the subject, having lived your entire life in the city," I replied.

"I managed to get out and about once in a while," Brodie replied.

"Crete?" I suggested. "Or perhaps, Brighton? Not exactly overrun by bovine creatures."

"Aye."

And it was just that simple, as we seemed to slip into our old selves once more with that easy camaraderie and banter.

He was dressed for the cold weather in thick worsted trousers and jacket, and turtleneck jumper in a dark shade that made his eyes seem even darker. There was a weariness there, and a look perhaps of things that had taken him to London, and answers after almost thirty years. But he was here.

His beard was slightly longer as was his hair that curled over the neck of the sweater. My instinct was to approach the usually "surly beast" and run my fingers through that thick dark silk, but I didn't.

"Are you all right?" he asked in an almost detached sort of way, as if we were old friends recently reacquainted.

I nodded. "Mrs. Hutton has said that the bruises will all be gone in another week, and I'm certain they would not dare linger a day more." The woman had been most adamant.

A faint smile then, and I discovered that I had been holding my breath as if waiting for a glimpse of the old Brodie I knew as he stared out across the pasture.

"Are you all right?" I asked in turn, a question that had far more meaning than a few bruises of his own, or the wounds he'd received.

He didn't answer for the longest time, and I thought he might not. Then, he slowly nodded.

"Aye."

And I knew that he would eventually tell me what he wanted

me to know. On other matters. Most particularly the matter of what Sir Avery considered the more important aspect of the Agency's on-going investigation of the Chief Commissioner of Police in Edinburgh.

He had used Brodie. Never mind that the two cases had intertwined with Burns' involvement in those decades-old murders along with the recent ones. It had been betrayal, that I sensed had been "discussed", but would not be forgotten.

"You met with Sir Avery while in London?" I knew that Brodie respected the man, however there seemed to have been a change in that.

He nodded. "We've agreed to disagree in the matter."

And future matters as well, no doubt. Brodie was after all, rather strong-minded about loyalty. He was thoughtful again, as he reached out and scratched the ear of a particularly curious Highland cow.

I could have sworn that she had a contented smile on her face. Shameless girl.

"I thought that once I had the answers that it would be enough," he continued then, staring out across the pasture and the long building of the distillery just beyond.

I understood as much as anyone might, at last having answers. But I sensed he wasn't looking for me to agree, or even say anything. It was something that he needed to say.

"I went to Greyfriar's after I returned to Edinburgh," he said then. "According to the records, my mother was buried in a common grave that was simply given a number."

I saw the change in his expression and sensed how difficult that must have been— a common grave, a number, and for many who believed in the necessity of a proper grave with a headstone... no way to properly mourn the loss of a loved one.

"I know that she's not really there; just a body," he continued. "If there is such a thing as the soul going on, she would already know that..." He shrugged. "But I wanted to tell her anyway. I suppose that was for me." He turned and looked at me then.

"But it wasna enough."

This was the part that I had silently feared, that it might not be enough, and he would close himself off with his anger and bitterness and simply go on his way.

I wasn't prepared for that.

"The past weeks since..." he continued, "when it was finally over, there was something else."

"Most people who go through these things are never able to move past it, ye ken. I've seen it. They become another victim. Thomas Eldridge over his sister, Calhoun perhaps with the burden he's carried all these years, young Mick Tobin's widow and the life she had once imagined but lost."

He shook his head. "I found that in finally having the answers, I wanted more."

There was a faint smile, the one at one corner of his mouth that had a way of making me forget something I might want to say.

"God knows that I have no right... some of the things I've done," he added.

"And I thought, this is where ye belong." He made a sweeping gesture with his hand. "And at yer townhouse in London with yer books, and off on yer travels...

"Yer a lady, and I'm from the streets."

I was holding my breath again, preparing myself for what I was certain he would say next; the usual things people got caught up in regarding titles, one's position in society, expectations.

I had been born to a title for all the good it did. There were certain expectations of society that I had stepped away from a long time ago. I didn't give a fig about any of it. And now?

I had to admit that I didn't want to hear what I was certain he was about to tell me.

"I have nothing to offer ye," he said then. "Only an office with the monthly rent, a cripple who lives below and insults just about everyone he comes into contact except for ye, that mangy beast ye've taken a likin' to, God knows what reason, and clients... "He shook his head. "Some which are as bad as the ones we make inquiries about...

"But I want ye. I want ye fiercely, more than I've ever wanted anything. Even with yer stubbornness, that temper of yers, and the way ye take yerself off and put yerself in harm's way, to drive a man crazy."

I let out the breath I had been holding and took another. He held up a hand. "Ye'll let me finish. It's not enough for me to be with ye, in that way, if ye get my meanin'.

"I want more, even as I stand here knowin' that I have no right and fully expect ye to say no, or in the very least to argue with me over it and tell me that I'm a fool, or worse.

"I want ye, God help us both, and I have nothing to give ye, except meself and this."

He held out his hand, the last of the day's light gleaming at the copper chain and medallion that hung from his fingers— the St. Christopher's medal his mother had given to protect him, something I knew was beyond priceless to him.

No flowers, no ring that others might have expected. Not even a formal proposal with dozens of people looking on.

Just Brodie, as he held out his hand.

Oh, bloody hell!

Author Note

Record-keeping, police archives, crime files, photographic evidence— all part of the story as a new century approaches.

However, the business of crime never seems to change. Lust, greed, and murder of course.

I've discovered that in my research for the series. And murder is a very nasty business that often conceals one's identity, until the murderer is exposed.

Only the names and the places seem to change. That is the story behind *A Deadly Vow*, a vow made a long time ago by Angus Brodie to find a killer, with its own twists, turns, deceptions, and conspiracy.

And with this, I thought it was time to give Brodie his own voice, with his emotions, what drives him, and his growing relationship with a woman who tests him at every turn, Mikaela Forsythe. Rather than through her viewpoint. He is after all, a man of his own. A bloody Scot! Something I know a little about.

So having given him that voice with his own chapter, I hope to have given you a bit of a glimpse of a man with his own history, who refuses to compromise, is constantly at odds with a woman far above him in class but one he's discovered that he wants, and needs.

How would he ever explain to the Mudger or Rupert, if he let her simply go her own way?

Not bloody likely.

Let me know your thoughts on that as I prepare to send Brodie and Mikaela off on another adventure of mystery and murder, and...?

And do be certain to look next for *DEADLY OBSESSION,* Angus Brodie and Mikaela Forsythe, Murder Mystery Book 6.

Carla Simpson
(And yes, I am married to a Scot... Oh my!)

A Sneak Peek...

DEADLY OBSESSION

Angus Brodie and Mikaela Forsythe Murder Mystery
Book 6

by
CARLA SIMPSON

Prologue

AMBER LIGHT GLOWED SOFTLY in the darkened room, the smell of chemicals thick in the air as the sheet of paper was dipped into the last basin and the image of a young woman appeared.

She wasn't pretty like the others who carried an air of privilege and wealth, with that certain expectation of young women who were seen in the society pages of the Times newspaper. But still there had been a sweetness in her features that contradicted the plainness.

There had been no protest, she hadn't made a sound or cried out. There was only that startled expression, surprise perhaps. But no words came with her last dying breath.

There was only that air of sadness about her, her image caught in that photograph—sadness and perhaps loneliness as she had left the dressmaker's shop.

"Soon," a voice assured her from the shadows, as if she could still hear beyond death as the photograph was removed from the basin and carefully hung to dry alongside the other photographs.

"Soon, the others will join you."

About the Author

"I want to write a book... " she said.

"Then do it," he said.

And she did, and received two offers for that first book proposal.

A dozen historical romances later, and a prophecy from a gifted psychic and the Legacy Series was created, expanding to seven additional titles.

Along the way, two film options, and numerous book awards.

But wait, there's more a voice whispered, after a trip to Scotland and a visit to the standing stones in the far north, and as old as Stonehenge, sign posts the voice told her, and the Clan Fraser books that have followed that told the beginnings of the clan and the family she was part of...

And now... murder and mystery set against the backdrop of Victorian London in the new Angus Brodie and Mikaela Forsythe series, with an assortment of conspirators and murderers in the brave new world after the Industrial Revolution where terrorists threaten and the world spins closer to war.

When she is not exploring the Darkness of the fantasy world, or pursuing ancestors in ancient Scotland, she lives in the mountains near Yosemite National Park with bears and mountain lions, and plots murder and revenge.

And did I mention fierce, beautiful women and dangerous, handsome men?

They're there, waiting...

Join Carla's Newsletter

Also by Carla Simpson

Angus Brodie and Mikaela Forsythe Murder Mystery

A Deadly Affair

Deadly Secrets

A Deadly Game

Deadly Illusion

A Deadly Vow

Deadly Obsession

Merlin Series

Daughter of Fire

Daughter of the Mist

Daughter of the Light

Shadows of Camelot

Dawn of Camelot

Daughter of Camelot

The Young Dragons, Blood Moon

Clan Fraser

Betrayed

Revenge

Outlaws, Scoundrels & Lawmen

Desperado's Caress

Passion's Splendor

Silver Mistress

Printed in the USA
CPSIA information can be obtained
at www.ICGtesting.com
CBHW070309180224
4418CB00010B/591